# Death in the Floating City

## Also by Tasha Alexander

*And Only to Deceive*

*A Poisoned Season*

*A Fatal Waltz*

*Tears of Pearl*

*Dangerous to Know*

*A Crimson Warning*

*Elizabeth: The Golden Age*

# Death in the Floating City

*Tasha Alexander*

Minotaur Books ✶ New York

DEATH IN THE FLOATING CITY. Copyright © 2012 by Tasha Alexander. All rights reserved. Printed in the United States of America. For information, address St. Martin's Press, 175 Fifth Avenue, New York, N.Y. 10010.

www.minotaurbooks.com
www.stmartins.com

Library of Congress Cataloging-in-Publication Data

Alexander, Tasha, 1969–
     Death in the floating city / Tasha Alexander.—1st ed.
     (A Lady Emily mystery)
         p. cm.
     ISBN 978-0-312-66176-2 (hardcover)
     ISBN 978-1-250-01103-9 (e-book)
     1. Murder—Investigation—Italy—Venice—Fiction.   2. Aristocracy
(Social class)—Fiction.   I. Title.
   PS3601.L3565D43 2012
   813'.6—dc23

                                                    2012025257

First Edition: October 2012

10   9   8   7   6   5   4   3   2   1

*For Andrew, who showed me Venice*

I stood in Venice, on the Bridge of Sighs;
A palace and a prison on each hand:
I saw from out the wave her structures rise
As from the stroke of the enchanter's wand:
A thousand years their cloudy wings expand
Around me, and a dying Glory smiles
O'er the far times, when many a subject land
Look'd to the winged Lion's marble piles,
Where Venice sate in state, thron'd on her hundred isles!

She looks a sea Cybele, fresh from ocean,
Rising with her tiara of proud towers
At airy distance, with majestic motion,
A ruler of the waters and their powers:
And such she was; her daughters had their dowers
From spoils of nations, and the exhaustless East
Pour'd in her lap all gems in sparkling showers.
In purple was she rob'd, and of her feast
Monarchs partook, and deem'd their dignity increas'd.

In Venice Tasso's echoes are no more,
And silent rows the songless gondolier;
Her palaces are crumbling to the shore,
And music meets not always now the ear:
Those days are gone—but Beauty still is here.
States fall, arts fade—but Nature doth not die,
Nor yet forget how Venice once was dear,
The pleasant place of all festivity,
The revel of the earth, the masque of Italy!

—GEORGE GORDON, LORD BYRON,
    *Childe Harold's Pilgrimage: Canto the Fourth*

# Death in the Floating City

# 1

"I'd expected jewel encrusted, not encased in a layer of dried blood." Almost cringing, I fingered the slim medieval dagger that felt heavier in my hands than its size suggested.

Tourists come to Venice, the city Petrarch called *mundus alter,* "another world," to take in the opulent beauty of the floating city's palaces, the soft colors and vibrant gold of St. Mark's Basilica, and the rich elegance of Titian's paintings. My trip, however, came without the prospect of such pleasant things. I was standing in a dark, musty palazzo with my childhood nemesis glowering over my shoulder as I inspected the knife an intruder had used to kill her father-in-law. An unpleasant sensation prickled up my neck as I stared down. Instruments of murder are not something with which a lady contends on a daily basis. Particularly not one still bearing evidence of its evil use.

"The police returned it to me in just that condition," Emma Callum said, wrinkling her nose. "I wasn't about to touch it. And the servants point-blank refused to clean it. I'd fire the lot of them if my Italian were better."

I liked to believe the majority of my fellow countrymen were excellent travelers abroad. Credits to the empire. An Englishman ought to conduct himself in a manner more likely to draw admiration than scorn, and should use his explorations of the world as an opportunity to expand his mind and improve his character. Emma showed no sign of such aspirations, a condition unusual in someone who has chosen to go beyond simple tourist and embrace the life of an expat. Then again, Emma had lived in Italy for three years without bothering even to learn the language.

My husband took the knife from my hand and studied it before laying it on a table. We'd been married just over two years, and Colin Hargreaves still took my breath away every time I looked at his preternaturally handsome face. Early on in our acquaintance (even before I'd abandoned my erroneous suspicion that he'd murdered my first husband—but that's another story altogether), I'd decided his perfectly chiseled features looked as if Praxiteles, my favorite ancient Greek artist, had sculpted them. His dark eyes and darker wavy hair lent him a romantic air that would set Mr. Darcy to permanent brooding and send Heathcliff stalking across the moors, never to return. No man, fictional or real, could compare.

Our hostess, however, was an entirely different matter. One might, perhaps, compare Emma to Miss Bingley or Mrs. Dashwood, but she did not quite reach the level of a great villain of literature. Still, nothing short of murder could have induced me to renew my acquaintance with Emma. We had never been close, and it was unlikely this would ever change. Put simply, she despised me, and I'm ashamed to admit I returned the feeling. When we were six years old, she destroyed my favorite doll, smashing its porcelain face with her boot. She scooped up the pitiful remains of the toy my father had specially brought for me from Paris and ran downstairs from the nursery to the conservatory where our mothers were having tea.

I will never forget the way the conservatory looked that day, the way the sunlight filtered through the leaves of my mother's precious lemon trees, and the scent of bright lilies, which forever after would seem to me heavy and cloying. Emma held out her bounty, her eyes wide with horror, and spoke, her voice trembling.

"Look at the terrible thing Emily has done," she said. From where she conjured her tears, I know not, but her voice grew even more pathetic as she continued. "I told her the dolly was pretty, but she insisted she wanted one with better curls. So she stepped on her. Crushed her head in with her foot and said now she knew she'd get a new one."

"Did she?" My mother's face was inscrutable, but I knew the trouble I was in for.

"It doesn't seem right," Emma said. "To destroy something only to be rewarded."

"I can assure you, Emma, that will not happen."

When I woke up the next morning, all my remaining dolls had disappeared from the nursery, and there was never another one seen in the house.

I knew better than to tattle and didn't even try to defend myself. Any attempt to do so would have been met with even more trouble. Emma and I continued to be thrown together throughout childhood due to our mothers' friendship, but I refused to engage in any but the most basic interaction with her. She did not improve with age. As a debutante, she barraged with attention any gentleman who showed even the slightest interest in me, culminating with a clumsy attempt to wrangle Philip, the Viscount Ashton and at the time my soon-to-be-fiancé, away from me.

It was unlikely our acquaintance would ever grow into a real friendship.

Now Emma needed me, and I was not about to walk away from her, despite our past. Her father-in-law had been murdered, and her husband had disappeared shortly thereafter, an act that, so far as the authorities were concerned, proved his guilt. She sent for me, begging for help. This, in itself, was proof of how desperate she was feeling.

Seeking our assistance was no rash act on Emma's part. My husband, an agent of the Crown, had a reputation for his ability to crack any investigation with his trademark discretion. And I, if I may be so bold as to give myself such a compliment, had proven my own mettle after successfully apprehending six notorious murderers. As a result, the day after reading her panicked wire, my husband and I traveled to Venice and, almost immediately upon our arrival, climbed into a boat and glided out of the slim canal that skimmed the side of the Hotel Danieli. The gondolier rowed us under a single bridge and into the lagoon before turning into the Grand Canal. Sunlight poured around us, its reflection dancing over the ornate facades of the buildings that rose, majestic, straight from the water. We passed the domed church of Santa Maria della Salute, built in the seventeenth century to give thanks for the end of the plague that had killed upwards of a hundred thousand people in the city, and we crossed under the Ponte della Carita, to my mind the ugliest bridge in the city. It was made from iron, did not have a graceful arching form like the famous stone bridges prevalent throughout Venice, and had been placed too low over the water, making it difficult for gondoliers during high tide. Around us, the canal was crowded with boats, the only method of transport in a place with no streets. I'd already decided I didn't miss them. I much preferred the sleek gondolas, with their singing boatmen, to the clatter of horse and carriage.

On both sides of us, glorious palazzi lined the water. Although built with precision, they had succumbed to centuries of shifting waters that left their facades with a pervasive asymmetry. This did not detract from their beauty. It only enhanced the feeling that one was gliding through something out of a dream.

As the elegant stone arches of the Rialto Bridge came into view, the gondolier steered us to the side of the canal and slowed to a stop in front of an imposing fourteenth-century palazzo, seat of the Barozzi family and Emma's marital home. I nearly lost my balance as I stepped out of the gondola onto the slippery marble pavement at the water entrance. My shaky legs told me I was nervous to meet my old rival.

A sinewy man opened a low wooden door and ushered us inside. "Signor Hargreaves?"

Colin nodded.

"*Buongiorno.* Signora Barozzi is expecting you."

Although Emma's husband bore the title *conte* even before his father's death (it was given as a courtesy to all of a count's sons), no one in Italy used the term in direct address. Emma, who had made much out of becoming a contessa—always using her title when signing letters and insisting that her parents' servants address her as such when she visited England—must be disappointed to be referred to as *signora.*

We walked along a dark corridor and up a flight of marble stairs into a dim room, the *portego,* which ran the entire length of the house. At one end was the Barozzi family *restelliera,* a display of swords, scimitars, spears, shields, and banners hanging on the wall, below which stood two suits of fifteenth-century armor. At the other, large trefoil windows looked onto the canal, the light pouring through them providing the only illumination in the room. Neither of the large lanterns hanging above us was lit. Portraits of the Barozzi ancestors, in dire need of restoration and cleaning, lined the remaining walls, staring down as if to assert the family's noble roots. The fresco covering the tall ceiling was showing signs of decay—the paint had started to peel—and the bits of terrazzo floor that peeked beyond the edges of a threadbare Oriental carpet had lost their shine. Eloping might not have served Emma quite so well as she had hoped.

Some years back, at the insistence of her parents, Emma had accepted the proposal of the younger son of a minor English nobleman. It had appeared, after several unsuccessful seasons, to be her only hope for marriage. She had resisted the gentleman's affection for months, and we'd all believed she'd done so because she harbored higher aspirations. Who could have guessed that all along the dashing Conte Barozzi had been wooing her from afar and that they had plotted their elopement almost from the time they'd met in a London ballroom?

After their secret marriage, Emma and her new husband fled to the conte's home in Venice, scandalizing the *ton*, everyone fashionable in society. Her family stood by her, and I'd heard rumors that her father, ever devoted to his difficult daughter, continued to offer her financial support. This gossip led in turn to stories about the conte's lack of fortune. But, as is often the case, trading cash for a title was not considered a bad bargain. Most people agreed the new contessa had done well for herself.

Emma rose from a seat near the windows and crossed the room to greet us. The bright yellow satin of her gown suggested time in Italy hadn't altered her taste in fashion. Garish had always been her signature. She was as skinny and angular as ever, all hard bones and frown lines. I pushed unkind thoughts out of my head, displeased that old habits had got the better of me. I was prepared to let go the troubles of the past. Emma and I were no longer sparring schoolgirls or rival debutantes. I was here to help her.

She did not meet my eyes but focused on Colin instead. My heartbeat quickened as I wondered if she would launch straight into her usual flirtatious ways or if marriage had tempered her.

"Darling Hargreaves," she said, holding a hand out to him. "It's so good of you to come. Both of you." She made a point of looking away from me. "I know I do not deserve your kindness."

"Think nothing of it," I said, feeling an unfamiliar warmth towards her. "It's time we move beyond our differences. We're not children anymore."

"Thank you, Emily," she said. "I simply had no one else to turn to. I suppose that ought not surprise me. After all, what lady of my rank would associate with persons who investigate crimes? That I know even one is astonishing. Two, if we count your charming husband."

She winked at him.

I pressed my lips together hard. "Emma, we need to know exactly what happened the night of your father-in-law's death." Exchanging social niceties with Emma was far less pleasant than thinking about murder.

"I had no idea anything out of the ordinary had occurred until the following morning," she said. "I'd seen Signor Barozzi before I retired to my room and he was in perfect health. The next morning, our steward informed us that he was dead. I know you'd much prefer it if I could give you some sort of juicy clue as to what happened, but I can't. I do hope having the murder weapon helps."

I took the slim dagger back into my hands. Its blade was eight inches long, and precious stones—diamonds, emeralds, rubies, and sapphires—encrusted its hilt.

"It belonged to my husband's mother," Emma said. "She kept it next to her bed."

"For protection, or just because she liked the way it looked?" I asked.

"Protection. It's an old family habit," Emma said. "You know how these Italians can be. Very passionate and very dramatic. Not at all like we English. It's quite alarming."

"Was anything else in her room disturbed?" I asked.

"I can't really say." Emma clasped her hands and looked down. "My father-in-law hasn't let anyone into her room since she died more than a dozen years ago."

"No one was allowed in the room?" Colin asked. "Not even servants to keep it clean?"

"No," Emma said. "He couldn't bear to have anyone touch her things. He dusted them himself and even went so far as to wash the floors."

"Have you gone into her room since the night he died?" I asked.

"I did, just to see it," Emma said. "Perhaps it sounds callous after having lost a family member, but I admit I was curious."

"If no one has been in the room for so many years, how can you be certain the knife came from there?" Colin asked.

"Paolo—my husband—recognized it."

"May we see the room?" I asked.

"If you wish," Emma said, "but you won't find anything of interest."

We followed her into an ornately decorated room where the frescoes on the ceiling were in slightly better condition than those I'd seen in the rest of the house. The furniture, some of which could have been original to the palazzo, was fashioned from heavy, dark wood. The bed was enormous, with a canopy high above it and long velvet drapes pulled to enclose it on three sides. Through the fourth side, where the curtain had been drawn, we could see the bedclothes of fine linen, still rumpled as if the bed's occupant were in the next room taking breakfast. There was still a slight depression on the pillow where Signora

Barozzi's head had rested on the night of her death. My skin prickled at the sight.

A quick search of the room yielded nothing of interest to our current case. Colin checked each of the windows and then asked Emma to show us where her father-in-law's body had been found.

"It was here." She had taken us back to the *portego* and pointed to a spot on the floor. "We believe his assailant entered the room through the window just above."

"Is it generally kept open at night?" I asked.

"No, but it was open when the servants found him. It had been shut the night before."

"It's possible the conte opened it himself," I said, pulling a notebook out of my reticule and starting to scribble in it. "Of course, that doesn't preclude the possibility someone else did."

Colin peered out the window. "It's a long way down," he said. "Someone climbing up from canal level surely would have been noticed, either by neighbors or boaters."

"The police looked into that," Emma said. "No one came forward to say they'd seen anything unusual, and it would be impossible to know who had been passing by at just the right moment. A hopeless business, really."

"You said in your wire there was a ring found with the body," I said.

"Yes." She pointed to a table on which sat a heavy gold band with a deep red corundum ruby set high in its center. "He was clutching it in his hand."

I took it from her. "It's medieval," I said. "Probably fourteenth or fifteenth century." I moved closer to the window, where the light was brighter, to read the inscription on the band.

*Amor vincit omnia*

"Love conquers all," I said. "A common phrase on poesy rings of the period. Is it a family piece?"

"No," Emma said. "I'm afraid there's not much family jewelry left. The house is expensive to run, and old fortunes . . . well, they don't often last. We don't know where it came from. Paolo didn't recognize it."

"Was anything tampered with in the rest of the house?" Colin asked.

"Nothing was taken," Emma said. "Nothing was disturbed. We all slept through without so much as noticing." Blotchy red streaks colored her face, and I felt a surge of compassion for her.

"Don't blame yourself," I said. "Whoever did this was careful not to wake any of you. We will do everything we can to identify the guilty party and bring him to justice."

"And Paolo?" she asked, her voice small. "He'll come back to me once he's exonerated. I know he will. He's innocent, Emily. He would never have raised a hand to harm his father."

"I believe you." I smiled in as reassuring a manner as possible. I hoped she was right. Her husband had disappeared mere hours after a maid had found his father's body. Why had he fled, without so much as a word to his much-adored wife? Would an innocent man have assumed he'd be implicated in the murder? I surveyed the room and shuddered, feeling suddenly cold, as if an oppressive evil were closing in around me. What secrets did this once-beautiful house hold?

# Un Libro d'Amore
# 1489

*Besina Barozzi always knew she was not among the fortunate—or un-fortunate, depending upon one's perspective—who could rely on beauty. She didn't possess it. It was her mind, not her too-long nose or thin lips, that would have to set her apart from the profusion of stunning girls for which Venice was famous. She might not be strictly any cleverer than her friends, the daughters of other noble families, but her brother, Lorenzo, had made her different, and for that she valued him above all others. He had taught her how to analyze art, how to paint, how to read poetry, and appreciate fine literature. And though she did not know it, he had also schooled her to have a wit as quick as the finest courtesan's.*

*The other girls around her had no interest in such things. They made lace and did needlework. They were pious. They did not aspire to be more than beautiful decorations that adorned their beloved city.*

*Lorenzo had ruined his sister for such simple pursuits.*

*As children, they were inseparable. Their indulgent nurse, half blind and generally good-natured, did not object when they pushed furniture together to form the walls of Constantinople and fought their way over* with wooden swords, or when they donned carnivale masks to act out elaborate pantomimes. Even later, when Lorenzo fell under the tutelage of a series of stern scholars, he managed to furtively slip each book he studied to Besina when he'd finished. His mother nearly caught him once, but he offered her reassurance by telling her the book was not poetry but psalms. As she could not read, she could not argue.

So, because of Lorenzo's influence, Besina Barozzi was in possession of an intellect unlike that of any of her peers on the night Nicolò Vendelino first saw her, at the Palazzo Ducale, in the midst of a party the doge was throwing to mark the wedding of his favorite granddaughter.

Besina was convinced she saw Nicolò first. He was dancing with a girl prettier than anyone else in the room, and Besina might have been jealous had she noticed, but she could see nothing but Nicolò's eyes, their blue brighter than the sky and framed by impossibly long lashes. His eyes locked onto hers as he continued to dance, ignoring his partner. He never missed a step and bowed when the music finished, but he did not divert his gaze from Besina to so much as glance at the beauty before him.

Besina did not know that Nicolò had already seen her, long before she had watched him dance. He had been standing nearby when she entered the room with her parents, and in that moment fell in love with her. It was her eyes, he said later, full of life and intelligence and curiosity, that won his heart, just as his eyes had won hers. As soon as she had passed from his line of vision, he had rushed from the glittering reception to the doge's chapel of San Marco, where he fell to his knees in front of the altar built to house the sacred body of the saint, raised his eyes to the glittering mosaics on the ceiling, and prayed she would love him as fervently as he already loved her. He didn't care that the Barozzis were his family's enemies, the feud going so far back that no one bothered any longer to discuss its initial cause. All that mattered now was to know that Vendelinos hated Barozzis and always would, but Nicolò was young *enough to think this wouldn't matter. His parents had indulged him, their long-awaited son, almost from the moment of his birth. And Nicolò knew one other thing. The Barozzis were rich.*

*Money, Nicolò believed, had the power to eradicate any feud.*

# 2

It took Colin and me most of the afternoon to thoroughly search for clues in the rest of Ca' Barozzi. The *portego* and the bedrooms currently in use by the family were in somewhat better shape than the rest of the palazzo, but their condition still confirmed what Emma had told us about the family finances. This was not the lap of luxury. The rest was sparsely, if at all, furnished, and many of the walls bore darker spots where paintings, now sold, had once hung. Current shabbiness aside, there was plenty of evidence to suggest the building must have once been spectacular. The terrazzo floors, when smooth and polished, would have glistened. The tapestries and silk that hung on the walls were of fine quality but couldn't be expected to last forever without care and restoration. The bits of medieval frescoes remaining on the ceilings all but broke my heart. They once would have been spectacular. Now they were all but lost.

Beyond observations about the house, however, our search turned up nothing of obvious use to the case.

"Divide and conquer the work before us?" Colin asked after we'd returned to the *portego*. Emma had abandoned us to lean out the open window and wave at a group of English tourists who were passing below, strewing colorful flowers into the canal and shouting wine-fueled greetings as they floated along the water. Her reaction to both her father-in-law's death and her husband's disappearance was increasingly difficult to gauge. She had seemed rattled by the murder and upset that Paolo was gone, but now she was laughing and gay.

"You speak to the police," I said. "I'll start digging for information about the ring. We can meet back at the Danieli."

He tilted his head to mine, our foreheads almost bumping. "What about Emma? Will she assist you?"

"Unless you're keen on taking her with you to the police," I said. "I can keep her with me, although suggesting she'll assist might be wildly optimistic."

He glanced at our hostess and, seeing her attention was still firmly focused outside, brought his hand gently to the back of my neck, sending a most delicious sensation through my body. "Not keen in the least. It's funny that two ladies with such similar names should have such wholly different characters. No one would ever mistake Emma for Emily or vice versa. I shall leave her to you," he said. He shot a quick good-bye to Emma, who pulled herself in from the window in time to have him kiss her hand before he exited the room.

"You're not interested in talking to the police?" Emma asked me once he'd gone.

"I'm more interested in the ring," I said. "You're quite sure no one in the house has seen it before?"

"Absolutely certain," she said.

"All the portraits in the *portego* are of men," I said. "They must have had wives. Surely Titian would have wanted to paint them. I noticed more paintings in another room when we were en route to your mother-in-law's bedchamber. Could you take me there?"

"The ladies are in the *camera d'oro*," Emma said. "It was the old conte's favorite place in the house. Why didn't you look when you were there before?"

"Before, Emma, we were doing a general search, wanting to keep our minds open to find anything that might be pertinent. Now I'm focusing on something specific."

Without further comment, she led me to a room off the *portego*, a chamber smaller than the one we'd just left but still of decent proportions, its walls covered in leather paneling that had once been decorated with gold leaf. Only remnants of it remained, but enough to give the room an opulence distinctly Venetian.

"The room was originally full of mirrors," Emma said, "and the most ghastly furniture you've ever seen. I'll never understand the Venetians. They're prone to such excess."

"They seem a delightful people to me," I said. "I've never been so immediately taken with a city."

"You don't have to live here. They all despise me."

She hadn't learned the language and, so far as I could tell, had made no attempt to embrace the culture. Had she done anything to endear herself to her new neighbors? Now was not the time to criticize her for any perceived failings. I studied the room. Instead of mirrors, portraits of varying size now hung at regular intervals, four high, throughout the room. I studied the ring, then held it out to Emma. "Look at each painting and see if you can find it."

We started next to each other at the back of the room and moved portrait by portrait, Emma going clockwise and I anticlockwise, so we would meet at the opposite end. The Barozzi women, at least the thirty-three I studied, were not a particularly attractive lot. The only ones whose faces weren't dominated by extremely long noses were those who had married into the family. The opulence of their jewels and the sumptuous fabrics of their gowns were indicative of the family's former wealth: crimson silk, gold trim, elaborate embroidery, heavy pearls, enormous rubies, and deep sapphires.

None of them was wearing the ring in question.

"She was the wife of a doge," Emma said, motioning to the portrait in front of her. "The Barozzis were quite an influential family in their day. Pity the money's gone now."

"You have the house."

Emma shrugged. "I don't know that it would be possible to find a buyer brave enough to take on the repairs needed to keep Ca' Barozzi from crumbling."

"You have the paintings."

"The good ones were sold years ago. There's neither Titian nor Bellini among them now," she said. "So what do we do next? Search more portraits?"

"No. It's time to speak to a historian."

.　　.　　.

I did not expect Emma would be able to direct me to anyone useful. Historians, I imagined, would be even less likely to win the acquaintance of a *lady of her status* than are investigators of murders. However, I didn't need Emma's help in the matter. A letter from a well-respected historian of Renaissance Venice who had recently retired from the Sorbonne had been waiting for us when we arrived at the Danieli. The man, Signor Caravello, had read about the case in the paper and was especially interested in the ring that had been found on Signor Barozzi's body—a detail Colin wished the police had kept from the public but that now could prove to benefit us. Shortly thereafter, a second article ran, one in which Emma bragged that one of Queen Victoria's favorite agents (she mentioned Colin by name but neglected to include me) was coming to Venice to assist in the investigation. Signor Caravello found out where we were staying and left a note offering to help us in any way he could.

Emma had no interest in coming along but directed a servant to hail a gondola for me. I gave the gondolier the address, wishing I could have simply walked to it. But the labyrinth pavements that cut through the city in seemingly random directions would require better navigational abilities than I currently possessed, and I had no time for getting lost.

It took nearly half an hour by boat to reach Signor Caravello. I had expected to be let off at a house, but the boat stopped in front of a small set of steps rising to meet the pavement next to the canal. The gondolier pointed me to a shop a short walk from where we stood. I thanked him and asked him to wait for me.

The canal was narrow, no more than six feet across. On one side, the buildings plunged straight down into it. On the other, where I had disembarked, a *calle* ran along a row of tidy-looking shops. Pleasant smells of fresh bread wafted from the door of a bakery, next to which stood a butcher. Farther along were a cobbler and a greengrocer, and just past them was Signor Caravello's bookshop. The front window was loaded with pile upon pile of leather-bound volumes, some new, some antique. The display was not quite so neat as those in neighboring windows, but it did suggest an admirable passion for reading. I opened the door. A bell tinkled, and I walked into the store, almost tripping over an enormous globe near the entrance.

"What a spectacular piece!" I said to no one in particular, unable to contain my enthusiasm.

"The globe?" A young woman was sitting on a tall stool behind a well-worn wooden counter. "Everyone loves it. It's ridiculously old. Fifteenth century."

"I've always loved antique globes," I said, bending over to examine the maps drawn on its surface. "I find them desperately romantic. They conjure up visions of explorers setting off in search of exotic riches in the New World. Can you imagine undertaking such a voyage?" I traced the lines marking latitude and longitude on the perfect sphere and pushed gently, feeling the surface brush beneath my fingertips. "I simply have to spin them. They lure me in and I'm incapable of resisting."

"I've never given that globe much thought beyond having to dust it. Perhaps I should reconsider. In the meantime, as I'm not working today, I'll fetch my father for you. Papà! Customer!" she called, turning her head to the back of the shop and raising her voice. "She's taken with your globe, so you're bound to like her." She returned her attention to the novel she held. Mary Elizabeth Braddon's *The Venetians*.

"I adored that book," I said in what could generously be described as passable Italian. "Braddon is my ultimate guilty pleasure. Although perhaps I shouldn't admit that before you give me your opinion of the story."

"It's not her best," the girl answered in flawless English. "*Lady Audley's Secret* was much better."

"My absolute favorite." I extended a hand to her. "I'm Lady Emily Hargreaves. It's a delight to make your acquaintance."

"Donata Caravello," she said, an elegant smile escaping her full lips as she raised her voice. "I'm always pleased to meet someone else who appreciates Braddon."

"I've come in search of Signor Caravello," I said. "I presume he's your father? He sent a note to my husband offering to help us learn more about a medieval ring currently in our possession."

"Of course," she said. "I remember him writing to you. His English isn't quite so good as mine, and he asked me to check the letter for him."

"Rot, total rot." An elderly, slightly stooped man popped his head through a doorway in the back of the store, just in view of us. He had started shaking his head the moment he spotted the book in his daughter's hand. "I won't have anything by that Braddon woman in my shop."

"Papà, don't be an old bore," Donata said. "This is Lady Emily, who's come about the ring. You remember the ring?"

"Ring? Oh yes, quite right." He shook my hand by way of introduction. "You don't approve of what my daughter is reading, do you? I thought I overheard some very unwelcome words coming from your mouth as I entered the room." There was too much jovial warmth in his voice for me to take even the slightest offense at his words.

"I do hope you'll overlook my fondness for sensational literature long enough to help me," I said.

"So long as you stop calling it literature I'll give you temporary respite." His accent was heavier than the girl's. "But you must promise not to encourage my daughter in her pursuit of mediocrity."

Donata rolled her eyes and closed the book. "No more criticism, Papà."

He threw back his head and winced in mock horror. "You see how she treats me? The disrespect? I fear for the future of my beloved city. How can it survive when our young people have no respect for anyone, even their parents?"

"He's still mourning the end of the Most Serene Republic," Donata said. "Please don't ask his opinion of the unified Italy."

"I shall do all in my power to resist," I said, suppressing a grin. "And you should know, Signor Caravello, I spend much more of my time studying Homer than I do reading sensational novels."

"A fellow scholar? That is more like it," Signor Caravello said. "You know the most ancient Venetians, the Veneti, claimed to be descended from Antenor, who they said brought them from the ruins of Troy. The citizens of Padua try to make similar claims, but we Venetians have never been put off by accusations that we are stealing from someone else's heritage."

"I find I like Venice more and more," I said, grinning.

"So what can I do to assist you, signora?"

"It's Lady Hargreaves, Papà."

The old man shrugged. "Forgive me."

"That's entirely unnecessary, I assure you. I'm Lady Emily but also Mrs. Hargreaves, and I think *signora* sounds much nicer than either," I said. I pulled the ruby ring off my hand (wearing it had seemed the safest method of carrying it while in a boat) and handed it to him. "I'm interested in what you can tell me about this. It's the ring in question."

"Yes, yes. I was surprised to read about it in the papers." He took a magnifying glass off the counter and held the gold band in a trembling hand. "It's Venetian. There's a mark inside identifying it as such. Mid-fifteenth century, I'd say. A popular sort of design, the kind of thing given by lovers to one another, though it was more common for the phrases to be written in French than Latin."

"Is there any way to identify the owner?" I asked.

"Ordinarily not, but in this case, possibly," he said, tipping the magnifying glass in my direction and motioning for me to come closer. "*N.V.–B.B.* Do you see it inside?"

"Yes," I said. The tiny, worn letters set next to the goldsmith's mark were almost imperceptible. I'd spotted no hint of them when I'd looked with my naked eye at Ca' Barozzi.

"N.V. undoubtedly gave it to B.B," Donata said, "but that's not much help, is it?"

"A little, maybe," I said. "This was found by the Barozzi family. B.B. might have been one of their ancestors, but I've got no idea who N.V. could be."

"The Barozzis are an old, noble family," Signor Caravello said. "I'd assume N.V. was of equal status, and probably a man."

"Ladies can't give jewelry?" Donata asked, her dark eyes flashing.

"They can and they did," her father said, "and a ring of this style would have been worn either by a man or a woman. However, it's unlikely a man could have fit his finger into a band that's snug on Signora Hargreaves's hand." He winked at me as he said my name.

"You're right," I said. "I can comb the Barozzi family records for someone with the initials B.B., but have you any suggestions as to where I might start searching for N.V.?"

"*Le Libro d'Oro,*" Signor Caravello said. "It is the book that contains the names of all the noble families of Venice. You can find it in the city archives at the Doge's Palace. You would have to pick a year, though."

"Papà, don't you think it would be too hard?" Donata asked. "To go through all those volumes?"

"I'm not easily daunted," I said.

Donata let out a long breath and smiled. "I am impressed."

"Mid-fifteenth century, you said, yes?" I asked, turning back to her father.

He nodded.

"I'll start with 1450," I said.

"You won't be able to just barge in and demand the book," Signor

Caravello said. "Donata, go with her. I will write a letter instructing that you be admitted."

"Papà can do whatever he wants in Venice," Donata said.

"I'm most grateful," I said.

"It is my pleasure to offer whatever meager assistance I can," he said. "It is a sad thing for such a beautiful piece to wind up in the hand of a brutally murdered man. So unfortunate. Signor Barozzi was a good soul."

"Did you know him?" I asked.

"Our paths crossed on occasion," he said. "I helped him to study the illuminated manuscripts in his family's collection. A magnificent lot. I do hope his son holds on to it."

"I'm sure he will," I said with a firm smile.

"I cannot have you start on illuminated manuscripts, Papà. The archives will close soon," Donata said. "We must be off." She kissed him on both cheeks and embraced him before pinning a once elegant but now out-of-fashion hat onto her head. A broad smile on her pretty face, she looped her arm through mine. "I take it that's your gondola waiting at the dock?"

"It is," I said.

"What a luxury," she said. "To have a gondolier at your disposal. We have a small boat, but Papà is too old now to row it, so the task falls to me. It does not make for shoulders that look elegant in a ball gown."

"I imagine not," I said. Donata may have believed her shoulders to be less than elegant, but no one would have considered her anything short of stunningly attractive. She was not delicate, but her curvy figure, mesmerizing eyes, and plump red lips more than made up for that.

"There's no easier way to get around the city," she said. "It's more than a hundred separate islands, and the canals make for smoother transit than bridges."

"Worth rowing, then," I said. "How long have you been back in Venice? I understand you were away for some years in Paris. Is that correct?"

"Yes," she said. "My father was a professor at the Sorbonne. We returned six months ago."

"I adore Paris. But it must have been hard to be away from your friends for so long."

"Not really." She fluffed the cushion on the seat and leaned back, smiling. "It's always been the two of us, you see. My mother died when I was born, and Papà quite depends upon me. I've not had much time for friends, at least not friends of my own. Still, it's not been much of a hardship. Papà is always surrounded by the most fascinating intellectuals, and I learned early on to prefer their company to that of fashionable ladies my own age."

"It sounds like a fortunate upbringing."

"It was," she said. "I wouldn't trade it for anything."

Our gondolier pushed against the wall of a building with his strong leg. "Ordinarily I prefer to walk when I come to a new city," I said. "I find it's the best way to get to know a place, but I like the idea of rowing myself."

"Rowing is exhausting," Donata said. "You'd be better off walking if you're bent on self-navigation."

"I fear I would get hopelessly lost in the tangle," I said, "and one would have to be devoid of all romance to object to going anywhere by gondola. Even so, I would very much like to learn how to navigate this city on foot."

"That, signora, would take a lifetime to accomplish." She smiled. "How long do you plan to stay in Venice?"

# Un Libro d'Amore

# ii

"Dance with me?" Nicolò took Besina's hand without giving her a chance to answer. She blushed and looked down but made no attempt to disguise her smile. The music was a padovana, its slow tempo suited for speaking to one's partner, but Nicolò and Besina remained silent, lost in each other's eyes, delighted to feel their hands together.

The dance finished, and Nicolò led Besina from the floor.

"Do you intend to talk to me?" she asked. "To tell me your name? To ask mine?"

"I know yours already," he said and suddenly found himself without words to continue.

"But I, kind sir, do not know yours."

"I am Nicolò Vendelino, and from this moment I pledge to love you for eternity." He half expected her to laugh or send him away.

Besina did neither of the things he feared.

"I was aware of that the instant I looked in your eyes," she said, "and I knew my heart would forever be yours."

*Lorenzo watched from across the room, uneasy to see his sister flirting with a family enemy. He frowned, his eyebrows twitching, and wondered if he should interfere. Family honor required that he stop any Vendelino from trifling with any Barozzi lady. But nothing in Nicolò's face suggested anything but emotions of the gravest nature. He appeared to have no motive beyond earnest sincerity, which concerned Lorenzo all the more.*

*He looked around for his father, unsure of what he should do, but could not locate him in the crowded room. When he turned back to his sister, she was gone. Along with Nicolò Vendelino.*

*Nicolò had taken Besina's hand and pulled her into the loggia overlooking the lagoon, but the space was already crowded with others looking for privacy. There were many couples hoping to steal a romantic moment, but even more groups of men engaged in grave discussions of business.*

*"Come," he whispered to Besina. "This is not private enough." With swift and elegant speed, they descended a staircase, left the palace, and crossed in front of San Marco, the doge's chapel.*

*"It's as if we've escaped some unimaginable but dreadful fate," Besina said, laughing as she struggled to catch her breath. "Silly, don't you think? But I feel invigorated."*

*The bells of the clock of St. Alipio rang, marking the quarter hour. The sound seemed to vibrate from the walls of the buildings that lined the long square, and it startled Besina. For an instant, she wondered about the path on which she was about to embark. It wasn't yet too late to stop, but it would be soon. She imagined her parents, her brother, and the rest of her family standing before her. And then she looked back into Nicolò's eyes and laughed more.*

*She never again considered stopping.*

*She took his hand and pulled him to stand with her under the arch nearest to them. She leaned against its pillar, inside the passageway that* ran the length of the square, hiding herself from the view of anyone who'd come to stand in front of San Marco. She raised her hand to Nicolò's cheek but did not touch it.

"Love in whom I hope and desire,/Has given me lovely you as my prize," she recited, quoting the poet Pier delle Vigne.

Nicolò could feel warmth emanating from her palm onto his face. His breathing quickened. "You woo me with the poetry of the damned?"

"You're a student of Dante?" she asked.

"You know the Inferno?"

"Love, which quickly arrests the gentle heart,/Seized him with my beautiful form/That was taken from me, in a manner which still grieves me./Love, which pardons no beloved from loving,/Took me so strongly with delight in him/That, as you see, it still abandons me not." She did not take her eyes from his as she spoke.

"I loved you when first I saw you," Nicolò said. "Now I know you will be the companion not only of my heart but of my soul. From you I must never be parted."

With that, he clasped his fingers around her hand, guiding her arm around his neck as he brought his lips to hers.

Never was there a kiss more ripe with innocence.

# 3

The instant I opened the enormous and dusty volume of the *Libro d'Oro* handed to me by a clerk in the city archives, I realized I'd taken on a task of only somewhat less than Herculean proportion. Donata's warning had not been for nothing, and the amusement with which the clerk met my request should perhaps have given me pause. The *Libro d'Oro* had profound significance in Renaissance Venice. Only those whose family names were listed in it could serve in the republic's government. It had started, in the early days, with a manageable group of families, the equivalent, I suppose, of the English aristocracy. Like the English aristocracy, it had expanded over the years as the number of influential and wealthy families in the city ballooned. Eventually, the *Libro d'Oro* had been closed to further additions.

The volumes through those we planned to search contained hundreds of names of every child born to every noble family. Donata threw up her hands and shook her head, a wide grin across her face. "All these children! Our work is before us, eh?" She barked something in Italian spoken too quickly for me to understand, and the clerk scurried off, returning with another volume that he placed on the table in front of her. "I'm taking December 1450. You have April, no?"

I nodded. "These are noble families, correct?" I asked her.

"*Sì*," she said.

"But they don't have titles."

"No. The Venetian republic had no interest in such things. If you did come across a titled person in this period, he would no doubt have been a foreigner. Even now, no one goes by titles."

Three hours later, we'd come up with six potential families. None of the entries showed a son whose given name began with *N* being born in the volumes we'd perused, but we were taking a wild stab at guessing dates. That did not concern me. I hadn't expected the identity of N.V. to leap out at us. All I'd hoped was to put together a list of the families whose name began with *V* present in the city during the time.

"We should turn to marriage records next," Donata said. "Find a couple with the right initials."

"That might be too difficult," I said. "Looking up marriage records would be good, but we don't know what year we need, and I imagine not knowing the groom's surname would be a considerable obstacle. I think we should focus on two things now. First, figuring out who B.B. is. Second, if that doesn't immediately reveal the identity of N.V., we can turn to the families whose surnames we've identified."

"So where to now?" she asked.

"Ca' Barozzi."

·   ·   ·

Emma knew almost nothing about her husband's family history but directed us to follow her to the library. Its windows overlooked a small courtyard, the only sort of garden one might have in Venice. This one

29

was not the haven of cool greens and bright petals one would hope to find in such a space. It was a shambles. Weeds choked the flowerbeds, climbing vines had lost all sense of direction, and the potted orange trees looked in dire need of water.

Donata sighed. "Beautiful." I wasn't sure if she was being facetious about the view outside or genuinely complimenting the lengths of shelves lining the walls of the room.

"What used to be in here?" I asked Emma, pointing to an almost empty glass display case. Emma had been leaning against it when Colin and I had searched the room earlier. I had glanced at it and seen the handful of glass animals it contained, but now closer examination revealed its velvet lining had faded around shapes distinctly like those of books.

"A collection of illuminated manuscripts," Emma said. "They're quite valuable."

They must have been the ones to which Signor Caravello had referred. "Why are they gone?" I asked.

"Mmmmm?" she replied, playing with the clasp of the elaborately engraved gold bracelet that hung around her wrist.

I wanted to shake her and force her to pay attention. "What happened to them?"

"It appears Paolo thought it best to keep them close, so he took them when he left," she said. "They've been handed down in the family since the fifteenth or sixteenth century or something. I'm not sure. Very rare, of course, and worth a small fortune because of the quality of the drawings. His father refused to sell them at any price. They're quite lovely. All of them done in Venice at a time when printers were taking over from copyists. I gather we're to think printing changed the world. Gutenberg and his press and all that."

"You're certain your husband took them, not the murderer?"

"Yes. One of the maids saw him removing them moments before he disappeared from the house."

"Are the police aware of this?" I asked.

"Yes," Emma said.

"Why did you not see fit to tell me this earlier?" I asked. "Colin and I were in this room only a few hours ago."

"I suppose it didn't occur to me," she said. "I'm not the one who's supposed to have the mind of a detective."

It had been a mistake not to ask about it before. I should have known better than to rely on her to point out pertinent information. "Do you know specifically what books they were?"

"Oh, yes," she said. "They were all done by the same man. Can't say I remember his name. Some Venetian monk. There's a Bible, of course, two Books of Hours, some extremely tedious Latin poetry—I assume it's tedious. It's Latin, after all. Dante's *Divine Comedy* and a collection of psalms. The drawings in all of them are beautiful."

"Why would Paolo have thought there was a pressing need right now to keep them safe?" I asked.

"I don't know," Emma said, "but I can't think of any other reason he would have wanted to tote them around."

"You don't think he would have sold them?" Donata asked.

"Never," Emma said. "He respected his father too much to do that. He knew how much the old man loved them."

"We shall discuss this further after I've spoken to my husband," I said, hoping Colin would have learned more from the police. I told Emma about the initials on the ring. "I chose to go to the city archives before returning here, as I knew they were closing soon, and I have identified several possibilities as to the family name of N.V. Now we need to see if we can figure out who B.B. was. I'm hoping that may prove easier. She may, after all, be a Barozzi."

"Whatever you think," Emma said. Donata looked at her with hard eyes. "There's a large book on that table." She nodded in its general direction. "It's a record of family births and deaths."

Although its dimensions were larger than those of the *Libro d'Oro*, this volume was considerably less daunting. It took me little more than a quarter of an hour to page through the records of the fifteenth century. The handwriting was difficult, but not impossible, to decipher. When I was finished, I considered myself fortunate the Barozzis hadn't had more of a penchant for alliteration. Only one entry had the initials B.B., that for a baby girl who had been born in 1474 and was called Besina.

·   ·   ·

It troubled me that Emma had failed to mention the missing books to us when Colin and I had been in the library earlier. It troubled me, too, that I had not taken better care at that time. Colin couldn't be held accountable. He wasn't the one who had inspected the case.

Donata, perhaps sensing my tense mood, suggested that we walk back to the Danieli. "You want to learn the city, yes?" she asked. "We should walk. I can show you the way."

The air had turned cooler, but it still had the heavy feeling of a hot summer day, and I welcomed the shade of the narrow passages Donata guided me through. I quickly agreed with my friend that it would take a lifetime to become competent navigating the labyrinthine *calli* of Venice, but I also knew it was a skill I wanted to master. I'd fallen in love with the ethereal beauty of the city. We were still hours from twilight, and yet the light around us seemed to have changed entirely from when we'd entered Ca' Barozzi. The shadows were darker, and

the sun had traded its white hotness for a more tempered gold. V[
like Paris, had a light all of its own.

"In Besina's day, noble ladies would never have walked anywhere," Donata said. "They took private gondolas and usually those with covered cabins so they would not be seen. They wouldn't have had any familiarity with these back streets."

"What about the men?" I asked.

"They, too, relied primarily on gondolas," she said, "but they would sometimes walk, I suppose. They could do what they wanted, just as men do now."

We crossed bridges, traversed narrow passages, basked in the light in large *campi,* and eventually emerged onto the Riva degli Schiavoni, only a short distance from the apartment where Henry James had finished writing *The Portrait of a Lady* more than a decade ago. Donata and I parted at the door after I thanked her for her assistance and sent my regards to her father. She hesitated before leaving me, and I wondered if I should invite her to join us for dinner. But as soon as I opened my mouth, she smiled, waved, and disappeared into the crowd filling the pavement outside the hotel.

"Ah, Signora Hargreaves," the concierge said as I stepped up to his desk. "You are not coming from the water entrance?"

"No," I said, smiling. "I walked. But fear not—I had a most excellent guide. May I have my room key?"

He reached it down from its space on the wall behind the desk. "Your husband returned some time ago and is waiting for you upstairs."

The Danieli was comprised of several palazzi, and our rooms were in the oldest of the group, built in the fourteenth century. I crossed through the ornate lobby with its gleaming terrazzo floors and huge floral arrangements and went up the marble staircase before turning into a corridor whose ancient wooden floors creaked in a most charming manner with nearly every step I took. Colin opened the door to our suite before I could place my key in the lock.

"You weren't despairing, I hope?" I asked, kissing him on both cheeks. "Hadn't begun to wonder if I'd never return?"

"Not in the least," he said. "I was looking out the window and saw you approach. Have you turned Italian? Not that I object to the kisses. I'm only hoping there will be more."

"Fear not," I said. I kissed him firmly on the lips and stepped inside the room. "I've made a new friend and already adore her. You'll have to meet her as soon as can be arranged."

"Caravello was a help, then?" he asked.

"Yes, but it is his daughter, Donata, who will prove the more useful to us."

Colin had flung open our windows and shutters and turned two pale blue silk-covered chairs to face outside. The noise from the wide promenade and the water below filled the room. Gondoliers called to each other, the beautiful tones of their voices evident even when they weren't singing. Tourists prattled, bright with the thrill of being in Venice. The occasional whistle from a steamship blasted in the distance. I loved the bustle and the excitement but was happy to sink, exhausted, into a comfortable seat.

"So," Colin said. "What did you learn since I saw you last?" He moved a small gilded rococo table between our chairs and sat down, a bottle of whisky and two glasses in his hands. He poured—a single finger for me, two for him—and passed me a glass.

"More than I expected to," I said.

He nodded, listening carefully as I recounted for him the details of my afternoon, staying silent until I mentioned the illuminated manuscripts missing from Ca' Barozzi.

"One of them has already been sold," he said. "I wired a number of rare book dealers throughout the Continent to inform them of the theft. The police had alerted their colleagues in other cities to Paolo's disappearance and gave them a description but did not get in touch with bookshops."

"Perhaps because they don't consider it a theft," I suggested. "Doesn't Paolo technically own the books?"

"One would assume so," Colin said, "but I read his father's will. It mentions the manuscript collection separately from the rest of the estate. The conte left it to Emma."

"Emma?" This surprised me. "She doesn't seem to have even the slightest interest in them. Regardless, she's not going to accuse her husband of stealing them."

"No, probably not," he said. "Still, he had no legal right to take them without her permission. Although so far as I know, Emma isn't yet aware of the bequest."

"Which volume did he sell?"

"A small Book of Hours. In Florence, two days ago, which suggests he hasn't traveled too far. The police have their counterparts there watching for anyone matching Paolo's description but have turned up nothing."

"I wouldn't expect them to," I said. "Surely he's moved on by now."

"A reasonable conclusion," Colin said. "One other tidbit from the book dealer. Paolo wasn't alone. There was a Benedictine monk with him."

"A monk?"

Colin drained his glass and set it on the table as a large ferry passed in front of our window, dwarfing everything around it. "He didn't enter the shop. Waited outside. The dealer saw them speaking before and after Paolo came in, and they left the street together. They make a striking pair, the monk in his robes and Paolo nearly a head taller than everyone else around him."

"Is it significant that he's Benedictine?"

"I don't know," he said. "It's possible. The Barozzi manuscripts are all fifteenth and sixteenth century, and there was an important scriptorium in Florence at that time run by Benedictines."

"Perhaps Paolo wanted to know more about the books," I said. "But what? Anything concerning their value he would have learned from the dealer."

"Precisely," Colin said.

"Between the books and the ring, I'm convinced this murder is as rooted in the past as in the present."

"Have you evidence or is this intuition?"

"It's primarily intuition at the moment," I said, "but the fact that I was so readily able to identify the owner of the ring seems to me to be a sign."

"You can't be certain the ring belonged to Besina Barozzi," Colin said. "All you know is that someone who shared her initials owned it at some point in time. It's entirely possible the ring came from someplace far from Venice and was sold to a jeweler who resold it to someone who gave it to a girl whose initials had nothing to do with those engraved inside."

"Possible," I said, "but that would be a rich coincidence. I do, however, take your point and will alert you the instant I have something more solid."

"I would expect nothing less from a lady of your skill."

# Un Libro d'Amore

Things became considerably more difficult for Besina and Nicolò after their magical encounter in the Piazza San Marco. Because of the vendetta between their families, they did not often attend the same social functions, so they could not see each other with the accidental ease so often relied upon by those newly in love. Although the feud was not at the forefront of either family's thoughts—it had been going on too long for that—it was prevalent enough to mean that none of the normal routines of courtship were open to Nicolò. He could not implore Lorenzo to help him press his suit. He could not call at Ca' Barozzi. Most significantly, he could not ask his father to begin marriage negotiations with Signor Barozzi.

Not again, at least.

At twenty, Nicolò was young enough to possess just a lingering modicum of the sort of naïveté that would have been utterly charming in a small boy. He believed his father would listen to reason, would respect love, and would agree that the significant dowry sure to be offered by a family of the Barozzis' wealth would go a long way toward ending any lingering feelings of ill-will harbored by the Vendelinos. He stood, full of hope, before the heavy desk in his father's office on the ground floor of their house, the room from which Signor Vendelino conducted business, where he met with merchants from the East and negotiated prices for their exotic goods. Where Nicolò used to come as a child, watching quietly and hoping to be given a sweet or a trinket from some far-flung land.

At first, it seemed his father wasn't even listening. He didn't look up from his papers until Nicolò revealed the name of his intended bride.

"That's quite enough," his father said, rising from his chair so quickly it toppled over behind him. "If you have an interest in pursuing a career in diplomacy—an avenue I would not recommend for a variety of reasons—trying to forge an alliance between warring families through an undesirable marriage is not the way to begin. We will discuss the subject no further."

"Warring? How are we warring with the Barozzis? I've seen no evidence of enmity beyond the occasional insult shot at them from within the walls of our own house."

"You know nothing about this." His father's voice was low and serious. "Speak about it to no one else, especially your mother. You will not marry a Barozzi. You will not speak to a Barozzi. And you will never, ever mention this again."

# 4

Colin and I were breakfasting on the Danieli's stunning rooftop terrace. The sweeping views of the lagoon below us and San Giorgio Maggiore with its imposing Palladian church across the water were breathtaking. My husband's coffee smelled delicious, but I had never acquired a taste for the bitter libation and was instead drinking a tall, cool glass of peach nectar.

"I would have preferred a full English breakfast," Colin said.

"What has come over you?" I asked. "This persistent jingoism does not become you."

"You know I'm an excellent tourist," he said, "and I have a great appreciation for other cultures. Nevertheless, when I am working, I like the comforts of home. They ground me and help my mind stay focused."

"So you seek out all things English wherever you go?"

"Precisely."

"I require the opposite," I said. "Immersing myself in another world helps me stay open to new ideas and keeps me from searching for the familiar."

"*Buongiorno!*"

I recognized Donata's bright voice as she stood at the entrance to the terrace and waved for her to join us. I had asked her to meet us here, thinking it always a good idea to have a partner-in-sleuthing when one is working in a new city and unable to depend upon one's most capable spouse to always be on hand. Happy though I was to work on my own, I realized it was not always the safest of decisions: A solitary lady can be a target for unwanted attention. Before arriving in Venice, I had assumed Emma would want to accompany me, but she had proven disinterested on that count.

"I was so pleased to get your note. You are kind to invite my help," Donata said, taking a seat as soon as I'd introduced her to Colin. I'd stayed up much of the night going through books about Venetian art and guides to all the museums and galleries in the city, doing what little I could in the hotel to trace possible paths for information about Besina. "My father confirmed your suspicion. He believes there is a portrait of Besina Barozzi in the small museum you mentioned to me." She was eyeing the platter of pastries on our table. I lifted it to her, and she took a jam-filled *cornetto*.

"I'm as keen as the rest of you to see what she looked like," Colin said, "but is it the best use of our time at the moment?"

"Have you a more pressing plan for the day?" I asked. "I don't mean that to be glib. Learning more about Besina may be our best way forward. The ring may be an old family piece that's been out of the Barozzis' possession for so long they didn't recognize it as theirs. Why is *this* what the conte was clutching when he died?"

"Because the murderer gave it to him," Colin said.

"But why that specific ring?" Donata asked.

"It had to signify something," I said. I gave my husband a pointed look. "Before you ask, I have no idea what. It could have something to do with the family finances and why the Barozzis were forced to sell off valuable possessions, but it also could be something particular to Besina."

"It's possible," Colin said.

"Which is why you should begin by speaking with whoever handles the Barozzi finances and why I should find out more about Besina."

"Darling." He reached across the table and squeezed my hand as he flashed a wry smile. "I know how difficult it is for you to leave the enticing world of banks and accountants and ledger books to me. Are you sure you don't mind? As the finances are something into which we must look, I've already made an appointment with the director of the Bank of Venice. I'd so hate to miss it."

"Don't tease," I said. "Your extremely rational nature makes you the perfect choice for analyzing such things. I do better where creativity is required. Besides, I manage all our household accounts. I deserve a break from the tedium."

"You are a most competent manager. If you require a break, you shall have one." He smiled. "I've no doubt you will excel at constructing a full picture of the life of Besina Barozzi. I know I can count on you to abandon the effort if you begin to sense it's not relevant."

"Of course," I said. "I am well aware of the gravity of what we are doing. Our only goal is to discover who killed Emma's father-in-law."

"And making it safe for Paolo to return to his wife," Donata said, her smile almost hesitant. "I'm a romantic."

"I just hope that's a viable end to the story," Colin said. "Do not think me cynical, Donata. I am at least as romantic as you. At this point, though, we have no reason to think Paolo has the slightest interest in returning to his wife."

He rose from the table, kissed me, and took his leave from us, heading for the bank.

•   •   •

Donata and I stopped at Ca' Barozzi to see if Emma would like to accompany us to view Besina's portrait, but she declined our invitation, explaining her morning was already fully booked.

*Booked how?* I wondered. *With something more important than trying to clear her husband's name?* Of course, I was not being fair. Emma had sent for me because she did not know how else to help her husband. That she did not want to include herself in the work at hand ought not to be held against her. I certainly hadn't expected we would become fast friends, brought together by a mutual goal.

Perhaps, though, I had hoped.

I wished I could shake all lingering naïveté from myself.

Our gondola slowed, depositing us at the small building that housed the pet project of an Englishwoman who had left the sceptered isle to take up permanent residence in Venice. She'd founded and abandoned theater companies, acted as patron for any number of artists of modest talent, and, at last, found what she hoped would be her lasting legacy: a museum dedicated to the ladies of her adopted city.

The gallery encompassed the entire ground floor, which would have originally served as warehouse space and offices for the family who lived above. The low beamed ceilings and lack of natural light in the space did little to enhance the displays. Now, paintings covered the walls. They weren't Titians, Carpaccios, or Bellinis, but they were solid, credible works: some portraits, some depictions of the, shall we say, *extravagant* lifestyles of courtesans, and a handful of canvases that had been painted by women. Below them, display cases lined the perimeter of the room. I peered into the one nearest to me and saw a pair of shoes with staggeringly high heels.

"I can't imagine anyone actually wearing them," I said. I'd read about them, the chopines that had been popular with both courtesans and patrician ladies during the Renaissance, but had only seen drawings of the towering platform shoes. Confronted with the ten-inch cork soles in front of me, I gasped. "It would be impossible to balance, let alone walk. Surely they were just . . . ceremonial?"

"Not at all," Donata said. "Servants or ladies-in-waiting would take the arms of the woman wearing them and keep her upright if she required help. They'd go all over the city in them. Wore them to parties."

"It must have made for an inelegant gait."

"To be sure," she said. "At least until the wearer learned to be steady on her feet. But it also made her rise above everyone around her. Imagine being ten—or even twenty—inches taller than the rest of a crowd in the Piazza San Marco."

"I can't imagine it would be worth it," I said. "Although we aren't much better now, are we, with our tight corsets and ridiculously wide sleeves? And I'm not confident there's ever been a fashionable shoe that could be described as comfortable."

I continued my survey of the room. Other cases contained pieces of jewelry, rosaries, prayer books, and miscellaneous articles of clothing. Fascinating though they all were, I kept my attention on the larger paintings, searching for Besina. Donata, however, paused in front of a grouping of miniatures.

"What I would like to find is a portrait of Besina carried by N.V.," she said. "His dearest treasure, with him always."

"You are a romantic," I said and stepped to the next case.

"It infuriates my father," she said, "but there's nothing I desire more than finding perfect love. What could be superior? Not his academic pursuits."

I smiled. Donata looked as if she were designed for love, like a stunning portrait of Venus. I hoped she would find her perfect love, and I was about to say so when I came to a painting whose card read:

*Portrait of Besina Barozzi, 1489*
*Artist Unknown*

Her brown hair, a light chestnut shade with hints of red, was braided and wrapped around the top of her head, accentuating her large forehead. A long, thin nose dominated her narrow face. Her mouth was unremarkable, but her eyes, hazel with bright rings of gold around the pupils, made the portrait come alive. I called for Donata to come look.

"She certainly wasn't a beauty," Donata said.

"Her eyes are stunning."

"This dashes all my fantasies about N.V. carrying a smaller version around. What a travesty."

"That's unfair," I said. "Physical beauty may attract a person initially, but it's hardly the only thing that can take away one's breath."

"Easy words for a woman whose husband is the image of Adonis's better-looking brother." She stepped closer to the painting. "It's not a bad dress." The bodice, a rich wine-colored velvet that neatly complimented the color of Besina's hair, was elaborately embroidered with gold thread.

"I was hoping we'd find some indication of her married name," I said.

"She might not have ever married," Donata said. "Dowries were an expensive business at the time. Families—even the wealthiest ones—often allowed only one of their daughters to wed."

"Conserving their resources?" I asked.

"Precisely." Donata nodded. "The rest of the girls were sent to convents."

"It's always harder for ladies than men, isn't it?"

"In this case, not always," she said. "The men were no better off. They weren't allowed to choose a bride. Marriages were strictly family alliances, and often sons were forced to remain bachelors, with all of the family fortune and influence saved for one chosen daughter and one chosen son."

"Even so, I imagine bachelor life in Venice was far superior to being shipped off to a convent," I said.

"You don't know much about medieval Venetian convents." A sly smile escaped Donata's full lips. "But that's a topic for another day."

"A day to which I will look forward," I said. "In the meantime, we need to learn everything we can about the provenance of this painting." I sought out the woman who sat at the entrance of the museum. She knew very little about the portrait of Besina but asked us to wait while she summoned her supervisor.

Her supervisor, it turned out, was the very Englishwoman who had founded the gallery.

"Yes, Besina," she said, after I'd explained to her what I was hoping to learn. "There's not much to say in terms of the provenance of my painting. I bought it directly from the Barozzis some years back. There is, however, another portrait of the same girl, done when she was a bit older. Are you acquainted with Signora Morosini?"

I admitted I was not.

"It is of no consequence," the woman said. "Write to her at her Brenta estate. That's where the painting is, and that's where the signora can be found in the summer. Her villa is one of the most pleasant places you can find near Venice. I've no doubt she would be pleased to welcome you there. I will give you all the information you need."

.    .    .

After leaving the museum, Donata and I parted ways, promising to rejoin forces when I'd wrangled an invitation to call at the Villa di Tranquillità on the banks of the Brenta River, not far from Venice on the mainland.

The gondola returned me to the Danieli, where I retired to our sitting room to jot down notes from the morning on the page next to the sketch I'd done in the museum of Besina's portrait. That finished, I pulled out a sheet of stationery and penned a note to the owner of the Villa di Tranquillità, hoping my request would not be refused. This was a time when I was grateful for my rank. If it could open doors for me, I would not disparage it, regardless of the inherent unfairness of any system based on hereditary aristocracy. The letter finished, I flipped through my slim leather-bound journal until I found the list of *V* names I'd taken down from the *Libro d'Oro* and went to the lobby to speak to the concierge.

He shook his head as he looked at the names. "Some of these? No problem," he said. "I can easily direct you to the houses. The families would be pleased to receive a caller of your status. The rest? I'm afraid some of them have long since disappeared from the city."

"I suppose I shall have to limit myself to those still here," I said, smiling. "Thank you for your assistance." Armed with calling cards and the gondolier on whom I was coming to rely, I set off to myself to Venetian society.

*     *     *

I knew, of course, Venice was a popular destination for my fellow countrymen, not only for casual visits but also as a second home. It was a place full of expats and tourists, permanent and transient. Only a few years ago Robert Browning had died in his palazzo on the Grand Canal. Georges Sand had begun her infamous affair with her soon-to-be-former lover's doctor in a room not far from mine in the hotel. Painters could not resist the lure of Venice, and Lord Byron's exploits in the city were the stuff of legends.

As I set off to make my calls, I found myself once again captivated by the beauty around me. The city was magic, almost unreal. It should have been impossible to build on these sandy islands. Venice should have sunk into the lagoon. Yet here it stood, against all reason, glimmering and magnificent, built, in the words of the famous archivist Marin Sanudo, "more by divine than human will," and today was hardly changed from its glory as a Renaissance power.

Hardly changed if one looked only superficially, that is. As I was welcomed into palazzo after palazzo, I saw the decay that lay beneath the surface of beauty. Like many estates in England, these enormous houses could prove an unmanageable burden to the families who owned them. The facades stood proud, seeming almost to hover above the water, but they had lost some of their ornamentation. Gilt paint had worn away, and bricks showed evidence of wear, but inside I saw spectacular chambers with exquisite views of canals, the rooms filled with large mirrors and furnished with the flamboyant rococo elegance that defined the city's style. I could not help but wonder how many rooms in each of these palazzi stood vacant and in need of restoration. One did not require an entire house to show one's status to friends.

The families I met charmed and delighted me with colorful stories of their ancestors and of the most glorious days of the Venetian republic. However, it was not until I reached the third household I'd visited that I found anyone who'd heard of Besina Barozzi.

"*Sì, sì,*" my hostess said. "She came to ruin and disgrace, you know. Sent to a convent by her husband. My many-greats grandfather married her husband's sister. We have the letters she wrote to him. They are full of complaints about the indecent behavior of her sister-in-law."

"Do you know the name of Besina's husband?"

"No, I don't remember that," she said. "I don't even know her married name. Only that he was displeased with his wife."

"I don't suppose I could read them?" I asked. I had assumed, perhaps naïvely, that N.V. must have been Besina's husband and had imagined for them a grand and passionate love affair. Now, though, I found myself disappointed to learn that the marriage about which Donata and I had such romantic ideas had not been a success.

"I would be pleased to show them to you," she said, "but to read the old Venetian dialect is not so easy. Come, though. We can try."

The letters, their edges crumbling, the words faded and smeared, would have been difficult to read in any language. My hostess offered what help she could but relied more on family lore about what the pages of old vellum contained than on transcribing the actual sentences. I ran my fingers gently over a sheet, feeling the ink, breathing in the slightly musty smell of the well-worn leather folio in which the missives were stored. I wanted to know every word.

"Would you trust me with these?" I asked. "If I were to borrow them? I promise you I'd treat them with the utmost care and would ensure they come to no harm. I've a friend, Signor Caravello, a renowned scholar, who could help me with translating them. We could return them to you with a complete transcription."

"I see no problem with that," she said. "The end result could be amusing."

I had not finished calling on all the families on my list but decided the rest could wait. I'd found documents that would confirm the identity of Besina's husband, and I'd found his family's descendants. Who knew what further treasures would be uncovered when I had full translations of these letters? Still, a pervasive sadness consumed me.

I'd wanted Besina's marriage to have been a happy one.

I was at least as romantic as Donata.

# Un Libro d'Amore

*Nicolò knew better than to go against the will of his father. He spoke no more of Besina. He did not ask again for permission to marry her. He knew that was not possible, at least not now. Still, he did not give up hope that someday she would be his wife. In the meantime, he had to find a way to court her.*

*He wrote to her twice a day, hiring gondoliers, the most discreet men in Venice, to carry his letters to the servants' entrance at Ca' Barozzi and to wait for her reply. Every word she wrote in return was, to his mind, a beautiful rhapsody. He went about his business in the city with a light heart, fueled by the knowledge that the girl he loved returned his feelings. She would wait for him.*

*While Nicolò was all brash confidence in the face of implacable adversity, Besina found it more difficult to be separated from her love. His letters made her weep and turn to poets whose lines equaled the sadness that filled her heart. She sat at a window in the first-floor loggia every afternoon, pretending to make lace, watching boats pass by on the canal.*

At three o'clock, Nicolò, in his gondola, would glide in front of her house, careful not to look directly at her.

Besina did not have to pretend she didn't see him. No one in the household paid close enough attention to her to take notice of why she found the view of the Grand Canal so alluring at that particular time of the day. She scrutinized Nicolò for the few moments he was in her sight, trying to reassure herself that his health remained good, that his face was as handsome as she remembered, and that the studied nonchalance in his eyes as he avoided hers still spoke of his deep love for her. Six months passed, then nine. They had not spoken to each other since the night of their first meeting.

This physical separation did not quench their desire for each other. It served only to heighten it. Letters flew between them at an ever increasing pace, but Nicolò wanted more than words. He remembered too well the softness of Besina's lips, the smooth porcelain skin of her cheeks, the touch of her small hand. He forced himself to be patient, difficult though it was, and eventually he fell into a routine that, for him, was very nearly peaceful.

Besina was not so calm. Her father had called for her, summoning her to his library. She'd been down at the water entrance to her family's home, Ca' Barozzi, the most opulent palazzo on the Grand Canal, pleading with Lorenzo to procure for her another book of Petrarch's poems. He promised, then urged her to rush to their father, who never liked to be kept waiting.

Besina hurried up the marble steps to the portego, nearly sliding on its gleaming terrazzo floor, slowing down only when her mother stopped her as she reached the door to the library, a room with maps painted on the walls, maps that had tempted her, when she was younger, to want to explore the world.

"Calm yourself, child," her mother said. She tugged at Besina's gown and brushed her daughter's long hair back behind her shoulders. "You must behave like a lady, not a wild girl." She opened the door and pushed Besina into the room ahead of her.

"Besina!" Her father beckoned to her to come close so that he might kiss her. "It is a great day for our family. Your marriage contract has been signed. The engagement will be announced by the end of the week."

For an instant, Besina slipped into a pleasant daydream in which Nicolò would be her groom, but she knew it could not be.

"Uberto Rosso could not be a better choice for a husband," her father continued. "He will manage your dowry well, as he did that of his first wife."

"First wife?" Besina asked.

"She died some years ago," he said.

"I don't even know him," Besina said, her heart pounding as sweat beaded on her forehead.

"You'll recognize him," her mother said. "You've met him before. He's a very distinguished and well-respected man."

Besina felt as if she could not breathe. She could not marry this man, this stranger, not when she loved another so deeply as she did Nicolò. Her father had already turned his attention to the papers before him on the table. Her mother's expression was stern, devoid of concern.

"No." Her voice was small. She was afraid to speak but knew she had no choice. "I will not marry him. I will not."

"There's nothing to discuss," her father said. "We've signed the contract. You will do as you're told."

Besina knew she should be grateful. She had known for years that marriage was expected of her and had once been pleased that she would not be sent to a convent. That was before she knew what it meant to love someone. Now her familial duty felt like punishment.

"But I—"

She stopped. Upset though she was, she knew confessing her love would only make the situation worse. She steeled herself and forced her mind to stop reeling. She would pretend to go along with it.

Until she could escape with Nicolò.

# 5

As soon as I left the palazzo, I had taken the letters to the bookshop, knowing Signor Caravello would have no trouble deciphering the old Venetian dialect. I was convinced something in Besina's life would explain why the conte was holding her ring when he died. The old man was only too pleased to assist me and promised to start translating at once, assuring me it shouldn't take him long to complete the work. Donata's eyes went wide when she saw what I brought, and she demanded her father let her help him. Even so, she was not all wanton optimism.

"Just remember, Emily, letters like this may be full of nothing more than inaccurate gossip," she said. "We must not put too much stock in them."

She was quite right, but her admonitions made no dent in the excitement I felt when I thought about reading whatever it was they contained. I thanked the Caravellos and set off to meet my husband.

Colin and I rendezvoused in front of St. Mark's, where high tide had made its way up through the marble drains of the square, flooding patches of it. We strolled around the piazza, able to easily avoid the pooling water—this was not, after all, the famous *aqua alta* that submerged bits of the city at regular intervals during the autumn and winter—and decided to stop for a drink at Caffè Florian, as charming a spot as I'd ever seen. The restaurant was made up of a series of small rooms, each running into the next, with dark parquet floors polished to shining. Red velvet-upholstered sofa benches lined the walls. In front of them stood delicate marble-topped tables and elegant, slim chairs. Each room had slightly different decorations. Some were filled with paintings of figures famous from Venetian history—Enrico Dandolo, a powerful doge, and Marco Polo, the explorer, for example. Others featured frescoes that brought to mind the greatest Venetian artists. But the weather was fine, puddles notwithstanding, and Colin and I decided to take a table outside, near the orchestra whose jubilant sounds filled the square.

"The Barozzi family's fortune has been in steady decline since Napoleon gave Venice to the Austrians," my husband said as we took our seats.

"Do they have enough to survive?" I asked.

"Emma's father gives her a generous allowance—she's lucky he's so tolerant of her having eloped—but it's not enough to make them solvent."

"I'm sorry for her," I said.

"Most troubling for the old conte's estate is the amount of debt he carried. He had several large loans that wouldn't normally be out of the ordinary for someone of his rank and situation, but he was incapable of paying them back."

Our waiter brought Colin a whisky and me a glass full of a

shockingly yellow liquid. I frowned. "One really ought to delve into the local culture when one travels, my dear," I said. "Could you not try limoncello in lieu of whisky?"

He glowered at me. I suppressed a smile as he ignored my reproof and continued as if I'd said nothing. "Paolo is the one most affected by the financial situation now that his father is dead. The debt falls onto his shoulders."

"So Paolo is the one least likely to have killed the conte."

"I wouldn't be so certain about that. A fortnight before the murder, Paolo pressured his business partner into making a bad deal that essentially bankrupted them both. They parted ways following the disaster, irrevocably dissolving their failed venture."

I sipped my liqueur, first tasting tangy lemon, then the sharp bite of alcohol. "How does that make you more suspicious of him?"

"There is an unusual asset coming Paolo's way now that his father is dead," he said. "Paolo's grandmother on his mother's side owned a substantial property in France. She left it to her grandson on the condition that he have no access to it while his father was alive. She worried the conte would pressure his son to squander the income on renovating Ca' Barozzi. By dissolving his partnership before his father's death, Paolo avoided having to use any of this new income to save the business. It won't be enough to solve all their financial problems, but it will take care of a significant portion of his father's debts."

"He wouldn't have had to do that regardless, would he?" I asked.

"The terms of their agreement required both men to put up their personal fortunes to save the company should it be in dire financial straits. The conte's death could not have been more perfectly timed."

"An unlikely coincidence, but not an impossible one," I said. "Why would Paolo run off and start selling family treasures if he's just come into a fortune that would put an end to most of his financial woes? And why would he have left his dying father with Besina's ring? Only to send us off on the wrong path?"

"It's possible, but I don't know yet," he said. "I'm going to focus on trying to find him. Can I count on you to continue following up on the clues from the murder scene?"

I nodded just as something caught my eye. Across the crowded square from us, a strange figure leaned against a pillar. He stood taller than everyone around him and wore a long hooded black cloak and an eerie white mask with a long beaked nose.

"What on earth is that?" I asked.

"A plague doctor," Colin said. "Very popular carnival costume."

"Carnival's months from now," I said.

"It's Venice, Emily. Yesterday I saw at least three gentlemen dressed like Casanova. Perhaps limoncello has a bad effect on tourists."

Now it was my turn to glower. "I'll brook no criticism from you, Mr. Hargreaves. I'm throwing myself into being as Italian as possible while we're here. It's disappointing you insist on remaining so very English."

"This whisky is from Scotland, my dear."

I swirled the limoncello in my glass and took another tentative sip. A shadow crossed my field of vision, and I looked up to see the ominous figure of the plague doctor standing above me. He dropped a heavy envelope onto the table and disappeared into the crowd without uttering a word. Colin leapt to his feet in a flash and followed him.

I opened the envelope. The paper within bore only three words, written in what looked like medieval calligraphy:

*Pericolo vi aspetta.*
Danger awaits you.

Colin returned, breathless, a few moments later. "No success," he said, dropping back into his seat. "Was able to keep sight of him until he turned in front of the basilica and started for the Doge's Palace, but then I lost him in the crowd. He vanished."

"Pulled off his cloak and mask and looked normal, I'd guess," I said. "Heaven knows there are enough people in the piazza to hide almost anything."

"Quite right."

"He left this thoughtful sentiment for us." I passed him the note. "We must be doing something right."

.  .  .

Colin and I were used to our work coming with threats, dangers, and any number of unpleasant side effects. We accepted the risks we took in search of justice and would not be daunted by a silly man in a ridiculous mask. After finishing our libations (my husband refusing to so much as taste my limoncello), we parted ways. He set off to gather further information about Paolo, while I had been charged with looking into the affairs of the old conte and continuing my pursuit of Besina's history.

I planned to start by collecting the letters I'd left for Signor Caravello to translate. I was beginning to feel more confident in my navigational skills and decided to walk to the bookshop rather than take a gondola. Map in hand, I plotted my course. To begin, I followed every PER RIALTO sign I saw. When I reached the famous bridge, I passed rather than crossed it, winding my way through a series of increasingly narrow passages. I had come away from the bustling shops near the bridge and entered a more residential area. Flowerboxes hung from windows, and the sound of family chatter escaped through shutters closed against the afternoon heat. I wondered what it would be like to live in such close quarters, surrounded by the good smells of baking bread and simmering sauces and the sounds of your neighbors' conversations.

I'd intended to plot a course parallel to the Grand Canal, but when I was stopped by the waterway at the end of the shaded *calle,* I knew my sense of direction had run amiss. Only a few steps ago I'd been on a crowded pavement, but now I was all alone. It was as if everyone had disappeared. I had not yet spent enough time in Venice to understand this was how the city streets worked. One was never more than a turn or two from utter isolation. The ornate facades of the palazzi visible from the canal were not matched by what I found here, at the rear of the same buildings. Behind, they were all brick or plain stone. No frescoes, no paint, no decoration at all. It was difficult to reconcile front with back. This was a city meant to be seen from the water, not from its hidden alleys.

I turned around, ready to retrace my steps. My heart quickened when I caught the flash of a black cloak and the long white hooked nose of the plague doctor's mask. He stepped out from a doorway, his hulking form blocking the center of the pavement not fifty feet away from me. He raised his arms, beckoning to me. I started to back up but knew there was nothing but the canal behind. Quickly weighing my options, I gathered my heavy skirts, lifted them, and ran, ducking into a *sotoportego* that veered to the left.

My heels clicked loudly on the pavement, and the sound reverberated against the solid stone of the narrow passage. It felt as if I were in a tunnel. My lungs burned and pain shot through my feet, but I did not slow my pace. I knew better than to look back—it would only slow me down. All I could do was chant a silent prayer that I could remain fleeter of foot than my would-be assailant.

Generally one is comforted by the certain knowledge that there is always a light at the end of the tunnel. I was looking forward to this certainty with indelicate ardor. But as anyone beyond the age of six knows, certainties are nearly always unreliable. My focus was primarily on the uneven stones beneath my feet. I couldn't risk tripping. Soon, though, the realization that there was not light ahead of me crushed my spirit. I was headed straight for another dead end.

Now panic engulfed me. I looked around for any way of escape, but there was nothing but the occasional closed door. There was no other direction for me to go. Perhaps I could rouse the residents in one of the houses, but I feared that would delay me too long. So I carried on until the last possible moment when, steps from the end of the path, I saw a narrow sliver of light coming from the right.

The *sotoportego* took a sharp right angle.

Six feet farther along, it opened into a bright *campo* full of people. Greeks in scarlet hats walked next to Turks in bright turbans and robes, both making the top hats favored by European tourists and Venetian gentlemen seem dull. I caught my breath as I threw myself forward with the last bit of energy I possessed, careening into the ancient well that marked the center of the square. I wanted to stop and try to slow my breath. Instead, I looked back from whence I'd come, fully expecting to see my pursuer.

He was not there.

A small boy rolling a hoop with a stick emerged from the *sotoportego*. Following him came a dour-looking woman who could only have been a particularly disappointing governess. She had a tight grip on the hand of a small girl whose face was smeared with chocolate. Emboldened more by the relative safety of the crowd around me than by any sense of fearlessness, I waited.

The bells in the square's church chimed the quarter hour.

Then the half.

Either he'd turned around or he'd disappeared into one of the houses in the *sotoportego*.

Half disappointed, half relieved, I did what any sensible lady would. I marched straight into a fruit shop and asked for directions, happy that my Italian didn't fail me.

.     .     .

"Horrible!" Donata winced as I shared the saga of my journey with her and her father. "But you can't really think it was the same person, can you?"

"Should I expect to encounter plague doctors on a regular basis when roaming the streets of Venice?" I asked.

"No," she said, "but it's not entirely unusual. Tourists like to dress up, even when it's not *carnivale*."

"You're more likely to find cads dressed as Casanova," Signor Caravello said, echoing my husband's earlier statement. "But I would not be alarmed, Signora Hargreaves. Venice is full of people in costume, and it's not unusual to be frightened when facing such a thing unexpectedly. There's always the appearance of menace in disguise, don't you think? Even when there's no real danger."

"That's certainly true," I said. "Fantasy and horror can so easily go hand in hand. Let's not dwell on this unpleasantness. I was hoping you could tell me about the letters."

"*Sì.*" He shuffled through several haphazard stacks of papers on his desk, grunting at regular intervals in a most displeased fashion. He shook his head and crossed to the shop's counter. "Of course. I was working here so that I might keep a sharp eye on two unruly Englishmen who were browsing earlier. Too many of your countrymen aspire to be Byron."

"I wouldn't object if they managed to succeed in style," I said, "but they never seem to, do they?"

"No one could." He adjusted his spectacles. "Now. Your friend Besina Barozzi. Not a happy woman in marriage. Her husband, who apparently had high expectations for the match, found nothing but faults in his wife. The letters were sent by the husband's sister. She writes in the insidious way used by those who care more about gossip than the truth."

"Are her complaints specific?" I asked.

"Alas, no, I am afraid," he said. "She has recorded a litany of small criticisms, most of which stem from Besina's education. Her sister-in-law felt Besina's knowledge made her seem more courtesan than wife. Yet despite that, she gave her husband only one child. A son."

"Courtesans would know better than to—" Donata stopped almost the instant she'd started to speak.

"But this woman is not suggesting Besina was a courtesan before she married?" I asked.

"No, she is not. Instead she suggests that Besina used poetry and literature as a way to seduce men. But not in . . ." His voice trailed.

"In a professional context?" I suggested.

"Exactly," Signor Caravello said. "In the end, her husband grew tired of the antics and divorced her."

"Divorced her?" I frowned. "I didn't know that was possible in the Middle Ages."

"Most likely you believe divorce began and ended with Henry VIII," he said. "Divorce was possible. Not common, mind you, but not unheard-of. Generally deserted wives were set up fairly well. Some even were allowed to keep their dowries. Besina, however, wound up in a convent after her divorce. A not unusual outcome, I imagine."

"Do the letters say which one?" I asked.

"San Zaccaria," he said, "but that is all I know. Once Besina was out of the family, she was no longer a topic of discussion in the letters."

"Donata told me Venetian convents weren't what I would expect them to be."

"Very true," he said. "Noble families typically married off only one daughter. Of the rest, one would remain home to look after any children in need of supervision in the palazzo, and the others would be sent to convents. When you fill such places with those who don't have a calling, the atmosphere often becomes more secular than spiritual."

"Many of them were like less fortunate courtesans," Donata said. "The church was willing to ignore what happened in convents in exchange for the money given by the girls' families to support them. It didn't matter if they chose to live the most debauched sort of lives."

"It was not all like that," Signor Caravello said. "Many girls studied music, and some of them did find a special devotion to God. Regardless, though, the letters don't mention Besina anymore after she'd become a nun."

I felt a pang of disappointment. I'd wanted the ring to signify real love. "What was her husband's name?"

"The letters never say. They are addressed to *my dear brother* and signed *your dearest sister.*"

"Perhaps the ring was not from her husband," I said.

"N.V. might have known her after she took orders," Donata said. "She could have been his forbidden love, doomed forever to a life of misery."

"Too much drama, child," her father said. "Stories like that only happen in your dreadful novels."

"And in Shakespeare," she said. "Surely you don't count him among the dreadful?"

# Un Libro d'Amore

## V

*Besina wept and wept, but Lorenzo would do nothing for her.*

*"Please, you must help me." His sister had fallen to her knees in front of him, begging. "I cannot marry this man."*

*He pulled her to her feet and dried her eyes. "There's no need for such dramatic display," he said. "Marriages are contracts. Father knows what is best for the family. You should rejoice he's picked you among all his daughters to marry. Our sisters are unlikely to be looking forward to convent life."*

*"So I'm to delight in having a slightly better prison than they will?" Besina asked.*

*"This is not a decision it is appropriate for either of us to make," Lorenzo said. "Do you think I have choices either? We are young, Besina, and we can't always see reason better than a four-year-old who truly doesn't understand why he can't eat sweets all day."*

*"I am not behaving like a four-year-old." Besina felt a pain growing in her head and raised her hand to knead the back of her neck. It was a motion she'd turned to all her life, almost without knowing she did it. To*

Lorenzo, it signaled how deeply she was upset, and it made him feel more helpless than he ordinarily did.

"Cara—"

She batted his hand away as he reached for hers. "I cannot think of a fate worse than marrying Signor Rosso. I'd rather die."

"Death is far more romantic in books than in real life."

Lorenzo didn't know Besina had no real interest in death. She was being melodramatic. But she also had no interest in marrying Signor Rosso.

As soon as her brother had left her, she pressed her mother for permission to visit her dearest friend. It was not an unusual request and was granted at once. The trip along the Grand Canal did not take long. Besina smiled at her family's gondolier, who used to tell her stories of his ancestors' escapades during the Crusades. When he stopped the boat at the slick stairs rising from the water, she stepped carefully onto the marble.

"Would you return for me in two hours?" she asked. "I'm sure to be at least that long. There's no need for you to sit waiting the whole time."

She stood in front of the door, pausing as long as she could before she made her presence known. When, inevitably, a servant greeted her, she excused herself, assuring him she would return momentarily.

She'd chosen this particular friend's house for a reason. It was on the Grand Canal, but there was a stretch of pavement next to it, running along the water, past a church and on toward a public gondola stand. Confident after taking a last look to ensure her own gondolier was long out of sight, she walked with what she hoped was an air of nonchalance in the direction of the boats. Her tall chopines clopped as she made her way to the end of the wooden dock that jutted out into the canal.

"I need your help," she said to the first gondolier who met her eyes. "You will be well paid for your trouble." She knew her secret would be safe. There was no one on earth more discreet than a Venetian gondolier. If any *of them dared tell of the trysts that went on in the felzi of their boats or of the sensitive messages they frequently delivered, their colleagues would drown them.*

*Besina sat in the center of the boat, taking a seat inside its felze and pulling the shutters closed, knowing she must not allow herself to be seen. While still at home, she had written a message. Now she pressed it into the gondolier's hand and had to trust that he could do with it what she asked. Never had she had to use more restraint than when she could hear him shouting to the servants inside the water entrance at Ca' Vendelino. She wanted more than anything to look out and see what was happening, but she did not move. She hardly dared breathe.*

*It seemed as if hours went by. Then days. She felt a sharp pain in her hands and looked down to see that she had clenched them so hard her nails had drawn blood from her palms.*

*It reminded her of the stigmata.*

*She stared at the blood till the gondola lilted heavily to one side. She closed her eyes and began to pray, beseeching the Virgin to send her love to her. "Ave Maria, gratia plena, Dominus tecum." Her whole body was trembling as she wondered if her prayer was a sin. She had been promised to another.*

*Then she heard Nicolò's voice calling to his mother as he stepped out of the house.*

*"Ciao, Mamma!"*

*And all worries of sin left her head in a flash.*

# 6

The next morning when the concierge at the Danieli handed me a thick pale yellow envelope, I'd nearly forgot I had written to the owners of the Villa di Tranquillità, requesting to see their portrait of Besina Barozzi. No sooner had I read Signora Morosini's response to my note than I rushed back to our room and grabbed Colin. Within minutes, we were in a boat headed for the estate on the banks of the Brenta River.

"The invitation said to come anytime," I said, sliding on my gloves only after I'd sat down in the vessel. "I'm taking Signora Morosini at her word."

"I don't know if I'd describe it as an invitation," Colin said. "She wrote to say someone has broken into her house and ruined the painting you'd hoped to see."

"Clearly she is in dire need of our help, whether she knows it or not," I said. "If that's not an invitation, I don't know what is."

The trip to the Brenta River was not a short one. Fortunately, the day was pleasant, if warm. I closed my parasol, welcoming the heat of the sun on my face. I tipped my chin towards the sky, smiling as I recalled the incalculable number of times my mother had warned me to be vigilant about guarding my complexion. This thought led me to remember the trouble I'd had running through the *sotoportego* away from the plague doctor. If I were going to abandon bits of my regimented upbringing, I might as well fling the bulk of it out the proverbial window and start wearing comfortable boots as well. It would be most conducive to my work. I would have some made as soon as we returned to England.

Our boatmen were singing, something from an opera I didn't recognize. They were glad, I suppose, that a steady wind was filling the sail and keeping them from having to row. The city, seeming to float above the glistening lagoon, had become almost too small to see, and a brisk breeze danced over the water. The sun felt even better against my skin. Colin touched my cheek, turning my head towards him. I sighed and let my eyes close as his lips brushed mine.

"When this tedious work is done, my dear, I'm going to have my way with you."

I pulled back in half mock horror. "What do you want the men to think when they see you kissing me? It's scandalous behavior in public."

"I'd hardly call a private boat public. And what I want them to think is that the fact we're English doesn't mean we're deficient in—" He paused, his dark eyes dancing. "Certain areas, shall we say?"

"Heavens," I said. "I hadn't thought of it that way. Well, if the reputation of the empire is at stake, God save the queen!" I leaned forward and kissed him. Our boatmen's song did not change, but I sensed a tremor of approval in their tone.

I liked Italy—and I found that extensive kisses make the time spent on a boat pass with remarkable speed. We reached our destination all too soon.

Used to splendor though I was, I was taken aback at the neoclassical magnificence of the Villa di Tranquillità. Palladio had designed it in the sixteenth century, and I couldn't imagine a better example of his work. A large dome, reminiscent of that on the Pantheon in Rome, rose from its center behind the long, elegant Ionic columns that fronted the home's perfectly symmetrical facade.

"We should think about abandoning Anglemore Park," Colin said, staring at the building before us.

"You'd never abandon the Hargreaves family seat," I said, not giving the slightest consideration to his comment. He was more attached to his country house than any other gentleman I'd ever known.

"I wouldn't have thought so until I saw this," he said. "Perhaps we could have Angelmore pulled down—"

"And reanimate Palladio and bring him to England? Unlikely, my love." One of the boatmen helped me out of the rocking vessel.

My husband was still studying the villa. "I could design it."

"Heaven knows you need something to occupy your idle brain," I said. "I've noticed that you aren't particularly industrious between the hours of three and four in the morning. Perhaps you could fill that time pursuing the study of architecture."

"Let me assure you, dear wife, that any occasion on which you've been awake to observe my state at such a time generally coincides with a great deal of industriousness on my part."

I blushed . . . and wished we were back in our rooms at the Danieli.

A servant welcomed us into the house, and we found that the interior of the Villa di Tranquillità matched the easy grace of its facade. Large, airy rooms opened onto two long loggias, overlooking the river, and it was on one of these that Signora Morosini received us.

"I admit to being most concerned when I received your message," I said, after making the requisite introductions. "Has anything else happened? Or was only the one canvas damaged?"

"Just what I told you in my note," Signora Morosini said. "Before I offer you refreshments, do let me show you what this vandal has done."

We followed her into the Palladian equivalent of a Venetian *portego* that, like that at Ca' Barozzi, was lined with fine oil portraits.

"I've always liked something about her eyes," she said, stopping in front of a large picture of a solemn-looking woman. "They don't match the rest of her expression."

Besina was older in this portrait than in the other I'd seen. Her skin was not quite so luminous, and her features were not quite so smooth, but Signora Morosini was right about her eyes. They hinted at a lively life behind a flawless impression of an honorable matron.

Or perhaps the impression hadn't been flawless. The painter might not have known what Besina's husband suspected of her.

Most striking was what the canvas had suffered. It appeared that Besina had posed clasping her hands together beneath her waist. A gaping hole now stood in their place.

"Can you remember anything about her hands?" I asked. "Was she wearing rings?"

"But yes, she is a Renaissance lady, very wealthy. Noble. She would have worn rings on every finger."

"Could this be one of them?" I held up the conte's ring for her to see.

She hesitated. "It's possible, yes. It looks familiar, but I cannot say I am certain. I've never much cared for old jewelry."

"Can you recall any details that had to do with her hands?" Colin asked.

"She was holding a rosary, but you can see that from what remains."

The crucifix and a length of beads were still visible at the bottom of the painting.

"The painting has been in your family for years, is that correct?" I asked.

"Some years, yes," she said, "but not in the way I think you mean. I bought it from Zaneta Vendelino. It was languishing in her family's villa, only a few miles from here. I spent a fortune having it cleaned and restored. And I suppose shall now have to do it again."

"Vendelino?" I asked. "With a *V*?"

"Yes," she said. "Is that important?"

"It may be extremely important," I said. "Do you know anything else about the painting?"

"Not really. The Englishwoman who suggested you visit me recognized the subject when she saw it at a party we had last summer. She said the Barozzis are an old Venetian family. But I need not tell you that. You are friends with Paolo Barozzi's wife, yes?"

Colin nodded. "It's quite possible that the ring my wife showed you is of critical significance to the murder that occurred at Ca' Barozzi. Can you try to remember anything about the rings on Besina's hands?"

"Two of them were sapphires. I know that as sapphires are my favorite," Signora Morosini said. "There was a ruby, I'm sure, but as to whether it's that particular one . . ."

"Is it true the Barozzi family once owned this house?" I asked.

"Oh yes, they did," Signora Morosini said, "but that was long after Besina would have been dead. I understand she came to disgrace and ruin before the end of her life. Her husband locked her up in a convent or did something equally dreadful to her."

"What had she done to merit such treatment?" Colin asked.

Signora Morosini shrugged. "It doesn't take much to aggravate a cantankerous husband, does it? And in those days, a man's power was absolute. I do not suggest things have changed all that much."

"It's intolerable," Colin said. "Then and now. Have you any other records or information about the time the Barozzis summered here?"

"Heaven knows what one might find in the attics, Signor Hargreaves. It's far too hot for me to be inclined to look."

My work, it seemed, was coming ready-made for me.

# Un Libro d'Amore

# vi

Nicolò climbed into the felze *and pressed his lips against Besina's so hard she struggled to breathe. Then, afraid he might have hurt or scared her, he took her in his arms and covered her neck with soft kisses. And then he began to work his way lower. She had never felt such pleasure, but fear mixed with it.*

*"Nicolò, you must stop," she said, her voice a trembling whisper. "We are not safe here."*

*He stuck his head out of the small cabin and murmured something to the gondolier that made him start rowing. Soon they were far from Ca' Vendelino, lost among the crush of boats in the Grand Canal.*

*"You were right to come to me," he said. "The situation is grave."*

*"I cannot marry him," Besina said.*

*"No. You cannot. I will find a way to save you from this fate. Are you prepared to act quickly?"*

*"I would go now were that possible."*

*"We will be together, my love," Nicolò said. "That I promise you. I*

will organize everything by tomorrow evening. Tonight will be the last you spend with your family."

"They will forgive us after we are married."

"Eventually, I hope." He kissed her again, this time gently, holding his passion inside, not wanting to frighten her. "But I care not for the approval of our families. All I want is your love."

After more kisses than Besina could count, Nicolò returned her to the house of her dearest friend, where she spent only a quarter of an hour. The other girl queried the source of her flushed face and bright eyes. Besina admitted nothing, blaming the unusually warm summer for the color of her complexion. Her friend had no reason to think there was anything amiss.

Besina returned home, not to spend a congenial evening with her family, but to suffer through a reception held in honor of herself and her would-be groom, a celebration of their engagement and a prelude to their imminent wedding.

Even those with the most generous of dispositions could not describe Uberto Rosso as the sort of man who might fuel the dreams of a young girl. He had not aged well, and his girth was matched in its obscenity only by his propensity to belch. He was a tall man, confident in his every movement, but incapable of grace. This was due not only to his size but to his disposition. He had no interest in beauty or elegance. His features did little to commend him, though his nose might be described as aristocratic. What little hair remained on his head had faded from jet black to a dull, greasy gray.

His hand was damp with sweat when he took Besina's and led her to dance. She wondered what she could say to him, knowing she'd spent the afternoon kissing Nicolò in a gondola, and worried her voice would somehow reveal her deception. It soon became apparent that she would not be required to speak. Signor Rosso showed no interest in any sort of *discussion. While Nicolò's touch had made her feel loved, her fiancé's felt like a show of ownership.*

*Ca' Barozzi was at its finest that night. No one could argue it was anything short of the finest palazzo in the republic. The family's wealth and influence shone from every bit of the house. Candlelight glimmered, reflected on gleaming terrazzo floors polished with linseed oil until they shined like mirrors, important works of art hung on the walls, and the frescoed ceilings were—so gossip said—more impressive than those in the Doge's Palace. The food served was the finest available, seasoned with exotic spices from the East. Music and laughter filled the rooms. The alliance between the Barozzi and Rosso families would be a triumph, bringing together fortunes and power. The doge himself was pleased at the news of the union. He said it would strengthen Venice.*

*Everyone was happy but Besina.*

*Until the messenger arrived.*

# 7

Colin and I played to our strengths as we set to work at the Villa di Tranquillità. Which meant I climbed a series of seemingly endless staircases to hot, dusty attics while my husband interviewed Signora Morosini's extensive staff about the damaged painting. The fact that this allowed him to explore nearly every inch of the property was a much-welcomed perk so far as he was concerned. He could bask in architectural heaven while I threw myself with something approaching wild abandon into the discovery of untold treasure.

"Treasure" might be too strong a word, but the delight I took in exploring the hidden bits of the Morosini estate could be matched only by the emotions I felt when I had first been able to read Homer in the original Greek. Armed with a maid ready to help me dust anything I found too odious to touch (Signora Morosini was more squeamish than I when it came to such things and insisted on sending a girl up with me), I surveyed the scene before us.

It would be unreasonable to expect the cast-off possessions of nearly four hundred years' worth of residents to be well organized, and the innumerable piles of trunks, the occasional mummified mouse, and the heaps of furniture in various stages of disrepair that filled the rooms did not disappoint me. I (figuratively) rolled up my sleeves and set to work, following a strategy of first trying to roughly identify the ages of objects before me. I would then focus on the oldest things.

Some of the collection predated the house itself. A Crusader's sword, for example. There were trunks full of rich fabrics now too fragile to touch—fabrics from the golden age of the Venetian republic: the finest silks, some plain, some embroidered, and heavy velvets whose bright colors had been protected from fading over the centuries.

"What Mr. Worth could do with something like these," I said, wishing my favorite dressmaker had access to such finery. "Nothing modern is ever so nice, is it?"

The maid asked if I'd like her to wash them. I shook my head, managing not to shudder at the suggestion.

Leather tubes held medieval maps, and a medium-sized trunk was full of ivory keys from a long-since-dismantled harpsichord. More than a dozen discarded paintings leaned against a wall. None was from the time when Besina was alive.

It occurred to me the Barozzis might not have kept anything of hers after she'd been unceremoniously flung from her husband's house, and even if they had, what were the odds that, generations later, those things would make their way to a newly constructed summer villa? The attics were unlikely to be of further use. Better that I search the hidden recesses of the convent in which Besina spent her final years.

I assumed she died in the convent, unless she'd managed to make a spectacular escape and run off to some far away place with the man she loved. Perhaps N.V. was not her husband. Perhaps he was the man who rescued her from a dingy existence in her small cell and gave to her the world. Thinking back, I now wonder if I might have applied myself with success to the art of writing fiction, so carried away was I by filling in the details of this woman's life. At the time, no such fancies occurred to me. Instead, with customary thoroughness, I searched the remainder of the attics, not surprised when I turned up nothing of significance.

By the time I descended to the cooler rooms of the house, Colin and Signora Morosini had returned to one of the comfortable loggias and were sipping prosecco.

"It appears that our plague doctor enjoys the occasional country retreat," my husband said as our hostess offered me a glass of the cool, sparkling drink. "Two maids and a houseboy insist they saw just such a figure the night the painting was vandalized."

"It may have been nothing," Signora Morosini said. "The child is often having nightmares, and those maids are particularly susceptible to suggestion. I wouldn't take anything they say too seriously."

"Any physical clues?" I asked.

"None," Colin said, "but the intruder came in through a first-floor window, just as the murderer did at Ca' Barozzi."

Signora Morosini blanched. "You think the murderer is the same person who destroyed my painting?"

"It is quite likely," Colin said.

"A murderer? In my house?" Horror gripped her. "Take that painting with you when you go. I don't want it anywhere near me."

.   .   .

Searching Besina's convent rooms had seemed an excellent idea until we learned that what remained of the building now housed police barracks. A perfunctory search of the spaces that had once housed the nuns—wild and debauched nuns, according to the young officer who escorted us through the place—revealed that too many changes had been made to offer us hope of finding anything of Besina's. I identified one brick that might have indicated a secret hiding place, but it was a false alarm and revealed nothing behind it but another brick.

"Perhaps we should go back to the villa," I said, frustrated, after we'd returned to the Danieli.

"You were extremely thorough, Emily," Colin said. "I've no doubt if there was something left to be found, you'd already have located it."

I sighed. "At least we know there is something significant about the ring. A serious error on the part of our miscreant. He's done nothing but draw attention to the object he wanted to hide."

"Unless the vandalism was meant to throw us off track."

I didn't like to admit that possibility, but had no choice. "I still think it's worth pursuing."

"Agreed," Colin said, "but you'll have a difficult time convincing me the solution to Barozzi's murder will come from the past."

"I won't have to convince you of anything once I've got the truth dangling in front of you."

"Not if I get to it first." He ran his hand through his thick, dark hair. "I've received word that Paolo has sold another book. This time in Padua."

"Any sign of the mysterious monk?"

"The monk completed the transaction himself this time. No one admits to seeing Paolo."

"Perhaps the monk is our murderer, and now that he's got his hands on the books, he's taken care of Paolo as well."

"I should like to be able to dismiss the idea out of hand, but can't," Colin said. "The only slim comfort is that—so far—no one has found a body matching Paolo's description."

"Does Emma suspect he might be in danger?"

"Not so far as I know," he said. "I'm going to Padua to speak to the man who bought the book. I trust you can mange things here?"

"Of course," I said.

"Keep watch for our plague doctor. I don't want to return to find you've been spirited off by some maniacal fancy dress aficionado."

His tone was full of jest, but his eyes registered concern. "I shall take extreme care," I said. "Perhaps I'll even manage to convince Emma to assist me with my work."

"I don't expect miracles, my dear."

&bull; &bull; &bull;

I expected nothing of the sort either but felt that a visit to Ca' Barozzi would soon be in order. Not so much to see Emma, but because I thought it possible Besina had returned there after her divorce. First, though, I wanted to find whatever concrete information I could, and I knew the city archives would be the place to start. They put to shame any I'd seen elsewhere. A clerk had told me they were second in size only to those in the Vatican but insisted that Venice's were more detailed. I had no reason to question him, as I could not have been more impressed with what I found. With relative ease, I'd managed to locate the record of Besina's divorce from a man called Uberto Rosso (not N.V.) and the record of her admittance to the convent. I wondered what Besina had done during the three-week period between the two dates.

As soon as I'd said good-bye to Colin, who was off to Padua, I directed the Danieli's gondolier to take me to call on Zaneta Vendelino, who was expecting me. As well as being the previous owners of Signora Morosini's portrait of Besina, the Vendelinos were the last of the *V*'s Donata and I had identified in the *Libro d'Oro*. Their palazzo, aptly called Ca' Vendelino, was situated on the Grand Canal not far from the famous Ca' d'Oro, and it provided a perfect contrast to Ca' Barozzi. While time had left an unhappy mark on the latter, Ca' Vendelino had been lovingly restored in the eighteenth century and taken exquisite care of ever since.

Six steps of perfect marble rose from the canal to a set of large doors covered in elaborate decorations of iron. They opened into an atrium of sorts, with a black and white tiled floor. This led to another atrium. From this, I mounted a wide staircase that took me to the *portego*. The room was enormous. Cavernous, even. Windows lined the walls on either end, and two huge lanterns hung from the ceiling. I followed a servant through a series of smaller square rooms, each decorated in pastel shades. Fine frescoes depicting scenes from Greek mythology were on every ceiling. More had been painted on the walls in some of the rooms, and the rest had walls covered in the finest silks.

"You like what we have done with the house?"

The voice came from a tiny figure sitting on a chaise longue in a square chamber done up in a soft, salmon color. She wore her hair, a perfect shade of the purest white, pulled back in a tight bun, and her clothing was more out of the romantic era than the present. Despite the warm weather, she pulled a long shawl made from Burano lace, with its famous Venetian points, around her shoulders.

"I shouldn't take credit, of course," she said. "Most of the work was done more than a century ago. Would you like a tour?"

I wasn't sure what to say.

"You are Lady Emily Hargreaves, I presume?" she asked.

"Yes," I said.

"You may call me Zaneta." She rose from her seat and motioned for me to follow her. "The frescoes are all by Tiepolo. The best. The ceilings are so high because we removed a floor. Very fashionable, yes?"

"It's lovely," I said, and it was. Beautiful. Tiepolo, considered by

81

many to have been the finest painter in eighteenth-century Europe, brought a grandness to his work that few others could achieve. His heroes appeared more heroic, his heroines more beautiful and vulnerable. There was no question the rooms of Ca' Vendelino were spectacular in their beauty. Yet there was something about the shabbiness of Ca' Barozzi that made me prefer it. I wanted to find the Renaissance in Venice, not something approaching the onset of the Regency.

"We have the most magnificent garden in the city," she said. "But you are not really here to see the house, are you?"

"I apologize if you thought I was," I said. "I meant to be quite clear when I wrote—"

"Yes, yes." She shook her head and turned around, taking me back to her salmon-colored salon. "You are interested in the painting of that Barozzi woman."

"Besina, yes. What can you tell me about it?"

"Very little, I'm afraid," she said. "How it came into our possession is unfathomable. The Barozzis are trash. Always have been."

Now I was at an even greater loss for what to say.

"You're not friendly with them." I felt stupid the instant the words fell from my mouth.

She raised her eyebrows. "Vendelinos do not speak to Barozzis. It has been this way since . . . oh . . . the thirteenth century at least."

"Six hundred years?" I asked. "Why?"

She blinked her eyes rapidly and shook her head. "Does it matter anymore? Such things are as they are. The reasons are unimportant."

"Are they?"

"Sit," she said.

I obeyed, lowering myself onto a delicate bone-colored chair with salmon velvet upholstery. "The portrait was, I believe, at your country house?"

"Yes. Well. Not in the house, per se. In one of the little-used out-buildings. That's why it went unnoticed for so long."

"How did Signora Morosini come to acquire it?"

"She saw it during a garden party I was hosting."

"In a little-used outbuilding?" I asked.

She raised an eyebrow. "You are savvy, yes? She was, I believe, involved in some sort of assignation with an unnamed gentleman. Why they chose to meet at such a place is quite beyond my comprehension."

"And she saw the portrait?"

"Apparently the gentleman is not entirely adequate in all areas," she said. "At least that's my judgment. I shouldn't want to be capable of noticing some old painting at such a moment."

"You're quite certain they were—" I stopped. This sort of gossip would get me nowhere. "I mean—"

"You're embarrassed."

Her words combined with the look on her face to make me feel slighted. "No. Not in the least, I assure you. I'm merely trying to imagine what it would require—or what would be omitted—to allow such a thing to happen."

Zaneta smiled. "Good girl."

"So Signora Morosini confessed all this when she asked to buy the portrait?"

"Not at all," she said. "The gardener saw everything. And he never keeps anything from me."

"So you sold her the painting?"

"Yes. As I said, it has no value to me. Once I knew I owned it, family honor required that I be rid of the dreadful thing at the first possible moment."

"You did look at the painting before you sold it?"

"Yes. If it were a Titian it would have commanded a higher price."

I pulled the ring off my finger. "Do you recognize this?"

Her manner changed in an instant. She sat upright, her eyes narrowed. "Where did you get that?"

"Signor Barozzi was holding it when he died."

"That ring belongs to the Vendelino family. It was stolen in the early sixteenth century, more or less."

"More or less?" I asked.

"Sometimes details aren't important," she said. "The material point is that it should come as a surprise to no one that it was the Barozzis who took it."

# Un Libro d'Amore

# vii

Lorenzo made the mistake of ceasing to worry about his sister halfway through the reception being held in honor of her impending nuptials. Besina had been sullen early in the evening, but now he could see she was blossoming. Her face glowed. Her eyes sparkled. Any beauty she ordinarily lacked seemed, as if by magic, to have been bestowed upon her. Though he found it difficult to believe, all Lorenzo could imagine was that Uberto Rosso had inspired the change.

Surely that was impossible.

He could think of no other explanation. This was, after all, the first time the betrothed couple had spent any time together. What else could explain Besina's transformation? Lorenzo was used to the idea that the moods of Venetians were like the tide, up for six hours, then down for six. Perhaps that accounted for the shift in his sister's demeanor. It was as reasonable an explanation as any.

So Lorenzo let go of his concerns with no regret and allowed himself to be swept up in a group of his friends, who, having indulged extravagantly in his father's finest wine, were ready to go elsewhere. Courtesans *were not where a man wanted to find love, but sometimes he had no other options.*

*And so Lorenzo departed, a feeling of relief rushing through him as he saw that Besina had, like him, accepted fate.*

*He could not have been more wrong.*

*An hour earlier, Besina's face had registered surprise when one of the servants handed her a sealed note. She thanked him, made her way through the throngs of dancers in the* portego, *rushed down the steps, and stole into the garden behind the house. No other garden in Venice compared to that at Ca' Barozzi. Her mother made certain of that. The sweet aroma of flowers filled the warm air, and the sound of water came from two directions—the canal in front of the house and the fountain in the center of the courtyard. Jasmine and roses bloomed in a profusion of color, songbirds in gilded cages ensured there was always music to be heard, and lemon trees in pots had been spaced among rows of boxwood hedges to create private groves.*

*Confident no one was watching her, Besina tore open the message, knowing full well it had to be from Nicolò.*

Tomorrow at midnight outside the rear entrance to your house. Too dangerous to try to leave via canal. I will be waiting there for you.

*Salvation was within her grasp.*

# 8

It took no small effort to keep Besina's ring out of Zaneta Vendelino's hands once she'd seen it. She insisted it was hers by right; I insisted the police required it as part of the murder investigation. Neither of us was being strictly honest. In the end, my will stood firmer than hers. Living with Colin had taught me well. I'd never once seen him back down on a matter of principle. Instead of becoming upset, he would appear to be almost serene. I did my best to mirror his technique, and it worked.

In order to save time, I took a gondola from Ca' Vendelino to Ca' Barozzi, where I wanted to speak to Emma and to see if I could eke out any useful information from the servants about her father-in-law. The question of the ring's significance had grown more and more cloudy. If the old conte had come upon it recently, and the Vendelino family had discovered this (I did not doubt for an instant Zaneta was perfectly capable of feigning surprise), would they have killed to get it back?

It seemed unlikely, but given my extremely limited knowledge of etiquette and procedure when it came to blood feuds and Italian families, I thought it best at present to pass no judgment on the matter.

Surely, though, if the murderer was a Vendelino, he would not have left the ring in the conte's hand?

"Please tell me you have some news?" Emma greeted me from the entrance of the *portego* before I'd made my way halfway up the flight of stairs. "I can't take much more of this."

"I've learned something about Besina's ring," I said.

"I don't care about the ring." She looked as if she might stomp her foot and have a tantrum. "What about my husband? When will he return to me? I can't bear being here by myself."

"Colin is focusing on finding him. I'm working elsewhere."

"Then you're of no use to me whatsoever."

I bit my lip, knowing it would be best to keep silent despite the fourteen quips that sprang to mind. "I don't have much use for you either. I need to speak to the servants."

"That's perfectly acceptable." She waved me away. "There's no need to even come upstairs, then. Go through the old warehouse. It's the side door from the water entrance."

With that she disappeared, not realizing that she'd inspired in me a new line of questioning for those in her employ. I wanted to know what it was like to work in the house.

The answer, shockingly, was that the servants were happy. Emma had managed the household from the time of her marriage, as her father-in-law wasn't much interested in domestic affairs. She wasn't a generous mistress, but she was neither stingy nor particularly demanding. The house was a shambles. She knew trying to keep it in order was a losing proposition, and the staff knew that so long as minimum standards were met, she wouldn't give them any trouble.

Except when it came to Facio Trevisani, who had recently lost his position.

Facio, according to the cook and three maids, had worked for the family for ages, since long before the old conte's wife had died. She had depended on him to maintain her garden. Given the current state of disrepair in the courtyard, I could only imagine that either he'd done an extremely bad job or its condition had deteriorated with an uncanny speed after he'd been let go. The cook gave me directions to his house. Acting on a strong suspicion that I wouldn't be able to follow them, I asked my gondolier for help. He, too, had difficulties but managed, in the better part of an hour, to find the grubby apartment for me.

The building that housed it was in alarming shape. I hesitated before climbing the stairs. The corridor was dark, and I thought about asking my waiting gondolier to accompany me but knew he was unlikely to abandon his boat. I heard a baby's cry coming from the floor above, and it gave me confidence. Surely no one would keep an infant in a place that was actually dangerous? Perhaps that question shows my naïveté at the time, but it nonetheless inspired me to take a deep breath, mount the steps, and knock on the door as soon as I reached the top of the third flight.

There was no response. I knocked again. And again.

Then, not wanting to leave without gathering any information, I went up another floor and knocked at the apartment from whence the cries of the malcontented baby came. A harried-looking young woman opened the door. I apologized for disturbing her and introduced myself as a friend of Facio Trevisani.

"You're a liar is what you are," she said.

The harsh words took me aback. "Why would you say such a thing?"

"If you were his friend you'd know why he wasn't here, wouldn't you?"

She had a point.

"I've not seen him for some time and am concerned about him."

"You're not one of those Barozzis, are you?"

"No, of course not. I told you I'm Lady Emily Hargreaves."

The baby started to cry again. The woman pursed her lips and tilted her head as she studied me. "I suppose you might as well come in."

Despite outward appearances, she had done an admirable job to ensure her home was warm and inviting. The windows were spotless, and there was not a piece of dust to be seen. Granted, her furniture was worn and mismatched, but she'd arranged it in an attractive fashion and was clearly house-proud. She picked the baby up from its cot in the corner. It calmed immediately, giving its mother a gurgly smile.

"What a beautiful child," I said. I knew extremely little about the raising of children beyond the fact that their parents enjoyed hearing them complimented.

"Thank you," she said. "You speak Italian well, but with an accent. You are French?"

"English," I said, suppressing a smile.

"How are you connected with Facio?"

"I know of his misfortune with his former employers and am worried about him."

"That wretch letting him go was the beginning of all the trouble," she said. "Wouldn't even give him a good reference. And you can't find a job if you can't present a character, can you? No one would hire him."

"I understand there was some trouble with the garden?" I was weaving fiction now, but it seemed a reasonable assumption. The garden was a disaster.

"That wasn't Facio's doing. The old man wouldn't let him do a thing. Crazy, that one."

Signor Barozzi must have refused to let him touch it, just as he'd done with his wife's bedroom. "But surely his son's wife, who managed the household, didn't hold him responsible for that?"

"It doesn't matter now, does it? Not with the poor child falling ill and no one to pay for medicine."

"So the contessa let him go?"

"No, not her. The old man. Yelled and bawled and threw him out of the house. And all the while he didn't give a care about what any of his other servants did. It's chaos in the household. I've heard all the stories. My heart breaks for that family. They'll never be happy again."

"The Trevisanis?" I hoped I wasn't revealing my complete ignorance, but it seemed unlikely, grammar aside, that she was referring to the Barozzis.

"Who else would I be talking about?" She shook her head. "When I think what that man's done, I'm glad he's dead. He deserved it. Stingy and mean he was."

"Facio?"

"No, the old man, of course. He's the one who's dead, isn't he?"

"Do you know where Facio has gone?" I asked.

"With his wife gone and no job, there was no reason to stay, was there? And the priests wouldn't give her a funeral in the church. No suicides, they said. No compassion, either. Who could blame her, with her only child taken from her just because they couldn't pay a doctor? It's no wonder Facio could face no more."

"Did someone take the child away?"

"No. The baby died, you see. Died of a simple fever because there was no money to pay for the doctor to come. Do you understand?"

I swallowed bile. The poor man, losing his child and his wife and all because of a shortfall of money. "I don't suppose you know how I could get into his apartment? I'd like to leave him a message."

"It won't do no good," she said. "He can't read."

"I know, but he'd recognize my handwriting, and he knows how to find me." Lies upon lies, all in the name of justice.

She paused, and I feared nothing good would happen. "He didn't lock the door when he left." Her cheeks colored, and I saw a flash of guilt in her eyes.

"Oh," I said. "I do hope you removed any perishable goods. It would be awful for him to return to rotting food."

"Yes, ma'am, of course." She all but stuttered. With her gaunt frame and a baby to feed, I could not fault her for scrounging for whatever nourishment she could find. If, indeed, that's what she'd taken from Facio's home.

"I won't trouble you any further," I said, "but, please, if you've any idea where he might have gone, do tell me. I want very much to help him."

She shook her head. But before I'd gone halfway down the stairs she called to me.

"Signora, wait!"

I turned back around. "Yes?"

"It's probably nothing, but I know he always wanted to learn how to build gondolas. Perhaps he's trying a new trade?"

"That could be," I said. "Thank you."

So far as I knew, a new trade generally didn't come with a new house. Although, having faced so much death, maybe he couldn't bear to return to what had been his family home.

Or perhaps he knew that returning could lead to facing charges of his own. Charges similar to those he had likely made against the old conte. I made my way down the steps and tentatively pushed against the heavy door of Facio's apartment, unaccountably frightened of what I might find inside.

No one—at least not recently—had looked after these rooms with the sort of tender care exhibited by the woman upstairs. Every surface was coated with a thick layer of grit and grime, the sort that accumulates at an alarming rate in old buildings. I opened the windows and the shutters both to let in light and to let out the heavy, oppressive air that filled the apartment. I wondered if this was what the Middle Ages smelled like.

I pulled out my notebook and jotted down my observations, starting at the door and moving clockwise through the room. Beneath the filth, the furniture wasn't in bad condition. A pair of glass candlesticks, no doubt made on the nearby island of Murano, from whence all the famous glass came, stood in the center of a medium-sized table. Murano glass did not come cheap. Facio must have been careful with his money. This theory was confirmed as I moved through the rest of the house. The furnishings were modest, save a single object in each room. He and his wife must have saved everything they could to fund their occasional lavish purchases.

An empty, deserted house is always a sad place, but most heartbreaking was what I found in the bedroom. In a corner near the bed stood an empty cradle, beautifully carved from the finest wood, its painted decorations visible beneath a layer of dust not quite so thick as that covering everything else in the apartment. Facio must have kept it, and only it, clean until he left. I wiped every bit of grime from it with my handkerchief and shook the tiny bed linens (made from exquisite fabrics) out the window before returning them to the cradle.

Facio Trevisani had ample motive for murder.

Before I left the building, I returned upstairs and asked if the young mother would be willing to tidy up her neighbor's apartment. For her trouble, I gave her a sum that must have been worth more than I realized. Her face lit up and she reached out to embrace me.

"Grazie, signora, grazie. You cannot understand what a difference this will make."

Back on the canal, I queried my gondolier as to who makes the

boats. He rattled off the names of several boatyards,
rticular stuck in my mind: Domenico Tramontin e Figli,
er than ten years ago. Perhaps its relative newness meant it
ore likely to take on a man wanting to learn the art. I would
go there, but first I wanted to return to Ca' Vendelino. If Facio wanted
to kill the old conte, there might be others with equally strong motives,
and I couldn't think of anyone more willing to tell me every bad thing—
founded or not—about the former head of the Barozzi family.

. . .

Zaneta Vendelino insisted we drink coffee and nibble on crisp, almond-
filled biscuits before she would speak to me about anything of consequence.

"A lady must always take pleasure in the things she does," Zaneta
said. "So we will have pleasure before we turn to the serious."

We discussed literature and art for a quarter of an hour before I
felt I could change the subject.

"Tell me, Zaneta," I said. "Signor Barozzi could not have had a
flawless reputation. Who hated him? Had he enemies? Were there stories about injustices he'd caused?"

"You would trust me on such a topic?" Zaneta was incredulous.

"Not entirely," I said, "but I'm perfectly capable of verifying whatever you say. Lying would accomplish nothing but diminishing your
character."

"You assume sending you on a fruitless chase wouldn't amuse me."

"Indeed I do. You're not that sort of lady."

She snorted. "You do have a keen eye for judgment. A Vendelino is
always honorable. Unlike the Barozzis."

I could not help but smile. "So tell me the worst about your rival."

"He was a worthless businessman. You know the Barozzis once had a fortune that very nearly surpassed our own." She leaned forward, her eyes serious. "You understand this was hundreds and hundreds of years ago. They squandered it from the moment they got it."

"Were they merchants?"

"They were a noble family, in the *Libro d'Oro* from the beginning. You know this book?"

"Yes," I said.

"They would have also conducted business, but I can't imagine they earned much money given their complete lack of acumen for it. It must have come through marriages."

"How long ago did their financial difficulties start?"

She shrugged and pushed behind her ear a strand of white hair that had fallen loose from her bun. "Who could say? By the time the old conte inherited, there was close to nothing left, and whatever he tried to do only made the situation worse. Which makes Florentina Polani's attraction to him all the more unfathomable."

"Florentina Polani?" I asked. "Was Signor Barozzi having an affair?"

She laughed. "He was far too staid and boring for that. No, in typical Barozzi fashion he all but ignored her advances until *carnivale* last year, when he humiliated her at a ball."

"How so?" Now I leaned forward.

"He danced with her three times in a row, not knowing who she was. Everyone was in costume, of course, so he didn't recognize her. Her voice was unfamiliar as well, as he'd never paid particular attention to anything she'd said to him in the past. But as they danced, she believed he had started to care for her. I know not why—something that was said while they were in the ballroom, I suppose. They went onto a loggia, for a bit of privacy and fresh air. She took off her mask and tried to kiss him. What do you think of that?"

"I could hardly say. I know nothing of the lady's situation. Certainly, it's admirable that she took an active role in trying to secure her happiness—"

"Enough." She smiled—grinned, really—and continued. "That old fool saw it was Florentina and yelped as he stepped back from her. Can you imagine? A grown man yelping? Naturally the others who had removed themselves to the loggia for more successful romantic encounters all took notice. Florentina was mortified. She's still teased about it. You must know how merciless women can be to the other members of their sex."

"Quite." I was all too well acquainted with the subject. "Had the conte dallied with other ladies?"

"No. He makes an indecent show of grieving his wife's death. It is almost as if he attempts to emulate your Queen Victoria, the endless mourner. It's in very bad taste."

"Was society aware of his ongoing grief?" I asked.

"He made it impossible not to be aware of it."

"So why did Florentina attempt to embroil him in an affair? Surely she knew her attentions would be rebuffed?"

"We can't choose where we love," Zaneta said. "It's the worst tragedy of the human condition."

# Un Libro d'Amore

# viii

*Besina's last day at home was one of the happiest she'd ever known. No longer fearing she'd be forced to marry where she didn't want, her mood improved greatly, and she felt a deep affection for the members of her family. Although she carried some guilt at doing it, she gushed over the fabrics her mother had gathered for her to choose from for her wedding dress and helped her arrange flowers they'd picked together in the garden.*

*Her mother had sighed in relief, glad that her daughter was no longer being difficult.*

*Finished with the flowers, Besina went to her little sisters and told them stories, something she'd not done for weeks despite their incessant pleading. It was a bittersweet pleasure, as she knew it was unlikely she'd have the opportunity to do it again soon, if ever. The knowledge that she might never see them after she left with Nicolò tugged at her heart. It wasn't something she wanted, but she would give them up for love if that were what love required.*

*This thought brought with it a sliver of anger. She shouldn't have to effectively renounce her family to marry the man she loved. This situation was not of her doing. She blamed her father, blamed the doge, even blamed Venice itself. Then she quickly buried the feeling and sought out her smallest brother.*

*He was in the garden, playing with a set of wooden toy knights dressed for the Crusades. At his request, she flung pebbles at them, acting the part of the heretics defending Constantinople. The game brought to mind memories of those she'd played with Lorenzo, and a rush of love for him, her closest sibling, filled her. Her heretics soundly defeated by the righteous knights, she tousled her young brother's hair and went in search of Lorenzo.*

*For three hours before the family sat down to dinner, Besina and Lorenzo read poetry together. She demanded Petrarch first, then Dante. Lorenzo told her about a new poet he'd heard recite at a party and promised that he would find her a copy of his work as soon as it had been printed.*

*It pained her to know she wouldn't be here for him to give it to her. Perhaps Lorenzo would not begrudge her this marriage. Perhaps he, among all the family, would be the one who would accept her decision and agree to see her.*

*She tapped her feet and started to feel nervous. So much about her imminent adventure was unknown. She trusted Nicolò to take care of her and knew she had no need to concern herself with the details, but still she wondered where she would be living tomorrow. Perhaps they would go to Padua to be married and stay some days before returning to Venice. Perhaps his family would welcome them into their house.*

*No, she knew that to be impossible.*

*She made the decision to think about poetry instead.*

*In the days and years that followed, she couldn't remember what they ate that evening, or what was discussed at the table. She couldn't* remember what they all did before retiring to their beds. The only thing she held close was the memory of her mother kissing her good night.

It would never happen again.

Half an hour before she was to meet Nicolò, Besina slipped out of her bed and silently pulled on her simplest gown. She retrieved the small bundle that earlier in the day she had filled with her most precious possessions, and then she picked up her shoes. She wished she could kiss her sisters good-bye, the sisters with whom she shared her room, but feared she might wake them. In stocking feet, she made her way down the stairs to the ground floor of the house. Once in the garden, she slipped on her shoes but walked on her toes to avoid any chance of clicking heels revealing her presence.

She wasn't sure of the time. The bells in the nearest campanile would mark midnight. Nicolò was not yet there. She'd arrived early by design, knowing that rushing would likely lead to noise and mistakes. She couldn't risk discovery. Her heart pounded and excitement brimmed in her.

At last she heard footsteps.

Deliberately quiet footsteps.

She turned the key to the garden gate, praying it wouldn't squeak. She started to push it open.

But before she could slip through it, rough hands grabbed her shoulders and pushed her to the ground.

This was not Nicolò.

# 9

I hadn't expected Florentina Polani to be a married woman. There is no accounting for this fact other than my youth and a certain innocence that I can only hope, in retrospect, was charming rather than grating. Florentina and her husband, along with a brood of seven children, lived in Dorsoduro, near the mouth of the Grand Canal and the spectacular Santa Maria della Salute church. I regretted greatly not having time that day to see the Titians inside, but one must maintain one's focus on work in times like these.

Dorsoduro was a pleasant walk from the Danieli. I cut through St. Mark's Square, past the sounds of the competing orchestras at the cafés and the swarming hoards of pigeons omnipresent in the piazza and continued on to the *traghetto* near Campo Santa Maria Zobenigo. *Traghetti* are gondolas that go back and forth across the Grand Canal, saving pedestrians from having to make their way to one of the few bridges spanning the waterway. I pressed a coin into the gondolier's hand and took a seat on a bench that ran along the side of the boat. All the local men on board stood as we made the short journey, their arms folded, their faces stern and proud. I wondered if I had sufficient command of my balance to accomplish such a feat.

Some things are best not tried, and as I did not think showing up on the Polanis' doorstep soaking wet would endear me to Florentina, I remained in my seat until we'd reached the far side of the canal. I followed one *calle* to the next, admiring, as I walked, the many hanging baskets of flowers suspended from window frames. I own I was a bit nervous. Calling on a stranger to discuss her attempt at adultery is unlikely ever to be free from a certain degree of awkwardness. I didn't want to make it worse than necessary and braced myself for a broad range of emotions from my hostess: embarrassment, anger, even calm acceptance.

Jocularity, however, had escaped me as a possibility.

Florentina's laughter erupted the moment I mentioned the old conte. Not a little laughter. Not a modest giggle. A guffaw.

It seemed entirely appropriate coming from her.

I'd never much subscribed to the theory of physiognomy. A person's appearance might, on occasion, serve as a mirror into his character, but I considered that coincidence, not science. My views on the subject might have been different if I'd considered them only in reference to Florentina Polani.

She was no longer a young woman, though a gentleman at her age would be described as being in the prime of life. Her figure was pleasantly rounded, no hard angles to be found, and her face, with wide-set eyes, rosy cheeks, and full lips parted in what seemed to be a perpetual smile, seemed indicative of a happy soul.

"The poor man," she said, wiping tears of laughter from her eyes. "Forgive me if I seem callous. It's all so ridiculous."

"I'm afraid I don't follow," I said. "Ridiculous?"

"The idea that someone would bother to murder such a useless, base, incompetent fool."

So much for physiognomy.

"Clearly someone thought it worth the bother."

"I won't go so far as to say he got what he deserved, but I also can't say I didn't take satisfaction in his demise."

"Can you tell me what happened between you?" I asked.

"I fancied him," she said, as casually as one might admit to liking lemon ice or scones with cream. "Can't imagine why, now, but I did. He appeared a respectable man, from a good family—which meant he'd be discreet—and I found his devotion to his late wife rather romantic."

"Romantic?" I can't say I quite understood how anyone would find such a thing romantic in a way that would draw her to the person in question.

"It showed him capable of deep love. It also ensured he wouldn't become too attached."

"I see."

"Understand that I speak freely on this subject only because it is already publicly known. I am not the sort of woman who ordinarily puts herself on view in such a way. But given what transpired, I feel the need to defend myself whenever possible."

"Of course," I said. "His behavior towards you was—" I hoped she would interrupt me.

"Outrageous. Nothing short of it. We'd become friendly over the years. Not in an intimate way—we never so much as flirted—just from moving in the same circles. A few months ago we found ourselves sitting next to each other at La Fenice during a performance of Verdi's *Rigoletto*. Do you know it?"

"Yes," I said.

"It is a powerful story. Moving and scandalous and romantic. I adored it. As did Signor Barozzi. My husband had fallen ill earlier that evening after eating a bad oyster. When the conte realized I was on my own, he offered to escort me home. We stopped at Florian for a coffee on the way. It was all extremely chaste."

"Did you have feelings for him at the time?"

"Not before then, but that night changed everything. Have you been in San Marco at midnight, Lady Emily? Have you found yourself swept up by the music and the beauty of the piazza? Have you looked up to see a moon rising above the marble buildings, casting the whole city in a new, bright light?"

Florentina could certainly warm to a subject.

"I have not been so fortunate," I said. "As I explained when I arrived, I'm here to investigate a murder. The delights of the city will, alas, have to wait."

"More's the pity, then," she said. "Regardless, in those circumstances, it is impossible—*impossible*—not to fall in love with your companion. I had no choice. So I accepted it, and I loved him."

"And your husband?" I asked. "Forgive me, but I must ask. Did he become aware of your feelings?"

"Not until that cur Barozzi disparaged me during *carnivale*. His rejection was so public. He pushed me away and made a most hideous noise. It drew everyone's attention."

"What happened after that?"

"I threw myself on the mercy of my husband. What else was there to be done? It's not as if he hasn't had dalliances of his own—he was extremely understanding. It no doubt helped that Barozzi's behavior made it obvious my indiscretion had never been consummated."

"How did you learn of the conte's death?" I asked.

"By reading the paper, like everyone else."

"Forgive me, but I must ask. Do you remember where you were the night he was killed?"

"There's nothing to remember," she said. "We spent an ordinary evening at home. You aren't suggesting I could have murdered him?"

I smiled at her warmly. "Of course not. The question is a matter of simple procedure. Seeing as how you'd taken such an interest in Signor Barozzi, you might have the best insight of anyone when it comes to identifying his enemies. Does anyone spring to mind?"

"I admit I've thought about this long and hard. What else is one to do when a former love comes to such an ignominious end?"

Who could argue with such logic?

"And your conclusion?" I asked.

"There were rumors that he had unpaid gambling debts and had been threatened on account of them, but I think these claims were baseless. He never went to the casino. His son, Paolo, is a more likely suspect, I'd say. He's inherited everything, hasn't he? And isn't the person who benefits most likely to be the murderer?"

I wondered if she really had so little knowledge of the Barozzi family's financial situation. "So you think Paolo did it?"

"Well, he did run off, didn't he?" she asked. "Not the act of an innocent man. Still, I'm not sure it was he."

"Who, then?"

"He may have humiliated me, but mortification pales in comparison to ruin. He destroyed Caterina Brexiano."

"I don't know her."

"She was the most famous spiritual medium in Venice before she became entangled with Signor Barozzi."

"What happened between them?" I asked.

"I don't like to fuel gossip," she said, "but I've no doubt the woman herself would be more than happy to enlighten you."

"Where can I find her?"

"She lost everything, even her home, after what he did to her, and now resides in a house of ill repute."

"A house of ill repute?" I asked, leaning foward. "I don't suppose you know the address?"

* * *

Confident though I was in my investigative abilities, I realized there are some situations into which a lady shouldn't thrust herself alone. As my darling husband was still in Padua, I could think of only two people to whom I could turn: Emma and Donata. The idea of Emma in a brothel was unthinkable, and, at any rate, I much preferred Donata's company. She was smart, quick witted, and game for a laugh. Furthermore, she knew the city and had proven an able assistant in matters pertaining to detection.

I called for her first thing the following morning, after having decided I'd prefer not to visit the establishment in the thick of the evening rush.

"Is it wise to go by gondola?" Donata asked. "Mightn't we be seen going in?"

"The back entrance could prove more discreet," I said. We didn't walk, not wanting to waste any time, but had the gondolier drop us and wait at the nearest public dock. Hindsight suggests we made something of a spectacle of ourselves by having decided to pull veils over our faces to make sure we could not be recognized, but such are the follies of youth. In a short while, we'd reached our destination.

"Do we knock?" Donata asked.

As I was unprepared to burst into the building unannounced, I saw no other alternative. The door opened almost immediately. I started to explain what we needed, but the young woman standing before us required nothing of the sort. She smiled and invited us inside, showing not the slightest curiosity as to the purpose of our visit.

She didn't look like a prostitute. At least not what I imagined prostitutes to look like. She couldn't have been much over eighteen, her skin dewy with youth, her hair lustrous and thick. Her well-made gown was of the latest fashion, and she made several insightful comments on current political situations as she led us down a narrow corridor and up a marble staircase.

I realized I'd been holding my breath almost since entering the building.

At the top of the stairs was a gorgeous room, richly furnished and decorated. I had assumed it would be red. It was a deep emerald green. I had assumed any art adorning the walls would be openly erotic. Instead, I found myself looking at a magnificently executed series of paintings depicting Persephone's time in Hades. Perfect irony.

The young woman handed us over to someone older, an elegant, slim woman with kind eyes and a face that must have once been a picture of beauty.

"Lady Emily, what a delight to have you visit us."

"You know my name?" I was stunned. Donata stood beside me like a stone.

"I make it my business to know everyone of importance in Venice. How may I assist you?"

"I've come looking for Caterina Brexiano." Discomfort pricked along my skin. I hoped she didn't assume I wanted her for some illicit purpose.

"I'm not surprised, given her history. I understand you help your husband in his investigations. But this one is yours, is it not?" With the slightest movement of her hand, she summoned another young woman, bent towards her, and whispered something in her ear. "She will fetch Caterina for you."

"Thank you," I said. "I don't know that I'd describe the investigation as *mine*. Mr. Hargreaves and I work as partners."

"Of course." She smiled.

"What can you tell me about Caterina's past?" I asked. "Her connection to the matter in which I'm involved isn't obvious."

"That's because the wealthy rarely give much consideration to the less fortunate unless they have a specific use for them. Caterina, as I'm sure you are aware, is a gifted medium. Whether or not one believes it is possible to summon and communicate with the dead is irrelevant. Caterina could put on a show like no other and, more often than not, told her clients things about their deceased loved ones that she shouldn't have been able to know. Only the most cynical dismissed her as a fraud."

"Do you believe she speaks to the dead?" I asked.

"Does it matter? I believe she is good at what she does, and I believe she is sincere. She certainly didn't deserve the fate that man thrust upon her."

"What happened?" Donata asked.

"I shall leave it to her to explain," the woman said.

# Un Libro d'Amore

# ix

*Three days had passed and Besina had not been allowed out of the small room into which her parents had locked her. She did not sleep the first night, succumbing to exhaustion only after the sun went down the following day. Servants brought her food and drink at regular intervals, but no one in the family had come to her. No one had asked any questions. Her shoulders were bruised where her father had grabbed her, forcing her back into the house without uttering a word. She assumed he had returned to the calle behind the garden in search of Nicolò after he'd dealt with her, but she had no evidence to confirm whether he'd gone and if he'd found anyone there.*

*She was terrified of what he might have done to Nicolò.*

*A key clicked and then turned in the lock. Besina expected to see a skittish servant averting her eyes, silently leaving food for her charge. Instead, her father's long shadow filled the room as he stood in the doorway, pausing before completing his entrance.*

*"What could you have been thinking?" he asked, coming toward her. She crouched on the floor in the corner of the room and covered her face*

with her hands. "And what do you think I am going to do to you that you cower away from me?"

She burst into tears.

He picked her up, pulled her hands away from her face, and put her on a chair. "Where were you going?"

"I—I don't know," she said.

"How foolish do you think I am?" he asked. "Who was helping you?"

Was it possible he hadn't found Nicolò?

"No one," she said.

"Am I to believe you didn't know where you were going and you had no one to assist you?"

He didn't know. He hadn't caught Nicolò. Nicolò was safe! She could not let her father see the relief coursing through her. "I was so scared, Papà. I can't marry that man."

"You'd rather run away and find your own way in the world, taking only the clothes on your back?"

He must not have noticed her bundle of treasured possessions. "I would," Besina said. "I thought I could seek asylum in a convent. I thought I could hire a gondola."

There was a strength in her voice her father hadn't expected. "An unacceptable choice for you," he said. "You will marry Rosso as is your duty to the family, and you will do so before any whisper of this lapse in judgment can spread. It doesn't appear that anyone outside the family realizes what happened. You will wed tomorrow."

She could not breathe. Tomorrow? Was there any chance of escape? Sobs consumed her.

Her father slapped her soundly across the face.

"No more of that," he said. "Your mother will help you dress in the morning in time to leave for the church."

*Besina fell to her knees the instant he locked the door behind him. She prayed. All day and all night. She prayed for redemption.*

*It did not come.*

*The next morning, she stopped crying, never to start again. She bathed and was dressed and went to Santa Maria Formosa and was given to Uberto Rosso in holy matrimony.*

*Besina feared her soul was dead.*

# 10

When I consider the myriad experiences my work has afforded me over the years, I always count that day in Venice as one of the most unexpected. Drinking tea in a bordello is something I cannot, in conscience, recommend to the general public, but I must admit I found it most fascinating. So fascinating, in fact, I nearly lost focus on my investigation. Nearly.

Caterina Brexiano was no beauty. Her coarse hair hung wild down her back, and her skin couldn't have looked worse for wear if she spent two weeks in the Egyptian desert without a parasol. Yet there was something about her, something magical and effervescent that made her external appearance irrelevant. Donata and I went with her to a smallish chamber up two floors from where we'd entered the palazzo. The walls were covered in pale green silk, and the fresco on the ceiling appeared to be a nuptial allegory. More irony. An enormous chandelier of Murano glass *a cioca*—with clusters of multicolored glass flowers—was suspended in the center of the room. It looked too big for the space.

I took the chair closest to the room's modest (sizewise, not in terms of its marble splendor) fireplace, choosing it because it faced a highly polished wood door. I wanted to know, without having to turn to look, if anyone else should enter the chamber. Donata sat next to me, and Caterina called for tea, which arrived quickly, along with some almond biscuits.

"We've come to ask you—" I started but was interrupted at once.

"About Signor Barozzi, of course," she said. "We will, naturally, discuss him. That is a foregone conclusion. Yet there are so many other things for us to ponder, do you not think?"

I paused. "I'm certain there are, but at the moment—"

Caterina rose from her seat, crossed to me, and took my hand. "You and your husband suffered a great disappointment and were told you might never have a child. I am deeply sorry for that."

More than a year ago, in Constantinople, I had lost the child I carried. My mind reeled, wondering how she could know this. It wasn't impossible—the circumstances of the murder investigation during which it happened had precluded absolute privacy. Yet how had she heard about it? Certainly she couldn't know that the physician on hand had told me he wasn't sure if I would ever again be able to conceive.

"Thank you," I said, returning my teacup to the table beside my chair.

"And you." She turned to Donata. "You will not be sad forever. Your questions about love will be answered."

"My questions?" Donata looked as nonplussed as I felt. "I can assure you I am neither sad nor do I have any—"

Caterina returned to her chair and raised a surprisingly delicate hand. "There is no need for denials, Donata. I know all."

"This is fascinating, truly," I said, "but we really must—"

"Lady Emily, are you aware that your first husband is quite desperate to communicate with you?" Her words were slow and measured.

"Something about your second marriage and a concern he has that you worry he wouldn't approve. You lost him how many years ago?"

This sent chills—unpleasant ones—down my neck and my spine and my front and my back and everywhere else. "It's been more than five years," I said, hardly hearing the sound of my voice. My first husband had been murdered in Africa by a man he believed to be his friend. I had fallen in love with Colin while trying to determine who was responsible for having made me a young widow only a few months after I'd been a bride.

"He's concerned?" I asked, as if such a thing were even possible. "Does he approve?"

Caterina closed her eyes and rocked ever so slightly back and forth. A contented smile appeared on her face and she nodded. "Yes. Yes, he does."

I was about to question her further when I realized I was in danger not only of believing her but also of becoming hopelessly distracted. "Thank you," I said. "As for the conte—"

"No, not yet," she said, turning away from me. "Donata, you are right to be concerned about your father. He does not have much longer to live."

"My father?" Donata asked. "I never said I was worried. He's in perfect health."

"Health is not the only factor in determining long life," Caterina said, "and if you weren't worried you wouldn't be pacing at night instead of sleeping."

My friend winced. "How could you know that?"

Caterina shrugged. "It's a gift."

Common sense returned to me. Everything Caterina had told me she could have learned from newspaper reports. Well. Almost everything. One tabloid in particular had made vague suggestions about my condition that she could have picked up on. Even if she hadn't, Colin and I had been married long enough that most people assumed we had children. The fact that we didn't could easily lead someone to believe there had been disappointments. As for Donata, it would be reasonable to assume a woman of her age would have romantic hopes. Anyone could see she looked drawn and tired—suggesting she hadn't been sleeping was laughably obvious. Her father was elderly and alone. Of course she worried about him.

"Lady Emily is skeptical," Caterina said with a wry smile. "I am used to that. We will speak of Signor Barozzi if you wish, and then we will return to other subjects."

"How long did you know him?" I asked.

"I spent exactly two evenings with him," she said. My face must have registered surprise. "Not like that. He hired me to contact his dead wife."

"Were you successful?" I asked.

"I was," she said, "but he was not happy with the result."

"What was the result?"

"She wanted him to let her go, to set her free. His continual mourning had trapped her spirit in that wreck of a house."

Donata laughed. "Is that so?"

"You find such a plight amusing?" Caterina asked.

"I wouldn't if for a second I believed it to be possible," Donata said. "As it is, I'm far too rational to be so deceived."

"What did Conte Barozzi think?" I asked, wanting to remain focused on the topic at hand.

"He was affronted and demanded his money back," Caterina said. "I refused, of course. I'd done what he'd requested. It was not my fault if he didn't like what his wife had to say. But I did agree to come back a second night. That time, she sent him a warning."

Caterina was extremely good at what she did. A consummate performer. She leaned forward, clasped her hands, and lowered her voice. The light in the room seemed to dim.

"His path was full of danger and hurt," she said. "His wife begged him to change course."

"What path?" I asked.

Caterina sat back up straight and flung her hands in the hair. "How am I to know? I only report what I'm told, and I'm not always given details."

How convenient.

"The conte did not react well to this?" I asked.

"Far from it," Caterina said. "He shouted and bawled at me and then unceremoniously expelled me from the house. The next day, he was denouncing me all over the city. My career was ruined. No one would hire me, and I could find no other work."

"I'm sure there are some people in Venice who would still hire you," Donata said.

"Not ones who can pay what I require," she said. "That is how I came to be here. It was the only asylum offered me."

"I don't understand why he reacted so severely," I said. "Or, to be quite candid, why he took so seriously what you said. I mean no offense, Signora Brexiano, but if he didn't like what he heard, why didn't he simply ignore it?"

"Because he knew it to be true," Caterina said. "That much was apparent."

"Can you remember specifically what he said regarding his path?" I asked.

"Yes," she said. "It was striking. He insisted—to his wife, you understand, through me—that this was the only way forward if he were to save the family, and that some wrongs are too serious to let go uncorrected."

115

"Was there anything else?" I asked.

"No. When his wife didn't agree with him, his temper got the better of him. That's when he snapped."

"And did—"

She interrupted me again. "That is all I have to say on the subject. But I do wish to return to you, Lady Emily."

I was conflicted. Like Donata, I was too rational to really believe Caterina could communicate with the dead. At the same time, it was so tantalizing to think that maybe, just maybe, she could. Only imagine the possibilities! To ask Cleopatra for the location of her lost tomb. To discuss military strategy with Alexander the Great. Most of all, to make sure your actions hadn't hurt someone you didn't realize you loved until it was too late.

I shook myself back to the present. No, I didn't believe Caterina had special powers. Nonetheless, it never hurts to try every avenue. I slipped Besina's ring off my finger and handed it to the medium.

"What can you tell me about this?"

Caterina's entire body shook violently as soon as she touched it. "No," she said. "This is an extremely bad thing. Get rid of it at once. It brings with it nothing but misery and death. It was not meant to be found again. Destroy it."

With that, she flung the ring onto the floor.

"I'm sorry, Lady Emily," she said, all the sparkle gone from her voice. "I can offer you no more today. This sort of communication takes a toll on the messenger. I'm afraid I must retire to my bed."

I watched her leave the room. "Do you think she'd object to me eating the rest of the biscuits?"

———

I had not intended to be glib by finishing the biscuits. They were delicious, and it seemed a shame to let them go to waste. Besides, I needed to do something to maintain normalcy in the face of such disturbing revelations. Donata, however, had no such compunctions. She had abandoned her claims of rationality by the time we exited the bordello.

"You must get rid of the ring," she said. "I don't believe in any of that talking-to-the-dead nonsense, but her reaction to the ring? That wasn't staged. There are objects that bring evil, and we've nothing to suggest this isn't one of them."

"Surely you're not so superstitious?" I asked.

"I didn't think I was until now," she said. "But consider the evidence. The ring reappears in the hand of a dead man. It didn't bring him light and happiness. It certainly didn't bring it to Besina, either."

"We don't know that," I said. "We don't have a clear picture of the rest of her life. Maybe she did find love after she went to the convent. Maybe she was happy. All we have is bits of her husband's account, which may be miles from her own experience. As for Conte Barozzi, my guess is that he would have been delighted to get the ring. If nothing else, it's a valuable piece he could have sold to stave off bankruptcy for another few months. The ring didn't kill him. His murderer did."

"Well, I wouldn't wear it if I were you."

"Caterina has done a masterful job on us," I said. "She had us so distracted we didn't even ask where she was the night of the murder. She's planted seeds about our personal lives designed to make us lose focus, and she's got us talking about the theoretical evil powers of an inanimate object. When all the while she has clear motive for wanting to kill Barozzi."

"You are right," Donata said as we approached our waiting gondola. "Should we go back and question her further?"

"Not at the moment. I want to think about her some more. She's canny. Canny enough to have broken into the Morosinis' villa and defaced the portrait, and canny enough to have seen the value in the act. Not only did it give additional significance to the ring, it also plays into her story that, in effect, it's cursed."

"True," Donata said, "but that doesn't mean she's not right."

"Florentina Polani's motives are not quite as strong as Caterina's," I said. "Something's nagging at me about her, though. Doesn't it seem too neat that her husband so quickly forgave her interest in Barozzi?"

Donata considered my question for a moment before answering. "Maybe not. He has a reputation for being something of a would-be Casanova. It's possible he has no objections to his wife seeking affection elsewhere."

"Possible, yes," I said. "It's also possible he was furious and that he killed the man who humiliated his wife."

"Why didn't he kill his wife instead?"

"Because he blamed Barozzi. What if Florentina had always been devoted before her encounter with the conte in La Fenice? What if her husband believed Barozzi had tried to seduce her, not because he wanted to have an affair but to toy with her and reject her in some sort of twisted game?"

"Also possible, but less likely."

"Even if he didn't believe that, I don't think it's a stretch to say a man whose wife has transferred her affections to another man would want to lash out."

"Very true," Donata said.

"Or even want to kill his wife's lover," I said. "If he acted on this urge, and Florentina knows it, she could decide to protect him. Which would explain her trying to laugh off the affair."

"But it wasn't really an affair."

"That's what we've been led to believe," I said. "That doesn't mean it's true."

# Un Libro d'Amore

## X

*For two months, Besina lived with not a single word from Nicolò. She was able to ascertain from Lorenzo that her love had come to no harm that night in the garden, but she knew nothing more of him. An older and wiser woman might have wondered if he had stayed true to his word and come for her, but Besina never doubted him. Not her Nicolò.*

*Her faith in him was justified. Nicolò had arrived soon after Besina's father had forced her back into the house. He had missed the confrontation entirely. It is impossible to know whether he might have doubted her, whether he might have believed she had lost the courage to run away with him. There was no moment in which he was forced to entertain the notion of doubt. He had found the small bundle abandoned in the garden and opened it. Inside were a single change of clothes and a copy of Dante's* Divine Comedy. *He knew Besina had tried to keep their appointment.*

*Nicolò had fingered the knife on his belt, wondering if he should force his way into the house. Whatever had transpired before his arrival, nothing good could have happened to Besina. Yet he knew he could not take on the whole Barozzi family by himself, and surely they were now armed and waiting for him. He would have to devise another plan. Somehow, he would find a way to be with her.*

*He remained full of hope for three days. On the fourth, he heard that the daughter of his family's enemy had married the wealthy and powerful Uberto Rosso. Rumors flew through the city about the rushed nature of the ceremony and the stony countenance of the bride, but no one took particular notice of either. They were all too used to marriages of duty and were inured to the emotional effects of them. Their attention was soon diverted by the next quasi-sensational bit of news circulated for their amusement.*

*Six more days passed before Nicolò's father came to him with an announcement of his own. He'd begun marriage negotiations for his son. The exchange between the two began similarly to the one had by Besina and her father. This one ended quite differently, though. Growing more and more agitated by his belligerent son, Signor Vendelino rose from his desk, demanding obedience.*

*"I will never do it, Father," Nicolò said. "I will never marry."*

*Nicolò misunderstood his father's motivation for standing. It was neither for emphasis nor for purposes of intimidation. It was a vain attempt to counter the pain shooting up his arm and through his chest. He turned a dark shade of red, clutched at the air in front of him, and collapsed. Nicolò fell to his knees next to his father, feeling his cheeks and his forehead and trying to rouse him.*

*And then Nicolò called for help.*

*But not even the best physician in Venice could bring the dead back to life.*

*Which left Nicolò the head of his family and master of his fortune. He was a man in charge of his own destiny—and he knew exactly what he was going to do.*

# 11

I left Donata off in front of her father's shop before returning to the Danieli, so immersed in thoughts about what I'd learned that I didn't notice the handsome figure standing in the lobby until he took me by the arm and pulled me to him.

"Is this any way to greet your husband?" Colin asked, a wicked smile on his face. He kissed me quickly on the lips. "I do love to see you so deep in thought that you lose all sense of your surroundings."

"Would that I were lost in the study of Greek rather than that of murder," I said.

"I have much to tell you," he said. "And we are expected at Ca' Barozzi. I sent a message to Emma saying we'd come the second you returned."

I looped my arm through his, retraced the steps I'd just taken from the hotel's water entrance, and within seconds was comfortably settled in a gondola.

"Have you found Paolo?" I asked as we pushed away from the hotel.

"No," he said, "but I found the monk. He's an expert on the restoration of medieval manuscripts."

"Restoration? That's interesting. Does he know where Paolo is?"

"He claims not to."

"You don't believe him?" I asked.

"I think he is a devout man of God and stays true to the literal facts," Colin said. "I asked him if he knew how to contact Paolo. His answer was no, but he did admit that he expects to hear from him soon."

"Where is this monk now?"

"Secured in our suite at the Danieli."

"Why, then, are we leaving?"

"Because at the moment, speaking with Emma is more important than continuing a less than satisfactory conversation with him."

Once he'd briefed me on the situation, I couldn't have agreed more.

Emma received us on the loggia, where she was sprawled out on a bench paging through *Godey's Lady's Book*. Personally, I didn't find that American fashion measured up to Parisian, but to each his own. We refused her offer of refreshment. We refused even to take a seat.

"Do you care to explain these?" Colin asked, dropping a bundle of letters on the table next to Emma's seat.

"All of your correspondence with a private investigator from Padua," I said. "Apparently, you suspected Paolo of having an affair?"

Emma sighed. "You don't understand. Everyone here has affairs. It's almost as if they are French."

"If it's so commonplace and socially acceptable, why were you so worried?" I asked.

"Because." She stopped. "Because. Oh, I don't know. Is it really so difficult to comprehend?"

"It's not difficult in the least when considering ordinary circumstances," Colin said. "This doesn't fall into that category. You were pressuring Paolo's father to leave his estate to you."

"That's a ridiculous claim," she said, waving a dismissive hand. Her voice turned to sugar. "Colin, you must help me. It's been so hard, living like this. I had no idea what I'd got myself into when I left London. I thought I was joining one of the most prestigious families in Venice. Instead, all I got was a moldering old house and a husband who doesn't care for me in the way I thought he did. Have you no compassion?"

Emma had a full stock of feminine wiles and knew well how to use them when she wanted to. The fact that she was neither conventionally beautiful nor particularly charming never deterred her. Unfortunately for her, Colin was utterly immune to all such maneuvers.

"I don't believe for an instant you got anything less than you both expected and demanded," he said. "Explain yourself, Contessa. Explain why your husband thought you were trying to steal his inheritance."

"Paolo never thought that," she said.

"Is that so?" I asked. "The thing is, Emma, we have not only your letters but his as well. He had hired a lawyer so that he might discuss the ramifications of divorcing you. The fact that his father had already altered his will in your favor was of great concern to him."

My words clearly stung. Emma swallowed hard and looked up and to the side, a technique I was all too familiar with for trying to stop tears. Perhaps her selfish machinations had finally caught up with her.

"Where were you when Conte Barozzi died, Emma?" Colin asked. His tone was soft and gentle now as he crouched next to her chair and took her hand. "I cannot help you if you don't tell me the truth."

"I was here," she said, tears flowing down her face. "I swear it. But Paolo wasn't, and there's no one who can corroborate my story. I was alone in bed while someone snuffed out the life of the only person who could have saved this sorry situation."

"How could the conte have saved it, Emma?" Colin asked. It was as if he were speaking to a child.

"I don't know exactly." She sniffed. Colin handed her a handkerchief. "But he promised me he could. He'd discovered something that would make all the difference."

"What had he discovered?" I asked, my tone sharper than I had intended. I was not so skilled at feigning calm as my husband.

"I don't know!" She pushed Colin away from her, stood up, and stormed away from us. "He wouldn't tell me. I thought if the finances were better worked out, things between Paolo and me could improve. And I knew that if my husband were in charge of the money, we'd be in more trouble than we already were. That's why I turned to his father. I wasn't trying to take anything away from my husband. You must believe that. I was trying to secure his future."

"That's why he wanted to divorce you?" I asked.

"No, Emily." She spat the words. "He wanted to divorce me because I cannot give him a child. Are you satisfied now? Have you humiliated me enough?" She closed her eyes, her face a mask of boiling rage. "I should never have asked you to come here."

# Un Libro d'Amore

A girl of Besina's age and experience could hardly have been adequately prepared for marriage, especially marriage to a man like Uberto Rosso. He had no interest in cajoling her or humoring her or even making her think he cared for her. She was a means to an end. She brought him money and power and she would give him an heir. He came to her nearly every night, taking her with rough hands and no regard for her own pleasure. He drank too much and said terrible things to her. She couldn't stand the stench of him on top of her and was thankful she could hold her breath almost as long as it took him to finish and roll off her.

Then he would take his leave without uttering so much as a word to her.

Besina hated him.

For two months she did nothing but wonder about Nicolò. Dream about him. Pray that God would release her from this hell—either into the arms of the man she loved or by bringing her a swift death. She did not think she could bear much more. Until the letter came.

It wasn't written in Nicolò's hand. She imagined he thought that *might be too dangerous. If it were intercepted, someone might be able to identify him as the sender. It was a single page, lavishly illuminated by the Benedictine monks in the scriptorium at Santa Maria degli Angeli in Florence. Besina didn't know that. She only knew that the sheet of vellum contained the most beautiful poem she'd ever read and that it had been sent by her love. She knew this because she found the small N.V. hidden in the illustration, hardly noticeable in the sea of flowers surrounding a young maiden listening to her love playing the lute.*

She welcomed him out of love;
But if she had strong love for him,
He felt a hundred thousand times for her.
For love in others hearts was as nothing
Compared to the love he felt in his.
Love took root in his heart,
And was so entirely there
That little was left for other hearts.

*Besina did not recognize the poet's name. It did not matter. Nicolò still loved her, and that meant life was once again worthwhile. From that moment, everything changed. No longer did she mope around the house, scurrying away at the slightest hint of her husband's presence. She kept out of his way with a flurry of productive activity. She ordered and oversaw extensive renovations to the palazzo. She became a conscientious maker of exquisite lace and excelled at needlework. She studied the Bible. She put the fear of God into the servants, of whom almost nothing had been expected before her arrival in the house.*

*She made every appearance of being a good wife.*

*But at night, after Uberto had left her, though she was still repulsed by his touch, Besina no longer closed her eyes and prayed for salvation.*

*She locked her door, lit a small lamp, crouched over her desk, and composed joyous letters filled with love to Nicolò. Each day the pile she hid in the wall behind her bed grew larger. And each day she wondered how she could get them delivered. She could not risk trusting any of her husband's servants, even the gondolier.*

*So deep was the connection between Besina and him that Nicolò anticipated her difficulty. In the midst of a set of needlepoint threads recently delivered that she had no recollection of ordering, Besina found instructions from him. She read them, then burned them and, with no hesitation, gathered the letters from her room, concealed them in her voluminous skirts, and marched to the water entrance of her marital home.*

*"I want to go to church."*

*The gondolier nodded. This was not an unusual request. His mistress was known to be devout. She had never returned to Santa Maria Formosa since the day of her wedding, always requesting instead to be taken to Santa Maria dei Miracoli. She had chosen that among the many churches of Venice because she had been in desperate need of a miracle of her own.*

*Now she knew it was coming to her.*

# 12

Emma was a bit of a mess when we left her. I was truly sorry for her, but she didn't pull me all the way into her web. I knew we could not entirely trust her. Much of what she said may have been true, but until Colin had verified each and every bit of it, I would take it no more at face value than I had Caterina Brexiano's supposed conversation with my deceased husband.

Which is to say I almost believed some of it.

Without so much as pausing for breath, Colin and I returned to the Danieli, where my husband introduced me to Brother Giovanni, who looked a little the worse for wear after having been lashed to a chair in our suite. I admit to being somewhat mortified by this. He was a holy man, after all. My husband, though not a bit religious, had at least managed to show our guest some compassion. He placed the chair so that its occupant might look out the window across the room. The view, it could not be argued, was spectacular.

"Am I under arrest, sir?"

I winced at Brother Giovanni's politeness, feeling we might be unworthy of the implied respect. A monk! Tied to a chair.

Colin crossed his arms. "As I have already explained, you are not under arrest. You are being detained by me, an agent of the British Crown. Would you care to see my credentials again?"

"No."

"I would have preferred not to tie you up," Colin said. "However, you made it clear you had no intention of waiting for my return, and I have not finished interrogating you."

"I was only being honest," the man said. "I could not lie and let you think I would stay of my own volition."

"Nor could I let you walk out when you have information critical to a murder investigation."

"I do understand, sir."

"You restore manuscripts, is that right?" I asked, pulling a chair close to his and sitting in it.

"I do, madam."

"That must be fascinating work. I'm a scholar of the ancient world and wish more than anything that I could hold and read the original scrolls of Homer's epics."

"The stories were told orally, madam," he said. "Homer never wrote anything down."

"I am aware of that," I said. I pressed my lips together and took a deep breath. "I meant the first written versions, but that does not matter at the moment. I'm interested in why Paolo Barozzi required your services."

"He has a lovely collection of books," the monk said.

"A collection that, so far as anyone is aware, is not in need of any restoration," I said.

"Correct."

"So why did he require your services?"

"He did not need a restorer, per se," Brother Giovanni said, "but . . . how to explain . . . he . . . he was looking for something. Something he thought was hidden in one of the books."

"Which book?" Colin asked.

"Unfortunately, he was not sure of that."

"Did you help him find this elusive information?" Colin asked.

"I was trying," he said.

"What about the books Paolo sold?" I asked. "Did he not suspect the information could be found in them?"

"As best as we could ascertain, there was nothing to be found in either text."

"Do you have any idea as to what the information pertains?" I asked.

"He told me it was too dangerous to let me know," the monk said.

"Surely you would have known the subject once you found it?" Colin asked.

"Of course, but he wanted to protect me as long as possible. His father was killed over it. He's afraid he will be, too."

"What is your method for searching the books?" I asked. "It seems more likely that he would have hired an expert in codes than a restorer."

"I will not argue with whatever you choose to believe, madam."

"A little more explanation, please." My sympathy for the man was growing thin. I was beginning to understand why Colin had tied him up.

"Paper—vellum—was an expensive commodity in the Middle Ages," he said, "and it was often reused. Written over again, resulting in what's called a palimpsest. Paolo had me looking for evidence of this in his books."

"Was the vellum reused?" I asked.

"In all but the two he sold."

"Is it possible to read the original text?" Colin asked.

"Sometimes," the monk said, "but only after having removed the newer paint and ink. It's a delicate process. That is what I was going to do for Paolo."

"That would ruin the books," Colin said. "Why should I believe Paolo is not pursuing this in an attempt to destroy coded messages in the later text?"

"Because if that's what he wanted to do, he would have burned them and been done with it in an instant," the monk said.

"Would he?" Colin asked. "When the collection is the most valuable thing the family now possesses?"

"I can only tell you what I know. I apologize if you find that unsatisfactory."

"How did Paolo plan to get back in touch with you?" I asked.

"We have an arrangement," Brother Giovanni said. "But it will only work if I am back in Padua."

"What is it?" I asked.

"I cannot say, Lady Emily. I gave my word to Paolo that I would never tell a soul. Not even the Grand Inquisitor could get it out of me. Were there, that is, still a Grand Inquisitor."

Somehow, I did not doubt that.

It meant only one thing: Colin would have to take him back to Padua at once.

·  ·  ·

"I can't say I regret bringing him here," Colin said. "It was worth it to see you, if only briefly. And he admitted more here than he did when I questioned him in Padua. Perhaps the journey softened his will. Or at least made him take the situation more seriously." Brother Giovanni, his hands tightly secured and under the watch of a stern boatman, was waiting for my husband in a gondola that would take them to the railway station.

"It was well worth it," I said. He pressed me against the wall of the narrow corridor leading to the water entrance and kissed me. "I'll expect much more of that when you return."

I took a seat in the hotel lobby, where Donata had agreed to meet me so that together we could go to the Tramontin boatyard. I'd made further inquiries about Facio Trevisani and found he had sought work with several other households in the city, as well as in at least seven hotels, where he'd made it clear that he would take any position, down to the lowliest. He was desperate, and he was denied everywhere. No one would take him without a character written by his former employer.

The walk, a pleasant one, took us half an hour, across the Ponte della Carita and along the Fondamenta delle Zattere with its spectacular views of the Giudecca Canal. Donata replied to my good-natured attempts at conversation with minimal answers. It was not like her.

"What is troubling you?" I asked. "You're hardly yourself today."

"I saw something when I was coming to the hotel," she said. "It was probably nothing more than coincidence, but I admit it rattled me. Your plague doctor. Someone in the costume was standing in the center of the bridge nearest my father's shop. He was standing there, watching me."

"Did he follow you?"

"No," she said, "but he nodded when I saw him. It felt like he was putting me on notice."

"You don't have to continue helping me, Donata. I don't want to put you in an uncomfortable or possibly dangerous situation."

"I'm not worried. Not exactly. It unnerved me, that is all. I've en-

joyed assisting you. It's much preferable to sitting in the shop and arguing with my father. Still, I think it made me reconsider how serious
what we are doing is."

"It is serious, Donata. Terribly serious."

"Then I cannot abandon you." She smiled. "I may, however, choose
to take gondolas over walking when I'm alone."

"A wise decision," I said. "One can never be too careful."

Domenico Tramontin was not expecting us, but he could not have
been more gracious. Justifiably proud of his work, he showed us the
tools used by the *squeraroli,* the gondola builders, and explained how,
with water and fire, they curved the long planks to the elegant shapes
required for the boats. He then ushered us into his office, sat us down,
insisted we be brought coffee, and asked how he could help us.

"I'm curious to know if an acquaintance of mine, Facio Trevisani,
has come to you looking for work."

"*Sì, signora.*" He nodded enthusiastically. "He did, but I cannot
give him work. He has no experience, no training, and I am too busy
to take on a new apprentice. It is unfortunate. He was most enthusias-
tic. I did not want to discourage him, but I had to tell him it was unlikely he could find the sort of work he wants. He was a gardener
before, so I suggested he see my friend who lives on Giudecca."

"Is your friend a gardener?" I asked.

"No," he said, "but his sister's husband works as one on a huge estate on the Brenta. La Villa di Tranquillità. I thought perhaps they
could use an additional hand."

"Do you know if he took your advice?" I asked.

"He did, he did. I was most pleased." Domenico's smile was infec-
tious. "I told him I would give him a good word, as there had been bad
blood between him and the Barozzis. I know a good man when I see
one, and I've never trusted a Barozzi. Facio is a good man."

"Should we find a boat and go to Brenta at once?" Donata asked as soon as we'd left the boatyard.

"No," I said. "I shall send a message to Signora Morosini and inquire as to whether Facio is working there."

"Then we will go?"

"Yes, if he's there."

"I've always wanted to visit a grand villa on the Brenta," Donata said. "Are you sure we can't manufacture a reason to meet with Signora Morosini in person?"

"We don't have time for such things now. I'm sorry."

"Never mind," she said. "I was only half serious. Not about wishing we could go, but about suggesting we do so when it's not necessary. Domenico Tramontin is a well-respected man. His backing of Facio may have made all the difference. I wouldn't be surprised in the least if he got the job, which is why my inclination was to go at once. Especially given the significance of the villa to our present investigation."

"Believe me, I'm equally tempted," I said. "If Facio is employed at the villa, it will make me all the more suspicious of him. He could easily have been the one who destroyed the painting. But why? I don't know how to connect him to the ring."

"Perhaps we need to learn more about his family," Donata said. "What if they were once great, and brought low by the Barozzis, centuries ago? It would give him even more motive for murder."

"A delicious suggestion, Donata, but unfortunately we've no evidence to support it. Do you think you could research his family? And if so, how long do you think it would take?"

"It would be no problem at all. I will enlist my father's help—he loves feeling useful. It couldn't take more than a day or two."

"Excellent," I said. "I'll count on you. Before you start, though, I need you for one more thing. You've no commitments tomorrow, have you?"

"None." Donata grinned. "And I find I, too, like feeling useful."

"Do you like minding the shop?" I asked as we walked to the nearest public gondola and hired a boat.

"It's not bad," she said. "I can read while I do it, which I like. It's what I'd be doing if I weren't minding the shop, so I can't complain. When my father's gone"—she crossed herself—"his customers will already be used to me and won't balk at finding a woman running the business. Of course, I hope that will be a long time from now." Her eyes grew a bit misty, but she pulled herself up straight and smiled. "Where are we going tomorrow, Emily?"

"I'm sure I've told you before, I believe we have more to learn from the Polanis."

"You have indeed," Donata said, "and I imagine this would be an excellent time to speak to Signor Polani? To see what he has to say for himself?"

"Quite. If we're fortunate, he could prove most enlightening."

"And if not, you will at least have met Casanova's successor."

"You know him?" I asked.

"I do," Donata said. "I delivered a book he ordered from my father not long ago. He insisted on personal delivery, and I can't say his intentions appeared honorable in the least."

"Good heavens!"

"Fear not, I escaped unharmed. Although if it's all the same to you, I'd prefer to distract his wife while you seek him out. I've no interest in a repeat performance."

# *Un Libro d'Amore*

# xii

Miracles could happen anywhere in Venice, but Besina knew that many had been attributed to the intersession of the Holy Mother. And many who received the Blessed Virgin's help prayed before the image Francesco Amadi had commissioned nearly a hundred years ago for a tabernacle in front of his house. In time, the number of pilgrims coming to the portrait grew so immense that the Senate of La Serenissima was forced to take action and ordered Amadi to build a more fitting place for his treasure. The people of Venice threw their support his way, collecting funds to finance the construction of a magnificent new church, Santa Maria dei Miracoli.

Today Besina knelt in that church on the bottom step of the tall staircase that led to the altar, over which hung the famous portrait. It was here that she prayed, not at a kneeler or in a seat. The hard marble pushed against her knees, but she rejoiced in the discomfort. It brought her closer to the Savior, purified her, and, she hoped, would make it more likely that Mary would intercede on her behalf.

She came no fewer than three times every week. When she'd finished her prayers, she sat where the congregation would for mass. This church was the only place she could find peace. The only place where she could let herself believe that, someday, light and beauty, like that in this holy space, might return to her life.

Today she prayed longer than usual. When she was nearly finished, she asked for forgiveness for what she was about to do.

And then, for the first time, she mounted the steps and walked all the way to the altar, bowing before it. She paused, at once afraid and compelled to raise her eyes and see the image of the Madonna. It was even more beautiful close up. She whispered a quick prayer to the Virgin and then turned to the left, going to the marble bench that lined the walls behind the altarpiece.

She sat on the bench, her heart pounding. Would God strike her down for what she was about to do? Writing to a man who was not her husband? She waited, making sure no one else was in the church to see her. She bent over slowly, a small piece of paper, folded and sealed, in her hand. It was the letter she'd written the previous night. There wasn't space to leave all the ones she'd brought, and she decided this was the one she wanted Nicolò to receive. She slipped it beneath the decorative legs of the bench, in the space left by a crack near the curve of the marble near the floor. She walked out of the church on trembling legs, hoping she had not put in danger her mortal soul. The remaining letters were still hidden in her skirts. She would burn them when she reached home.

Nicolò knew Besina's habits. He might have no longer had reason to sit outside her parents' house in his gondola, hoping to catch a glimpse of his love, but he did, on occasion, slow his gondola as he passed Rosso's palazzo. One day he had seen Besina leave and followed her, just to be near. He watched her from the window of the felze on his gondola, safe behind its narrow walls, hidden from view. When he saw the tranquil expression on her face when she exited Miracoli nearly an hour later, *and then repeated the same sequence day after day, week after week, he knew that this was a place they could use to exchange letters.*

*So on this day, waiting three hours after he knew Besina had returned to her home, Nicolò followed her steps, collected the paper, and replaced it with another. They would repeat this three times a week. Besina had not changed her routine. Uberto would never notice.*

# 13

Donata and I met in the lobby of the Danieli and hired a gondola to take us to the Polanis' house. There, when I asked Florentina if Donata and I might have the pleasure of being introduced to her husband, she apologized with great panache for his inability to see us. She was all sweet smiles as she explained how busy he was, buried under a mountain of work from which she could only hope he would free himself in time to dine with his family that evening. I did not believe a word she said. I had learned everything I could about him before returning to the house. Signor Polani had no work. He ran no business, he managed no estate, and he involved himself in no charitable activities. His only occupation was gambling. As the casino was not yet open for the day, I also knew he could not yet be at his favorite chair at his favorite card table.

Furthermore, the gondolier to whom I'd slipped a tidy sum to keep an eye on the house had assured me the signore had not stepped outside. Deduction is all well and good, but it never hurts to also acquire solid information.

I had anticipated being kept from Signor Polani. It fit neatly with my idea that his wife was protecting him. Which was why, as I'd instructed her, Donata was prattling on with Florentina, discussing everything from art to fashion to politics while I did my best to appear glum and distracted.

"Is your investigation stalling, Lady Emily?" Florentina asked. "You're positively out of sorts. I much prefer seeing you happy and smiling."

"I'm afraid my role in it will be sadly limited by things my husband has discovered in Padua. It's likely that's where the killer is," I said, lowering my voice to a whisper. It wouldn't hurt to let her think suspicion was far removed from her. "I will be glad to see justice served, of course, but can't help wishing my role in it hadn't been so diminished."

Florentina smiled. Smugly, I thought, which was not her usual jovial mode. "Padua, you say?" she asked. "How interesting. Can't say I like the place. Too many students."

"The university there is excellent," Donata said.

I let Donata get halfway through a speech she'd prepared on the relative merits of the courses before rising from my seat. We'd planned to bring the conversation around to Padua.

"Ladies, I beg you forgive me," I said. "I'm afraid I have no heart for socializing today."

"You're not leaving us?" Donata asked, her face all sincere concern. The girl would make a fine actress.

"I'm afraid I must. You're both so lively. My mood can do no one any good."

"Is there nothing I can do to cheer you up? Would you like gelato? Some biscotti? Anything?"

"No, Signora Polani," I said. "There's nothing that can entice me."

"Such a pity, Lady Emily," Florentina said. "You will be missed."

"Don't get up." I gave them a wan smile. "I can find my way out."

The statement was true. However, I had no intention of leaving directly.

So far as I could tell, Venetian palazzi all had similar layouts. The large *portego* on the first floor was the showcase: the place where the family exhibited signs of its wealth and influence. Off this room, one would find numerous smaller ones, each connected directly to the next, with no corridor joining them. When Donata and I had been led to Florentina, we'd passed through rooms that all had a decidedly feminine air to them, but I'd noticed that what I could see of the chambers on the opposite side of the *portego* was decorated in an entirely different fashion.

Deducing that this side of the house was most likely to be where I would find Signor Polani, I strode forward with confidence through two rooms and into a red salon overdone in exactly the manner I had expected to find at the bordello where Caterina Brexiano now lived. A gilded plaster rose filled the center of the ceiling and was surrounded by frescoes that could only be described as blatantly erotic. I moved on as quickly as I could, feeling my face grow hot with embarrassment. Beyond this chamber was a library that contained only two medium-sized bookcases, a large globe that caught my notice at once—it was even more spectacular than the one in Signor Caravello's shop—and an enormous table at which sat the man of the house.

I'd expected to find him—needed to find him—and should not have been surprised to succeed. Nonetheless, I gasped at the sight of him. While he was dressed by every technical definition of the word, he was not in a state to be viewed by the public. At least not the female public. He'd removed his jacket, rolled up his shirtsleeves to above his elbows, and unbuttoned his shirt almost to his waist, revealing that he had forgone putting on any sort of undershirt, an act I can only imagine stemmed from an effort to combat the warm summer weather.

"Forgive me." I averted my eyes and started to back out of the room. He put down the newspaper he had been reading, jumped from his seat, and came towards me.

"No, no, it's no problem," he said, buttoning up his shirt without the slightest sign of fluster about him. I remembered Donata's comment about him being a would-be Casanova. Perhaps he was used to ladies stumbling upon him in such a condition. "I am so pleased you have come. Beautiful ladies always manage to find me. It is my greatest blessing. You will sit?"

"You . . . you were expecting me?" I asked, hesitating to accept the chair he'd pulled out from the table. "How is that possible?"

"No, not expecting, of course, but I am delighted. Please, I insist you sit. Who are you? You are too delicious to have escaped my notice. You are new to Venice?"

"Yes, I—no, sir, I was calling on your wife and took a wrong turn leaving the palazzo. My name is Lady Emily Hargreaves. I'm assisting my husband in the investigation of the murder of Conte Barozzi."

"Of course." He smiled widely. "Florentina raved about you. And you have a friend—Donata Caravello, I believe? Pretty enough girl. Too smart for my taste, but there is someone for everyone, is there not?"

I thought it best not to respond to any of this. "I'm pleased to make your acquaintance. I didn't realize you were at home."

"Florentina always tries to keep me away from her attractive friends," he said, again flashing his captivating smile. "I can't blame her." His eyes were dark and liquid, his shoulders broad, his teeth white and even, and, dear me, I still had the image of his half-bare chest in my head. I was chagrined. "Please, now, you must sit, signora."

I obeyed him, quickly regaining my composure. There is no need,

when one has a husband as handsome as my own, to take much notice of other attractive men. I acknowledged his exquisite beauty and
moved on.

"I apologize for having to be so direct," I said, "but I'm very curious about what transpired between your wife and the conte."

"Ah." He plopped onto the chair next to mine, leaned close, and
took my hand. "Oh, you are beautiful, are you not?"

"Signore." My voice was firm.

"Yes. Barozzi," he said. "He was a fool. Nothing happened between
them. I cannot imagine what the man was thinking. Florentina is not
young anymore, but she is—"

I pulled my hand away from his and interrupted him, not wanting
to hear the rest of the sentence. "Does it not bother you that he trifled
with your wife?"

"Look, signora, I know how these things happen. Florentina will
have her flirtations as I will have mine." He paused and looked deep
into my eyes. "I think I would like to have one now."

I admit I was flattered. Who wouldn't be when faced with a man
handsome and strong and in the prime of life? But tempted? Never. I
stood up. "You must behave, signore. And you must tell me where you
were the night the conte was murdered." I closed my eyes, worried my
tone sounded flirty.

"You are most interested in everything I do, aren't you?"

He had a flair for looking at you in a way that made you think he'd
never seen something quite so captivating before. The sort of flair
mastered by politicians early in their careers.

"No, sir, I can assure you I am not," I said, crossing my arms firmly
across my chest. "Where were you?"

"I was at the casino rather late. Then I accompanied a friend home."

"Was your wife with you?" I asked.

"Heavens, no, signora. What sort of man do you take me for?"

I wasn't entirely sure what he meant but could tell I should be horrified.

"Can anyone corroborate your story?"

"My friend." He smiled. "You would not want to make her do that, would you?"

"You don't know me at all." Now I smiled.

"You would eventually break my heart if you let me love you," he said, rising and stepping close to me.

I admit my heart rate increased. Just a bit.

"You'll never find out." I removed myself to the far side of the table, deciding that keeping a large object between us was a wise idea. "Who is your friend?"

"You already break my heart. Come back here."

"No." I was growing tired of his game. "Tell me her name."

"Margarita da Forli." He must have recognized the change in my tone and grew more serious himself. "I apologize if I alarmed you."

"Thank you," I said. "Both for the name and for the apology."

"You cannot fault me for wanting to try. You are a beautiful woman. I am a man who is not dead. Obviously we should be together."

"That's quite enough, signore. I thank you for your time and shall leave you in peace now."

He crossed to me and kissed my hand. "We will meet again, and I promise, signora, I will do nothing to make you feel even the slightest bit uncomfortable. I am aware of my tendency to be, shall we say, overeager. I do hope you can forgive me."

As I was leaving the room, I paused at the globe that had caught my notice when I first entered. "This is an amazing piece," I said, gently touching its smooth, round surface.

"It's been in the house since the sixteenth century," he said. Now his tone was all business. Perhaps I should have shown interest in the globe earlier. His comment about Donata indicated a lack of attraction to women who showed signs of intelligence.

"I can never, ever resist spinning them," I said. I pushed against the surface but found it would not move. "Is it broken?" I asked.

"No," he said.

I crouched down to check if the metal support that held the globe in place had become bent, feeling with my fingers to determine if there was too little space between it and the sphere. As I reached the bottom, I found something stuck in it, and I tugged to pull it out. "Here's your problem," I said. It was a slim roll of canvas, the kind an artist would use, and it felt stiff enough to be covered with paint.

I unrolled it. It had been cut from a painting. Two hands, clasped, with a clear depiction of Besina Barozzi's ruby ring on the first finger of the right hand.

&bull; &bull; &bull;

"I swear I've never seen it before." Signor Polani had lost all manner of a lover. "I have no idea how it got there."

His wife, whom I had summoned, was sitting in the chair I'd so recently occupied at the table. Donata stood behind her.

"Why would we want such a thing?" Florentina asked. "Who would keep it? It's trash."

"It's a picture of the ring Signor Barozzi was holding when he was murdered," I said. "The painting from which it comes was vandalized at the Villa di Tranquillità only a few days ago."

"Signora Morosini?" Signor Polani asked, a knowing glimmer of recognition visible in his eyes.

Of course he knew her. She was of more than average beauty. I

145

had no doubt he had found her even more captivating than he'd found me.

"You are familiar with the place?" I asked.

"I may have been once or twice for a party."

"Did you remove this piece of canvas from the house?" I asked.

"Why on earth would I do that?" he asked.

"To keep us from learning the identity of the woman who originally owned the ring," I suggested.

"Why would I care?"

"He wouldn't care," Florentina said, resting her hand on his arm and smiling. "We've no interest in history whatsoever."

I tried very hard not to lose my temper. "I don't believe you really need me to explain this further."

"It's irrelevant, Lady Emily," Signor Polani said. "We were in Rome until the evening before you first called on my wife."

"Rome?" I asked.

Donata sighed and rolled her eyes.

"Yes, Rome." Color brightened on Florentina's cheeks as she nodded with great vigor. "We'd gone to shop."

"Did you buy anything?" I asked.

"Sadly, no," her husband said. "There was nothing beautiful enough for my darling girl."

"What a shame," Donata said.

"You traveled by train?" I asked. He nodded. "Do you have your tickets?"

"I never keep such things."

"If I were to interview your staff, would they be able to confirm the details of your excursion?"

"But of course." Signor Polani oozed confidence. No doubt his servants were well trained to give just the right sort of answers to prying questions. His amorous habits would have required it. "We returned to Venice the evening after the incident occurred at the villa. It's a long journey from Rome, as I'm sure you know."

"Yes," Donata said. "Arduous, too." The Polanis did not appear to take notice of her sarcasm.

"We won't trouble you any further at the moment," I said. "I do apologize for any inconvenience we've caused, but I am certain you appreciate the gravity of the situation."

"We do indeed," Signor Polani said, "and we are, of course, at your service should you require anything further. Anything." He looked at me tellingly.

I couldn't remember the last time I was so pleased to leave a house.

"Why did you let them off so easy?" Donata asked. "And shouldn't we be speaking to the servants?"

"The servants wouldn't give us any information of use," I said. "I'll notify the police, and they will follow up. Do you really believe the Polanis were in Rome?"

"No," she said.

"If the servants corroborate your belief, would it change how you think we should proceed?"

"It would allow us to confront Polani again. I'm convinced he's our killer."

"He very well may be," I said, "but he would give us nothing but more denials if confronted again. We have to approach this from a different direction, Donata. We need to seek evidence that places either or both of the Polanis at the villa the night the fragment of painting was stolen."

"Or that puts them at Ca' Barozzi the night of the murder," Donata said.

"That would be even better."

# Un Libro d'Amore

# xiii

*Nicolò's letters brought Besina great comfort and much joy. Nevertheless, as time marched ruthlessly on, she lost hope she would ever see her love again. She accepted this, content with his words and his promise that he would never marry so long as she could not be his.*

*Was it wrong of her, then, to wish God would take her husband from her soon?*

*Besina hated Uberto more each day, resenting what he had made her become. She wanted to be a devoted wife. She wanted children. But on those counts, nothing could go right. Three years had passed since she was forced to marry this odious man. Since then, she had three times been with child and twice given birth to infants who did not survive their first night. The first was a girl, with a thick crop of dark hair. The second, another girl, this one with the thinnest wisps of red-gold curls.*

*If Uberto was disappointed, he did not register his opinion with his wife. It was only when his son was born that his manner changed.*

*When the midwife sent a serving girl to tell him the news following* the third confinement, Besina did not expect any response. He'd never bothered to come when the others had been born. He took no notice until they died, and even that did not appear to affect him much. He stood beside his wife at their funerals but offered her no comfort and showed no emotion, neither in private nor public. He never spoke to her more than necessary and apparently did not deem the death of a child a situation that required conversation. Having failed twice to provide him with an heir, Besina knew it unlikely that she would change in his estimation, but this brought her no pain. She had settled into a routine that required nothing from Uberto. The less notice he took of her, the happier she might be.

This time, though, the third, he came storming into her room and ripped the baby from the arms of the nurse into whose care he had already been entrusted. He held the small, frail boy above his head and bellowed two words.

At last.

Besina fell asleep almost as soon as he'd left, but her slumber was not restful. She was afraid of what the morning would bring. Much though she hated her husband, much though she hated that her children were half his, she could not help but love them. She could not bear losing one again, could not bear the site of tiny fingers, stiff and blue, of a swaddled bundle placed in a tiny wooden coffin. The pain would be too great.

To her relief, the following morning brought no bad news. She held the boy, stroking his soft cheeks with her finger, until the nurse insisted he needed to feed. Then she gave him up with great reluctance, wanting to keep him close to her. For sixty-three days she had him. She counted each one. On the morning of the sixty-fourth, he did not wake up, and the house, once again, fell into mourning for an innocent soul.

This time, Uberto took notice.

149

*This time, Uberto cared.*

*He came to Besina that night, smelling of wine as he staggered into her room.*

*"Puttana." He uttered only the single word, his voice a low growl.*

*"I am no whore," she said.*

*He raised his hand and brought it down hard across her face. "You will not speak unless I tell you to." He hit her again. And again. And then more times than she could count. And then he dragged her from the bed and flung her across the room and into the wall. Besina slunk to the ground, too afraid to call for help.*

*Even after this, Besina did not cry. She knew then what had been true the day her father had dragged her from the garden and away from Nicolò. She would never cry again.*

*Besina cowered on the floor, bracing herself for more blows. Uberto kicked her twice, then picked her up and shoved her back onto the bed. She didn't feel his hands on her body as he ripped her nightclothes from her. She didn't feel anything as he forced himself on her. His touch could no longer affect her. She kept her arms at her sides. And she prayed.*

# 14

After we left the Polanis, I brought Donata back to the Danieli with me. With Colin in Padua, and Emma being Emma, I had no one with whom to dine. Donata balked at the invitation, insisting her dress was not fine enough for the hotel. I told her she could borrow one of mine and insisted that she join me. She drew a sharp breath when she entered our rooms, crossing at once to the window and admiring the view across the lagoon to the great church of San Giorgio Maggiore.

"This is a nice life, no?" she asked.

"I'm very fortunate," I said, suddenly feeling self-conscious. "Come, let's find you a gown."

She was shy at first but relaxed after a few minutes, and soon had picked a stunning claret-colored creation of Charles Frederick Worth. Tiny beads of the same shade sewn onto the silk made the dress shimmer, especially in candlelight. As Donata's fetching figure was far curvier than mine could ever hope to be, my maid had to loosen several seams before lacing her into the dress. Then she did Donata's hair, taking it from a simple chignon to a low coiffure, artfully pulling a few loose, dark curls to hang down her neck. When Donata stepped into the restaurant, she was a vision. There was not a gentleman present who did not take notice of her.

"This is a treat unlike any I have known, Emily," she said. "Thank you."

"It's nothing," I said. "It is I who owe you thanks for all the assistance you've given me. I truly appreciate it."

We dined on the most delicious fish I've ever eaten and drank prosecco until dessert, when we switched to limoncello. It was late when we finished, but before I put Donata in a gondola to go home, she insisted we walk through St. Mark's Square.

"It's the most beautiful place on earth at night," she said, "and the moon is almost full."

The campanile was striking midnight as we crossed in front of the basilica. The moon hung bright over the southwest corner of the piazza. Music from the orchestra at Caffè Florian washed over us. They were playing Mozart and then moved on to a Strauss waltz, and a rush of couples made their way to the space beyond the tables and into the center of the square to dance. Warm gaslight, golden compared to that of the silvery moon, illuminated the windows of the surrounding buildings, and in front of it all, the basilica rose, glorious, from this land stolen from the watery lagoon.

It was magical.

Yet it sent a sharp pang of sadness through me. I missed Colin.

"How have I not come out here a single evening since I arrived?" I asked.

"You've been too focused on work," Donata said. "Well, not *too* focused. Just as focused as necessary, I mean. Venice will still be here when you're done."

"And I shall have to take full advantage of it. For now, I cannot allow myself any distraction. There is too much at stake."

·   ·   ·

It would have been easy to miss the very slight hesitation, mirrored by a very slight coloring of her cheeks, when I asked Signora Morosini the next morning at her villa if she was acquainted with Signor Polani. She acknowledged that she was fairly certain he'd been to a party or two at the estate. She smiled. The guest lists were often large, we were to understand, and she wasn't always good at keeping track of her husband's acquaintances.

She was more forthcoming when it came to discussing her newest employee.

"I can't say I've ever been more disappointed in someone," she said. "Apparently he's an extremely gifted gardener. At least so my staff says. And of course he came highly recommended. I had extremely high hopes for him. Many say I am something of a visionary when it comes to landscape design, you know, and I had been told he would work miracles. I never spoke to the man myself, of course. There would have been no need for that. But he disappeared, just like that. Unreliable."

"When?" I asked.

"Two or three days ago," she said. "The head gardener can give you more precise information if you require it."

The head gardener did have more precise information but could only offer what little he knew. Facio had worked hard, harder than most. He'd shown insight and a head for design. He wouldn't talk much to the other servants. He was perpetually glum.

"He recently lost his infant son and his wife," I said.

The head gardener shook his head. "That makes more sense of it. Poor soul just lost his will, I suppose. He dined with the rest of us three nights ago as usual and was gone in the morning. Shared a room with another undergardener who didn't hear a sound."

Donata and I interviewed the undergardener, who confirmed that he had not been disturbed by his roommate's sudden departure. We searched the small, tidy chamber. Facio left nothing behind. Finally, we questioned the rest of the staff once again about the night of the vandalism to the painting, this time prodding to see if any of them might recognize Signor Polani. It was to no avail.

We boarded the boat back to Venice. Donata had been quiet all morning, hanging back more than usual while I was asking questions.

"Is everything all right?" I asked.

"No," she said. "My father has told me I should not help you anymore. He thinks I'm at the Danieli with you right now. I promised him I would go no further."

"Why?" I asked. "Has something happened?"

"I do hope you're not angry," she said. "I'm afraid I ruined your gown. When I went home last night, I . . . I met with some trouble."

"What happened?" I took her hand, worried.

"I'd got off the gondola and was walking to the shop. I could see Papà was still awake—the lights were on upstairs. You know what a short distance it is to go from the boat, but in that space a man stepped out from the shadows and in front of me. He tried to grab me, and I ran. I managed to get inside more or less unscathed, but he had got hold of the dress and ripped it terribly. I'm so sorry."

"I don't care at all about the dress," I said. "What about you? Were you hurt?"

"Not really. I twisted my ankle a bit, but it hardly hurt this morning. He came out the worst of it. I pushed him, hard, and he smashed right into the corner of a building. I've never been so thankful for the strong shoulders that come from rowing my father around."

"Donata, I'm horrified. Did you contact the police? Was the man apprehended?"

"I didn't think I should do anything without first speaking to you," she said. "He was dressed in costume. I think you can guess as what."

"Our plague doctor is back?"

She nodded, her eyes wide and scared.

"It will be fine, Donata," I said, reassuring her. "Don't worry. I'm so glad you're safe, and I think your father is right to exercise caution. You've had no training in evasive maneuvers or anything like."

"I want to keep helping you." Her voice cracked, just a little.

"You can," I said, "but from the safe confines of the shop and perhaps the archives or library, if your father will allow it. We've still lots of research to do about Besina, and we know almost nothing about the feud between the Barozzis and the Vendelinos. You could work on all that."

"Really?" she asked. "I'm so afraid of disappointing you."

"Don't give it another thought," I said. "This will be of great use to me, and there aren't enough hours in the day for me to do everything I wish I could do. Colin and I always divide and conquer. You and I can do the same."

"You're very kind to make me feel not completely useless," she said, "but it seems like I learn so very little. I found out nothing about Facio's family no matter where I looked."

"That's not much of a surprise," I said. "Unfortunately there are few records when it comes to those who are not wealthy."

"A sad truth," she said. "But what about you, Emily? Will you be safe working without me?"

"I will," I said. "Colin has trained me carefully. You have nothing to fear on that count. I know my limitations extremely well and will take no undue risks."

"You promise?" she asked.

"I do."

"It feels wrong," she said. "That I am stopped because of potential danger and you're left to face it."

"We have two very different sets of experience, Donata. At any rate, Colin will return from Padua soon. He'll look after me."

.     .     .

Of course I was disappointed to lose Donata. It is always preferable to have a like-minded individual as a companion in work. Even so, I didn't regret it entirely. It would be a great help to have her doing research, and the wisdom of having her in this role became apparent in almost no time. She had discovered, in the famous memoirs of an eighteenth-century lady, reference to love letters found in a palazzo. Letters addressed to a man called Nicolò and signed by a lady called Besina. Furthermore, property records showed the palazzo in question had been owned, in the fifteenth and sixteenth centuries, by the Vitturi family, who were wealthy merchants before they were wiped out by the great plague of 1630.

Vitturi with a *V.*

In the sixteenth century, the head of the family was a man called Nicolò. He must have been Besina's N.V. That much was obvious.

I know now that I had fallen prey to the overconfidence of youth. It did not occur to me that there could very well be a different N.V. and that he, not Nicolò Vitturi, was the gentleman with whom Besina corresponded. At that moment, all I cared about was reading the letters.

It was an amateur mistake.

Donata pleaded with her father to let her search for them, but he refused. She was not, he said, to risk going into a house unknown to her and begging favors from a family about whom he knew nothing. In fact, there was no family from whom to beg anything. They'd died out centuries ago. A fashionable hotel now occupied the former Vitturi family seat. This information worked no influence on her father, whose inclination was to lock his indignant daughter in her room if that was what was necessary to keep her safe. I could not fault him for his concern, frustrating though it was for Donata.

The majordomo of the hotel was familiar with the memoir in question. Charles Morgandy, a handsome and capable man, didn't recall references to Renaissance love letters but assured me his guests were captivated by the lurid descriptions of the authoress's many indiscretions, most of them having taken place in the palazzo. It was scandalous fun, he assured me, and he pressed into my hands one of the copies of the book the owners of the hotel had printed so that they might put one in every room.

I showed him a list of names. "Would it be possible to determine if any of these individuals have recently stayed with you?"

"I will set a clerk to the task at once," he said. "Do you know the dates?"

I frowned. "Sometime in the past year or so, I'd think."

"It may take a while. Would you care for something to drink while you wait?" Signor Morgandy asked. "Or would you prefer I send word to you when we have an answer?"

"Would it be possible to see your attics instead?"

He balked at the request but agreed to it in the end, accustomed, I suppose, to the eccentric demands of English tourists. I spent a pleasant hour or so combing through the rambling rooms at the top of the hotel but discovered nothing of use. The space must have been cleared out during the palazzo's conversion from house to hotel. I found nothing that dated from earlier.

The heat and lack of ventilation must have taken a toll on my appearance, as Signor Morgandy looked a bit unnerved when I returned. He rushed me into his office with the air of a man who knew how to keep undesirables from the view of his guests.

"Forgive me, Lady Emily," he said. "I wouldn't want anyone to think you'd become so . . . disheveled as the result of an uncomfortable suite."

The dust that covered most of me would have been off-putting to the heartiest of travelers.

The majordomo handed me a card. "It appears our search was more fruitful than yours," he said. "She stayed with us only a few months ago. I've written all the details here. Would you like me to have the clerk continue to search for the other names on your list?"

I replied in the affirmative. It was unlikely two of them would have been here, but one should never take such things on assumption. Unlikely is a far cry from impossible.

"I do have one more favor to beg of you," I said.

Again he balked and again he acquiesced. The room in question was unoccupied at the moment. I was free to look around it. At initial glance, I found nothing out of place. Then I took a closer look at the chamber's walls. In the wide space opposite the windows that looked over the Grand Canal was a trompe l'oeil painting of a garden, beautifully executed. It felt as if one could step into the scene. To the far left, near the bottom, was a small shed in front of which stood two extremely happy-looking gardeners. When I looked closer, I saw the door to the shed had a lock on it, and when I raised my hand to the wall and touched it, I felt metal. The lock was not part of the painting.

I took a lock pick out of my reticule, silently thanking Colin for having trained me to carry and use it, and soon heard the clicks that told me my deft maneuvers were successful. Using extreme care, I pulled open the door to the shed. The hinges were hidden from view and creaked as they moved. Behind the door was a perfect hidden compartment.

A perfect hidden compartment that, much to my disappointment, appeared to be empty. Until, that is, I looked in it a second time and went over every inch of it with my fingertips until I felt a scrap of paper stuck in a crevice in the back corner. I tugged at it until I had released it from the crack, making certain not to tear the delicate parchment in the process.

Both sides were covered with writing, but as it was only the tiny corner of a page, most of it was illegible, nothing more than fragments of letters. Except for a single word: *Besina.*

Satisfied with what I'd found and feeling a thrill of excitement, I raced back to the lobby, thanked Signor Morgandy—he'd been extremely helpful—and immediately hired a gondola. If the boatman found anything strange in my appearance, he was too well mannered to comment, and I directed him to take me in a direction opposite from my own hotel. A change of clothes could wait.

First, Caterina Brexiano had a great deal of explaining to do.

# Un Libro d'Amore

# xiv

When he was finished with her, Uberto left Besina, battered and bruised, blood still flowing from her split lip, without uttering another word. As she always did, Besina moved to lock the door behind him as soon as he was gone, but this time every step was difficult to take. Pain rocked her body as she made her way back toward the bed. The gold crucifix hanging on the wall glimmered, and she turned her gaze from the holy image to the candle flickering on the table below it.

Then the light was extinguished and the room fell into complete darkness. There had been no breeze, no movement that should have caused it.

Besina knew it was a sign.

Without pause and working in the dark as quickly as she could, she dressed herself, took the crucifix from the wall, and stole quietly to the steps, stopping only to listen at the door to Uberto's bedchamber. He was already snoring.

She was safe from his brutal hands.

And she knew exactly where she was going.

Besina had never walked through the streets of Venice, and so the journey she took to Ca' Vendelino was longer than necessary, convoluted and full of dead ends and wrong turns. She was not used to the maze of her city, did not know where any given calle would lead her. She meant to stay along the Grand Canal, but it was not so easy to do this. Three times she convinced herself she was hopelessly lost. Twice strangers spoke to her, mistaking her for a courtesan.

Besina never entertained the thought of returning either to her marital home or to that of her parents. Nor would it have occurred to her to seek asylum elsewhere, because she did not want asylum.

She wanted Nicolò.

The palazzo was unrecognizable to her from the back. She made her way to the closest place she could on the canal and counted how many buildings down from it she stood. She found her way there. She banged on the gate, rattling the iron bars. She screamed for help.

She was loud enough to raise a houseboy. Who woke the steward. Who cautiously tapped on his master's door after he had sent someone to investigate the fray outside the courtyard below.

When Nicolò saw Besina he wept. He took her in his arms and carried her to the most beautiful bedroom in the palazzo. He called for water and wine and, most of all, privacy. He washed the blood from her face, almost afraid to touch her for fear of causing her more pain. He held the goblet to her lips, tilting it so that she might drink. He brushed her hair.

He removed her heavy brocaded overdress and the softer one beneath it and her underclothes. He lowered her into the tub of steaming water the servants had left him, and he washed her body. Washed Uberto off of her. Besina hadn't opened her eyes since he took her in his arms outside, but she was awake, awake and lost in the love she felt for Nicolò. He rubbed her dry with the most tender touch, massaged fine oil into her skin, and wrapped her in a soft linen cloth.

*When he lowered her onto the bed, she opened her eyes.*

*"My love."*

*It was all she could say. He brushed her damp hair from her forehead and told her to sleep. He kissed her gently and pulled a chair close to the side of the bed. "I will sit with you all night," he said. "You will not be alone."*

*Besina pulled him to her, unable to bear the thought of him even that far away, and she kissed him. Deeply and with a fire she had never before felt.*

*Nicolò did not retire to the chair.*

# 15

I did not go directly to confront Caterina Brexiano. First, I made a brief stop at the city archives to request all documents pertaining to Nicolò Vitturi. Then I continued on to the bordello, caught somewhere between amusement and chagrin that I had to visit such a place again. My arrival this time was not quite so welcome as it had been before. I mark this down to my appearance after crawling around the dusty hotel attic. I'd got funny looks at the archives as well but was not about to take the time to change my gown. Vanity has no place in a murder investigation. My dust-covered person (I realized later there was a shockingly long spiderweb hanging down the back of my hair), combined with the later hour of the day—and, therefore, the presence of, shall we say, *clients* on the premises—made my hostesses (if they could be called that) a bit agitated. I could not blame them. I met the eyes of every *client* I saw with a stony, disapproving glare.

I do not apologize for my actions. How often does a lady find herself in a position to show her pointed disapproval of such arrangements? If it was bad for business, so much the better.

Caterina met me in the large main room of the house and took me up a series of stairs until we reached her room, the place where she slept. It had none of the glamour of the lavish chambers on the lower floors. It was cramped, with a low ceiling and walls painted a dingy ecru. The single window was so small as to go practically unnoticed.

"Need to keep me out of view, do you?" I asked.

"Among other things," she said. "I wanted to meet with you privately, Lady Emily."

"Signora Brexiano, do not pretend that you have asked to see me. I am the one with questions."

"You think I do not already know that?" she asked. "Any more than I don't already know about the troubles you have had with—"

I was not about to get roped into this nonsense again. "That is quite enough. I am not here to discuss myself."

"Another time, perhaps."

"I was hoping you could tell me about the time you spent at the Hotel Vitturi. You seem to have forgot to mention it when we last spoke."

"Is it significant?" she asked. "I had lost my home, but at the time I still had some money. I lived in the hotel until I could no longer afford it. How does it matter?"

"I find it an unusual coincidence that the rooms in that particular hotel each contain a copy of this book." I held up the volume Signor Morgandy had given me. "Do you recognize it?"

"I have some vague recollection of seeing it before."

"Did you read it?"

"No. I didn't have much of a head for literature at the time."

"It refers to letters written from Besina—I presume Barozzi—to someone called Nicolò. Nicolò Vitturi lived in the house at the time."

"Fascinating, I am sure, if you're interested in such things. How does this pertain to me?"

"That's what I want you to tell me. When I was here before, you were full of warnings about Besina's ring. I feel like I've been played, like you were trying to send me off on a fruitless chase. Which makes me wonder what it is you have to hide."

"I have nothing to hide—and this, Lady Emily, I must say is a rather disappointing meeting. This paltry information has sent you careening in here in your current . . . state?" She looked with disgust at my dusty dress.

"I came here to give you the opportunity to tell me what you've been hiding. Not, I suppose, that a woman of your moral standing is much concerned with her reputation."

"I will not be insulted."

"And I will not be lied to." I stepped closer to her. "I, too, found the hiding place behind the mural, and I recognized the signs of it having been recently opened. There were small flecks of paint newly missing from around the door. You were careful, mostly—but you made two mistakes."

"Do enlighten me," she said.

"First, you specially requested that particular room," I said. "Second, you forgot to take one small scrap of paper when you left. It's so tiny it's no surprise you missed it."

"Let me see it."

"No," I said. "I wasn't about to risk you trying to destroy it. I don't have it with me." This was true. I'd left it, wrapped in a handkerchief, with my waiting gondolier.

"Where is it? What does it say?"

"It's still at the hotel," I lied, "and it only has one word on it."

"What word?" she asked, her voice too loud and too harsh.

"*Besina*," I said. "Now. Do you want to tell me what really happened the night Conte Barozzi was killed?"

"If I knew that I would have gone to the police at once," she said. She was doing a decent job modulating her tone, but she could not hide entirely the tension she was feeling. The veins in her forehead bulged, and her cheeks flushed.

"Then tell me about the letters. How did you find them? And where are they now?"

"You can't prove I've done anything," she said.

"I have enough evidence to make the police reconsider your potential role in the crime. You request a room in the hotel where we know Besina's letters were, because of this book." I raised it in front of her. "Besina's ring, missing for an untold number of centuries, mysteriously appears in the hand of a murdered man. A man who destroyed your life. A man who claims to have learned something before his death—something from the past—that would reverse his family's fortunes."

"I lost interest halfway through what you said."

"Your interest or lack thereof is irrelevant. I'll go for the police right now if you would like. Or you could talk to me."

"I don't want to talk to you."

"That's your choice. I'll tell them downstairs to expect the authorities." I moved towards the door.

"Stop," she said. "There is more to tell, but it doesn't have anything to do with the murder."

"Tell me."

"Barozzi believed there was something in his family's past that would bring him untold riches."

"Untold riches?" I was skeptical.

"Enough money at least to settle his debts and maintain a modest lifestyle without losing the palazzo."

"The ring is beautiful, but not that valuable," I said.

"Not in itself," Caterina said. "He didn't know about the ring then, of course."

"What did he know about Besina?" I asked.

"Well, he didn't exactly know about her. That came from me."

"How so?"

"She spoke to me." Her tone turned slow and dreamy. "Never have I heard a sadder voice."

On the one hand, I was captivated and wanted to hear more. On the other, I realized the critical importance of keeping Caterina from distracting me with romantic nonsense.

"What did she say?"

"Only her name." Caterina frowned. "That was part of the problem, you see. Signor Barozzi wanted more."

"And you couldn't give it to him?"

"No. Not through any spiritual means."

"What happened then?" I asked.

"After our second séance, he was extremely angry, but I didn't think he would take such drastic measures to harm me. When he did, I was terrified. I knew I stood to lose everything. So I found out whatever I could about Besina Barozzi."

"How?"

"No doubt the same way you did. I searched records. I read books—which is how I learned about the letters. That memoir is famous. It was one of the first things for which I reached when I started my search."

"Why?" I asked. "It's not contemporary to Besina's life."

"No, Lady Emily, it is not." She smiled. "But you forget the romantic notions travelers have when it comes to Venice. If they live in a palazzo while they stay here, they always search for hidden treasure."

"Do they?"

"Wouldn't you? When a family could no longer afford to maintain their home, they would sell it, and move somewhere smaller. Would you take the entire contents of your attic in such a situation? Most likely not, whoever resides in the house later may be interested in what's been left behind over the centuries. People want to find what was abandoned, centuries ago."

"You did not find these letters in the attic. Nor did the author of the memoir."

"That doesn't matter. The principle remains. People cannot resist searching for lost secrets. So I read dozens of books until I came to the right one and learned of the letters. Then I spent the last of my money at the hotel."

"How did you know what room to ask for?"

"You haven't read the book, have you?"

"Not all of it." *Any of it,* I silently corrected myself.

"That was the room where our debauched authoress mourned when her assignations inevitably ended. Where else would she store the evidence of such a sad story?"

"So you do have the letters—and you've read them?"

"I have," she said. "They very nearly broke my heart."

"May I see them? Please?"

"Unfortunately that is not possible. I gave them, and the ring, which was bundled in with them, to Signor Barozzi the night he was killed. But I assure you—I swear on it—he was very much alive when I left him."

.     .     .

Caterina's revelations left me reeling and not entirely sure how to proceed. Only for a moment, that is. Reason soon returned to me, and I did the only sensible thing. I took her to the Danieli and installed her in my rooms, telling her that if she tried to leave I would have the police arrest her.

"The last guest my husband and I hosted here required tying up," I said. "I hope I will not have to do the same to you."

Caterina raised her thick eyebrows. "I do not need to be restrained."

"If, as you claim, you are innocent, you have no reason to try to escape. Should your conscience tell you otherwise, you will be stopped by the guard who will stand outside this door all day and all night."

"How exciting," she said. "Will he pursue me through *calli* and canals? What if I make it to the campanile at San Marco and fly to the top, threatening to fling myself without ceremony into the piazza below if he does not let me go?"

"Do not irritate me," I said. Caterina did not look like she was listening. She was too pleased with her surroundings. That much was obvious. She was drinking in the luxury around her, inspecting the paintings on the walls, fingering the heavy velvet curtains. I stopped her when she tried to look under the furniture for the marks of its makers.

"Am I to have luncheon?" she asked, sitting down. "I've a long story to tell. You can't expect me to do it without food."

I ordered to be sent up an assortment of *cicchetti*, the most perfect food I've yet found when one requires not a whole meal but a light repast. We had balls of rice fried and stuffed with seafood, black and green olives, pieces of spicy salami, thin fingers of toasted sandwiches filled with prosciutto and melted cheese. Caterina's expression brought to mind sayings about cats and cream. She was most pleased.

"You know, this room has a magnificent history," she said, once she'd tucked into the spread of delights the server placed on the table in front of her. "It dates from the fourteenth century, maybe? I am feeling very distinct sensations of—"

"No, no," I said. "The letters. Tell me everything."

She sighed. "I suppose I have tormented you long enough. I will say you've been a good sport." She blotted her lips with a linen napkin. "They were all written by Besina—but you know that already. The earliest ones were the standard sort of romantic fluff. I can't live without you—you are my only joy—etcetera, etcetera. Tedious."

"I imagine Nicolò wouldn't agree with you."

"Probably not. From what I could tell, he was as insipid as she. As time went on, though, the situation changed. She'd been forced to marry someone else and was devastated and miserable. He was a vicious, cruel man. Eventually, he divorced her and her family, mortified, put her in a convent. She died there, still miserable and alone."

"I knew all that without the letters."

"Not the insipid part, surely?" Caterina asked.

"Nothing in what you said could have been of particular interest to Conte Barozzi. Not in regard to the current plight of his family."

"You do realize you're too clever for your own good, I hope?" She took another rice ball, chewed slowly, and swallowed before she continued. "I could only read so much into what Besina said. It's difficult to gather a complete picture without Nicolò's letters. But it seemed as if he was offering something tangible—money, I think—to her."

"Would she have needed money in a convent?"

"Do I look like a scholar of the Renaissance?" She took a deep breath. "Her last two letters contained references to something he'd written that she didn't understand. She asked him to clarify. Whether he ever did, I don't know."

"Could you make any determination as to the topic they were discussing?"

"Something to do with a legacy, I think. I don't have a legal mind, so the details were lost on me. As I said, I think it had to do with money."

"Was there anything else?"

"Only the saddest part," she said. "Along with the letters from Besina there were six written by Nicolò, letters that did not appear to have ever been sent. It was evident from what he said that Besina had died, but he kept writing to her anyway, knowing she would never be able to read his words." Tears filled Caterina's eyes. "It was the most painful thing I've ever seen."

This all seemed to corroborate what Brother Giovanni had told Colin—that there was some sort of information hidden away that could help the Barozzi family—but I didn't know enough about estates and legacies to have even the beginning of an understanding as to whether something from so long ago could make a difference now.

What was undeniable, though, was the tragedy of it. A girl forced to marry where she did not love, her life lonely and sad. The man she loved more than anything continuing to write to her after her death. It was too heart-wrenching to bear.

I knew I could not rest until I uncovered every detail of the remainder of the story.

# Un Libro d'Amore

## XV

*Besina had never even dared imagine such pleasure as that she experienced during the time she spent with Nicolò. The night was not long enough, nor was the following morning. Nor would eternity be. But as the blue of dawn gave way to the rose gold hues of early daylight, Nicolò began to worry. A violent man like Rosso would not well tolerate a missing wife. He knew he must take immediate steps to protect her reputation should Rosso find her before they could escape the city.*

*He woke his love with soft kisses and spoke nothing of his concerns until he knew they could be ignored no longer. He wanted to think only of love for as long as possible. When at last he had to face the inevitable and broach the subject of what they must do next, Besina listened to him, her eyes wide and serious. She agreed to follow his every instruction. She felt no worry. Nicolò would take care of her.*

*Nicolò wished the confidence he had in himself matched Besina's in him, all the while carefully guarding his doubts from her. She did not need anxiety added to the pain Rosso had already caused her. Besina dressed, and together they breakfasted. And then Nicolò slipped a gold* ring with a large corundum ruby in it onto the first finger on her right hand. It had belonged to his mother and had long been a family treasure.

"Amor vincit omnia," he whispered, reciting the words inscribed on the band. He kissed her soft lips and took her downstairs, where he put her in a gondola, promising to come for her as soon as he could.

His eldest sister, he told Besina, would be their accomplice. Lucia would do anything for him. Nicolò had never before exploited her loyalty or asked a difficult thing of her, but he needed her now, and she had not held back any assistance she could offer.

Lucia welcomed Besina to Ca' Vitturi, rushing her guest past her husband's closed library door without stopping to make an introduction. They could not risk having to answer any questions. Lucia's home reminded Besina very much of her parents', and she felt suddenly sentimental and sad, filled with a hopeless longing for things familiar that she feared she would never have again. Lucia comforted her, brought her sweets and wine, and sat with her all morning and all afternoon.

"It shouldn't take Nicolò much longer," Lucia said. "He must be careful to attract no attention to what he is doing and plan the financial side of things in great detail. It is sad enough to leave Venice in any circumstances. You would not want to find yourselves impoverished and without a home as well."

"We will go far from here," Besina said. "To Cologne, and be lost there. Lost to everyone we know."

Tears filled Lucia's eyes, and Besina realized the pain she would be causing, and not only to this lady who had not hesitated to help her, who had welcomed her into her home. Besina's own brothers and sisters and her mother would suffer as well, as would her father. They would all be disgraced by her actions. They would never see her again, would never be able to take even a shred of comfort in knowing she had at last found happiness. Besina wondered if what she was doing was right. How much *harm would she cause her family? And what of the Vendelinos? How much would they be hurt by Nicolò's disappearance?*

*"I am sorry this is bringing you undue pain," Besina said, reaching out for Lucia's hand. "Maybe it is not the right thing. Maybe I should return to my husband and cope the way other wives do. Is my plight worse than any other's?"*

*Lucia did not want her brother to leave. She loved him and her children loved him, especially her firstborn, a son she had called Nicolò after her beloved sibling. She had had no particular affection for her husband when she married him but had gone willingly to his house. It was better than a convent, and she was lucky to have been chosen as the daughter who would marry. Over the course of years, she had found herself growing closer to Signor Vitturi, just as her parents had told her she would, and she now was happily settled in a home far grander than the one she'd left. But when Lucia looked at Besina, the bruises on her face, her scabbed lip, she knew Besina was not an ungrateful girl unwilling to accept her station in life. Uberto Rosso was not a man to whom it would be safe to return.*

*"You must go," Lucia said. "It is the only way."*

*"I cannot do it," Besina said, her voice on the verge of wavering. "What will happen to my family?"*

*Lucia was never able to answer the question. The door to the chamber opened to reveal her husband and Uberto Rosso.*

# 16

After hearing Caterina's account of what Besina's letters contained, I considered my next steps with care, wanting to be thorough and efficient. I visited Donata and her father, asking their advice as to where I might find the last will and testament of Nicolò Vitturi. Signor Caravello directed me to the city archives and told me exactly who would be able to help locate the record of such a document. If, that is, it still existed.

I showed them the scrap of almost crumbling paper I'd found at the Hotel Vitturi. It was from the bottom right-hand corner of the sheet; the letters of Besina's name were small and close together, as if she had crammed as much as possible onto the page. This speculation was confirmed when I looked at the other side. Although the characters were largely illegible and formed only part of a word, their presence meant that she'd used both sides of the paper.

"I can't believe it's really her hand," Donata said, looking through one of her father's many magnifying glasses. "She actually touched this, held it."

"So did Nicolò," I said. "It makes it all so real, doesn't it?"

"It does. Papà, please, you must listen to reason—" Donata begged and pleaded that she be allowed to accompany me. Her father was unmoved, but he was not entirely without compassion. He brought his daughter six thick volumes of legal text from a bookcase in the far corner of the shop.

"Read these," he said, "and find out what you can about the potential legalities of a legacy so long unclaimed."

This mollified her a bit, but only a bit. Signor Caravello accompanied me to the door of the shop and opened it when I was ready to leave. Donata was already hard at work, searching the books for appropriate references.

"I give her this to occupy her," her father said, "but you should go see this man." He handed me a slip of paper. "He will be able to tell you off the top of his head what she will never find in those books."

"Poor Donata," I said, feeling truly bad for my friend.

"No, no," he said. "Do not feel so. She is not wasting time. She will learn much, and knowledge is never wasted."

I left him with his unhappy daughter and headed for the archives, deciding I should try to find Nicolò Vitturi's will before seeking legal help about the potential status of an ancient legacy. The clerk who assisted me was most helpful. What I asked was not easy, he said, but he was confident he could find the document in question. Three hours later he summoned me to a small room where, on a table, he spread a yellowed and fragile document. Weights held the corners in place so we would not have to handle it in order to study it. I pulled on the pair of soft cotton gloves he handed to me and bent over his find.

"It is a very ordinary will," he said, looking over my shoulder. I could read most of it, as the Italian was less colloquial than the letters for which I'd required Signor Caravello's assistance. "He left the bulk of his estate to his eldest son. His other children received small legacies."

"Is there any mention of a woman called Besina Rosso?" I asked.

"No." He skimmed the page in front of us. "I can check again if you would like, but I see nothing."

I couldn't find her name either. Perhaps leaving something directly to her would have been too obvious. I wrote down the names of each of Nicolò's heirs and hoped that Donata would be able to find out something of use about them. Then I read through the will again, as best as I could.

"You're quite sure there's nothing unusual?" I asked. "Nothing that, perhaps, suggests a coded alternate meaning?"

"No, Lady Emily," he said. "There is nothing of the sort."

I believed him but did not let go of the idea altogether. If we could get nowhere with what we learned about his heirs, I could always revisit the will. I thanked the clerk and headed to the law office Signor Caravello had recommended. He was correct—the man to whom I spoke answered my questions almost at once. A legacy, no matter how old, could be validly claimed, but only so long as it could be proved that it had never been collected.

Ca' Barozzi was my next stop. Emma did not meet me at the steps this time. She had kept me waiting for nearly half an hour before I decided to take matters into my own hands. I left the *camera d'oro* where a surly servant had installed me and went directly to the library. I had work to do and would not be distracted or delayed. When Emma found me there, twenty minutes later, she scowled.

"Have you decided to make my house your own?" she asked.

"You are the one who summoned me here to help you," I said. "Now you need to let me do just that. Unless there's something you don't wish me to find?"

"I haven't the slightest clue as to what you're talking about."

"What else was on your father-in-law's body when it was found?"

"Only the ring and the dagger, as you well know." She looked slightly ill at the thought of the blood-encrusted knife. "Why? Should there have been more?"

"Yes," I said. "He had in his possession a set of letters written by Besina. Letters that may prove the family is entitled to a large legacy, long since forgot."

"Really?" Her eyes brightened. "That's the best news I've had in ages."

"Not if we can't find the letters," I said.

"Letters can only tell you so much," she said. "Legacies require legalities. Can't you simply find the will in question?"

I was surprised by how readily the idea sprang to her mind. "I've already examined it. There is no mention of Besina."

"So why are you in my library? If it's not in the will, it's irrelevant. Which I must say is a great disappointment."

"There could be a codicil," I said. "If there is, we need to find it. The library seemed a reasonable place to begin my search of your house. I've contacted the police, and they are sending over several men to offer assistance. If there is something hidden, it will be found."

"What a disruption," she said.

"Do you want to make it safe for your husband to return to you or not?" I asked.

"I do," she said and sank onto a chair. "I know you think very little of me and that you believe Paolo and I do not love each other, but we do. Very much. His indiscretions—"

"They are none of my business, Emma," I said. "I do not doubt the sincerity of your affection for your husband. Nevertheless, it is essential that I know whether you are hiding something from me. Your relationship with your father-in-law is very unusual."

"We were united in a common cause—to keep the family from falling apart. Paolo is terrible with money. That is why his father left the manuscript collection to me."

"Did you see Besina's letters the night of the murder?" I asked.

"No. I swear I did not."

"Then we must tear apart the house looking for them."

Emma did not question this. I was silently thankful she hadn't noticed the lack in logic. If the murderer had taken the letters when he or she (I was not wholly convinced by Caterina's plea of innocence) fled from the palazzo, they would no longer be here.

Unless there was no flaw in my logic. Unless the murderer was someone who lived in the house. If Emma knew, or suspected, that, she might find it perfectly reasonable to assume the letters were still here.

The police did, indeed, send me several capable assistants who didn't balk at being asked to search a house they'd already searched the morning after the murder. It was different when one knew what one was looking for. We applied ourselves with focus and energy, and I do not believe any party could have been more thorough. In the end, we found neither Besina's letters nor a codicil to Nicolò Vitturi's will. We did find the old conte's correspondence, and as soon as I read it, I began to look at Emma in an entirely different light.

The conte was deeply concerned about his daughter-in-law's inability to have a child. I determined this from a letter he received from a gentleman with whom he obviously had extremely close ties. I was shocked that Paolo had confided this problem to his father, and shocked further that his father, in turn, had found it fit as a topic of discussion. Then I read on. Divorce, the conte's confidant said, was unthinkable. Annulment was the only way forward, he counseled, and he believed Paolo would have no trouble getting one granted.

Did Emma know about any of this? I needed to proceed with extreme caution. I wanted a great deal more information in hand before I confronted her again.

*       *       *

As I suspected, Paolo had not taken any formal steps towards starting the process of annulling his marriage. The family solicitors may have known of his plan (if indeed it was his plan) but, of course, couldn't tell me. Nothing, though, had been filed in the public record. With the letter I'd borrowed (with police approval) from Ca' Barozzi in hand, I set off to call on the missive's author.

It was easy enough to find his address, which I'd taken from the back of the envelope he'd sent the conte. As always, my gondolier delivered me to exactly where I needed to be. The house was in Santa Croce, near the church of Santa Maria Mater Domini. Its occupant was a distinguished elderly gentleman who expressed more than a modicum of surprise at finding me at his door.

"So you see," I said, after I'd both introduced and explained myself, "I was hoping you could further enlighten me on the advice you'd given your friend."

"This is a delicate situation, Lady Emily," he said, "and was discussed in confidence with a friend I've known for longer than you've been alive."

"I understand, Signor Sanuto. Truly, I do," I said. "But, forgive me, Signor Barozzi is dead, and if we are to seek justice for his murder, we have to know as much as possible about everything in which he was involved."

"He was fond of Emma," he said. "He found her Englishness most entertaining, and he liked her high spirits. But he needs his son to have an heir. You understand?"

"So Paolo should cast aside a wife who has done him no harm simply because she cannot bear a child?"

His shoulders slumped. "I know it sounds callous. I do. Still, *la famiglia*, it matters. How could I counsel my friend to knowingly sit back and watch it end?"

"Miracles do happen. No one can know for certain there would be no child."

"Some things are certain enough," he said. "Look, the Barozzis were one of the greatest families Venice has ever known. Do you know how many members of the Council of Ten they gave the city? They should not be allowed to die out. It is tragic enough to see them so far below their earlier station."

I fought to keep my growing anger from him. Venice was no longer a serene republic. It was a city in Italy. There would be no more doges and no more Council of Ten. And old families do disappear, leaving behind nothing but legend. Perhaps the Barozzis would prefer a less ignominious end, but fate does not always give us what we desire. Heaven knew there was little love lost between Emma and myself, but I did not think she should be thrown away by a man who had vowed lifelong fidelity to her simply because she might or might not be able to produce an heir.

If it were even her fault. Of course, it never seemed to cross the minds of men that they themselves might be to blame in this sort of situation.

My feelings on the subject were not important at the moment.

"Tragic, indeed," I said. "Such things are sometimes inevitable, though. Did you know that Signor Barozzi left the family's collection of illuminated manuscripts to Emma rather than to his son?"

He nodded. "I did. It was a wise decision."

"So he wanted to give her a measure of financial control, but he also thought the marriage should be annulled?"

"If the marriage were annulled, he would have changed the will."

"Wouldn't that be putting the family back in financial peril?" I asked.

"Yes," he said, "but what other choice did the man have?"

I would have liked to point out several other choices but knew it would not be fair of me to attack Signor Sanuto's opinions. Furthermore, it would accomplish nothing. I thanked him and took my leave.

How I longed for Colin to return from Padua! There was so much to discuss, and I found that, when embroiled in an investigation, I very much needed the sort of conversation that inspired and guided my work. Confident in the knowledge that Caterina Brexiano was safely ensconced in the Danieli, I directed my gondolier to return me to Signor Caravello's shop. There, in the warm glow of gaslight, I would have a meeting of the minds with my new friends and organize my thoughts. I leaned against the soft cushions on the back of the *careghin* on which I sat and closed my eyes. I hadn't realized how tired I had become.

I must have fallen asleep, for the next thing I knew I had arrived at my destination. My little nap had invigorated me. Both Caravellos were pleased by my return, and they insisted that I dine with them in their rooms above the shop. The beamed ceilings on the first floor were higher than those below, but otherwise the spaces were remarkably similar, both dominated by enormous quantities of books. Signor Caravello moved a tall pile of them off a leather chair and motioned for me to sit.

"Tell me what you have learned," he said.

"Not until I've returned!" Donata had gone into the other room in search of their maid so that she might inform her of their unanticipated guest. "I don't want to miss anything."

"Bring some prosecco, Donata," her father called after her. "It's too long since we've entertained."

She returned with a bottle and her father poured. We drank good wine, ate a magnificent *tagliatelle con granchio,* long ribbons of pasta mixed with the most delicious crab I'd ever tasted, and talked about everything, starting with the case. I told them about Caterina Brexiano and the others to whom I had spoken.

"I do find Caterina fascinating," I said. "I don't think a medium and fortune-teller would do quite so well in London as she did here before Signor Barozzi eviscerated her. Now, fallen from grace, she's much in demand in the bordello, or so I'm told. It's quite unusual. Who would have suspected men in search of female companionship would also have such great interest in having their fortunes told? Caterina's reputation may still be in tatters, but she's at least regained some of her income."

"That is Venice for you," Signor Caravello said. "The famous sixteenth-century playwright Aretino spoke of it. *Venice embraces those whom all others shun. She raises those whom others lower. She affords a welcome to those who are persecuted elsewhere.*"

"Perhaps that partly explains why I've fallen so wholly in love with the city," I said. From there, our conversation moved to other subjects. Love, books, friendship. The night was one of the happiest in my memory.

When at last I returned to the Danieli, two things were waiting for me: an extremely sullen Caterina and a telegram from Colin.

He'd found Paolo.

# XVI

*Lucia stood to greet her husband and the unwelcome Signor Rosso. Nicolò had warned her of this possibility. He had told her Rosso would have spies looking for Besina. And Nicolò had made sure Lucia knew what to do if they found her.*

*"You came sooner than I could have hoped," she said. "Have you told my husband what happened, Signor Rosso? I would have myself, but I didn't want to disturb him at his work. And Besina is safe now, though I don't see how we'll ever be able to find the men who did this to her. I would never have asked her to meet me if I thought something like this could occur. That such a thing could take place in front of a church. It is unfathomable."*

*"What church?" Rosso spat the words, making no attempt to hide the disdain he felt for his wife.*

*"Santa Maria Mater Domini," Lucia said. "We had to walk from where the gondoliers could leave us. Besina arrived before I did, and thugs set on her."*

*"What did they want?" Rosso asked, his voice dark.*

"How could she possibly know?" Lucia asked. "Look at the poor woman. They beat her to within an inch of her life. We are fortunate they did nothing else."

Lucia's tone, quiet and insistent, made it impossible for Rosso to do anything but go along with the story. Signor Vitturi, who knew his wife had not left their casa that morning, identified the story at once as a falsehood. The bruises on the face of the woman who was a stranger to him told him all he needed to know. He stood silent, aware that if he revealed the lie, she would suffer even more.

Rosso took hold of Besina's arm and wrenched her from her seat. He made no effort to seem gentle and concerned. He led her out of the room before she could exchange so much as a final glance with Lucia.

Besina felt no fear. She felt no shame. She felt nothing. Uberto threw her into his waiting boat, and they returned home in silence. He dragged her up the stairs and flung her into her room.

"You will never attempt to leave me again," he said. Besina cowered, but the expected blow did not come. Uberto did not raise his hand against her. Instead, he spat on the floor next to where she stood and stormed out of the room, barking orders at servants as he went.

He did not come to her that night. Nor the next. And when he finally did again, he treated her as he always had, using her roughly. It was as if nothing out of the ordinary had happened.

Besina was filled with hopelessness.

# 17

Colin had located Paolo. My mind raced, and I wished my husband had not kept his message quite so brief. *Found Paolo* did little but fuel my overeager imagination. Was he alive? Was he hurt? Had he admitted to a role in his father's death? Was Brother Giovanni with him? Did . . . I knew I would accomplish nothing by wondering. I gave Caterina, who had settled into the second bedroom of our suite, the novel I'd purchased from Signor Caravello's shop that night for her. A French translation of *Pride and Prejudice.*

"Don't say I didn't keep you entertained." I locked the door between our bedrooms, checked on the guard in the corridor outside, and retired. Sleep came more easily than I expected, and I rested, undisturbed by thought or noise, until morning.

The first train from Padua wasn't due for another two hours when I woke up. I considered going back to sleep, wanting the time to pass quickly, but then I heard the door to the room open. My husband sat on the edge of the bed, his arms crossed.

"I wasn't expecting to find someone other than you in a rather alarming state of dishabille when I entered our rooms."

I sat up fast. "Caterina."

"So she informed me. She complained that you're not giving her enough wine, that she's tired of the view, and that she thinks Lizzy is a fool for having turned down Darcy."

"Obviously," I said. "Though I will brook no criticism of the view. Tell me about Paolo. No. Kiss me first."

He satisfied my latter request with a skill, thoroughness, and vigor that left me trembling. He smiled, sat back up, and adjusted his jacket. A man pleased with a job well done.

"How did you get here so quickly?" I asked.

"Special train," he said. "I didn't want to wait any longer than necessary."

"Tell me everything."

"Brother Giovanni is honest to a fault," he said. "I never let him out of my sight. I followed him to mass—sometimes twice a day—into shops, and through parks, but nothing he did seemed pertinent to our case. Then last night Paolo came to him."

"Is he all right?"

"He is, at least in terms of physical health. Although I'm afraid he's not making a great deal of sense. I have not alerted Emma of his return. I think we should have a more thorough discussion with him—and his accomplice—first."

"You brought Brother Giovanni as well?" I asked.

"Yes. We've quite a menagerie. Perhaps I should speak to the manager about adding an additional room until we're finished with them."

"You don't want them under police custody?" I asked.

"Not at the moment."

"Do you think Paolo and Brother Giovanni killed the conte?"

"No," Colin said, "but they're up to something—and whether what they're doing is legal or not, it may help lead us to our killer. I would suggest that you get dressed before we proceed. Your current appearance would tempt a man of twice the holiness of Brother Giovanni. And that, my dear, is no small feat."

"I thank you for the compliment," I said. "Will you hold off on starting till I'm ready?"

"They can wait," he said. "I may just sit here and watch you."

•　　•　　•

I may not have dressed quite as quickly as possible, but I did not delay so long that it would compromise our work, only enough to give Colin something to contemplate for the remainder of the day. We agreed Caterina shouldn't be present during the discussion and we would speak to Paolo and Brother Giovanni separately. We sent Caterina to read in her bedchamber. Colin took the holy man into our room, and I took the chair across from Paolo's in the sitting room.

"Your wife will be very glad to hear of your return," I said. "Unless, of course, you were planning to move ahead quickly with annulling your marriage."

Despite his dark complexion, his face paled. "You know about that?"

"Of course I know about that," I said. "Did you expect to find me incompetent?"

"No," he said, bowing his head. "I am ashamed. It was what my father wanted."

"And now that he's dead?" I asked.

"I will not leave her."

I was pleased to hear that, but one could argue his statement gave Emma additional motive to murder her father-in-law. It gave Paolo motive as well, if it turned out he had opposed the annulment all along. "What were you doing in Padua?"

"I am in an exquisitely difficult situation," he said. "I do not know if you appreciate that."

"Make me appreciate it."

"For some months before his death, my father had started spending much time outside the house. I did not know where he was going or what he was doing, but I was pleased to see him actively engaged in any pursuit. He had become very introverted after my mother's death. He adored her, you see, and found life barely worthwhile without her. On occasion, I could persuade him to go to the theater or to a ball, but it always took considerable effort. Then, one night, I found him in the library with our precious manuscripts all around him on the table, his eyes burning with interest in a way I hadn't seen in years. He was looking at them, one after another, through a magnifying glass. Ordinarily, he would not let them be removed from the case. Ever. No one was allowed to touch them."

"Brother Giovanni told me you believe there's something hidden in them."

"Yes, I am convinced of it. When I confronted my father about what he was doing, he told me he was trying to find a way to reclaim our family's lost fortune."

"So what was that way?" I asked.

"Through an unclaimed inheritance. Sadly, though, I know nothing more about it than that. He would give me no details. Insisted it would be too dangerous. The afternoon before he was killed, my father had been out and came home in a state. He would not tell me what had happened but said he feared for his safety."

"Yes, you told that to the police."

"I did, but I did not give them this." He held out to me a page cut from an illuminated book. "It is from Dante. *The Inferno* from *The Divine Comedy*. He had the ring in one hand, but this was in his jacket pocket when we found him that night."

"Why did you keep it from the police?" I asked.

"I admit I had not taken my father's fears seriously. He'd become agitated in the past few weeks, but I assumed that it had more to do with his age and his mental condition than anything else. He had shown signs of being less lucid than he used to be. Nothing alarming. Not until then."

"Which doesn't explain why you hid what could be a crucial piece of evidence," I said.

"If he was right that this work he was doing could save the family and that it was this work that had placed him in danger, I thought this was a significant clue to whatever he'd found. If it was left to languish in the police station, we might never find out what it meant. Or, by the time we did, whoever killed him could have rendered it irrelevant."

"Why didn't you show it to the police and explain the situation?"

"I couldn't take the chance that they wouldn't believe me," he said.

"Why did you flee Venice? You do realize that makes you look guilty?"

"Guilty?" He looked truly amazed. "No one could think I would harm my father. Had I stayed in Venice, his attackers would only have come for me."

I studied the page closely, wishing I had a magnifying glass. It was gorgeously illuminated, with a blue border, intricately decorated with an ocean of tiny blue flowers around every page. The effect was stunning, but it seemed an odd choice for *The Inferno*. "Have you found anything on it that you think could be a clue?"

"No, nor has Brother Giovanni."

"Is it from one of your family's books?"

"No," he said. "I only know it comes from a copy of *The Inferno*."

"Where were you when your father was killed, Paolo?"

"I'm ashamed to say I was with another woman," he said, hanging his head low.

"Emma said you weren't at home with her."

"She spoke the truth."

"And no doubt wants to protect you," I said. "Can your mistress confirm this?"

"Yes. I've already given your husband her name. It's a bit embarrassing, and I'd prefer to say nothing further to a friend of my wife's. I do hope you understand."

"How do you feel about the fact that your father left the manuscript collection to the wife he was counseling you to leave?" I asked.

"I completely understand it," he said. "He explained it all to me before he made the change in his will. I know I'm a profligate and would no doubt have been tempted somewhere down the line to sell the books. Emma would have never agreed to it. She's much more levelheaded than I."

He seemed a bit too ready to accept this. Of course, there was no way of having anyone confirm his reaction. In fact, I found it hard to believe that so many people involved in this case were so nonchalant about so many things. *My wife was trying to have an affair? No problem! My father was leaving my wife the better inheritance? He was right to!*

Caterina alone had not expressed a similar sentiment, and one could argue she had suffered the most at the conte's hands. I couldn't decide if this made her seem guiltier or not. Just because she had a better motive didn't mean the others' weren't enough to prod them to murder. Then there was Emma. Had the conte lived and her marriage been annulled, she would have been in a disastrous situation, but un-like Caterina, she would face social rather than financial ruin.

We needed more evidence. Which was exactly why I wanted time to focus my attention on Paolo's manuscript page. Colin and I con-sulted each other after he'd finished with the monk. He'd also spoken with Caterina and felt that she was unlikely to flee the city so long as she knew the police were keeping her under close watch. He told her she could leave, but this did not please her in the least. She said she'd prefer to stay in the Danieli.

Rid of one of the superfluous individuals in our suite, I wondered what we would do with the rest. No doubt Brother Giovanni would do whatever Paolo told him to, and Paolo was the real problem. Fearing the men who killed his father, he did not want his return to the city made public knowledge. After a brief, quiet discussion, Colin and I decided we could let the pair of them stay in our second bedroom. It was not an ideal arrangement but would allow us to keep an eye on them and seemed to appease Paolo's fears for his own safety.

"I can bring Emma to you if you'd like," I said.

"No." He did not meet my eyes as he replied. "She cannot know I'm here. There are too many ways it could lead to unfortunate things."

"Such as?" I asked.

"The killers could come after her," he said. "Or what if she is the killer? You would be delivering her to the man who would have to be her next victim."

· · ·

"I've never dealt with a more melodramatic group of people," Colin grumbled, after confirming with the man posted outside our door that he and his compatriots would be required for the unforeseeable future. "Paolo afraid of his wife? I don't believe it for a second."

"You don't think Emma could be guilty?" I asked. "She's plenty of motive for the crime."

"That she does," he said, "but can he really be so thick as to believe that she'd kill him after we'd let her into a secured room?"

"It wouldn't suggest thickness if he had some firm evidence against her."

"If that is the case, he ought to tell us."

Much as I wanted to scrutinize the manuscript page, I knew we had other things that required our attention first. I'd asked Donata and her father to investigate the genealogy of Nicolò Vitturi. We hoped to be able to find a connection between any surviving descendants and the Barozzi family. Signor Caravello began apologizing almost before Colin and I entered his shop.

"There is so little, I am afraid," he said.

Signor Caravello had gone to the archives himself, taking Donata with him. Vitturi's heirs, it turned out, were his five daughters and his wife, who received back the dowry she'd brought when she married. Two of the children died in an epidemic only a few weeks after their father. Donata had pored over marriage records to learn more about Nicolò's daughters while Signor Caravello focused on their deaths. One entered a convent and had no children. At least no legitimate children. One married a duke from Milan. The other, Signor Caravello could find no record of beyond her father's will.

"Not even of her death?" I asked.

"No." The old man shook his head slowly. "It was so long ago, Signora Hargreaves, that things do go missing."

"She must be buried somewhere," I said.

"What good would finding her grave do us?" Colin asked.

"She might be interred near her children. There could be a family monument. We could find out her married name and follow the genealogy from there."

"Alas, no," Signor Caravello said. "Not in Venice. Bodies are buried on San Michele, near the main island, but there is not room to keep everyone there forever. So you stay a while and then your grave is exhumed and your remains taken to Sant' Ariano to make room for new burials."

"So we go to Sant' Ariano," I said.

"There are no graves there, signora," he said. "Just piles of bones."

"But surely someone from a noble family—"

"Their monuments remain longer, but not forever. What would be done with the newly dead if we kept them? There is no solid ground beneath us, signora. Venice floats on the foundations her people have built."

"Is no one buried in the churches? In a stone crypt?"

"A few," he said, "but I would not bother to look. A woman married to a minor nobleman would not have received such an honor. Her family may not even have wanted it. How long do we need reminders of the dead? Certainly not more than a few generations."

"I know it sounds strange," Donata said, "but there is truly no other way here."

"I don't like this," I said. "Something doesn't feel right. Maybe we're on the wrong track entirely. Why would Nicolò have agreed to marry someone else when he was so in love with Besina?"

"You know well there would be plenty of reasons for him to marry, Emily." Colin put his hand on my shoulder, his tender touch meant to be soothing. "The same reasons are in full force today."

"Nicolò wouldn't have married," I said. "He loved Besina too much. He would have refused to take anyone else as his wife. I've never been more certain of anything in my life. He was the head of his family, was he not? He could have decided for himself."

"Yes," Signor Caravello said, "but the fact that he was the head of the family would have made it all the more important to ensure that he had a legitimate heir. Besina could not give him that."

I felt tears smart in my eyes and was angry with myself. Why was this affecting me in such a fashion? I was embarrassed and needed to stop letting myself get distracted by romantic nonsense.

"All right," Colin said. "Time to step back and start again. While I agree there is something to this notion of the past being significant to this case, we have very little else to consider in that regard at the moment—and we've plenty of work to do with people who are still alive."

So it was decided. Colin did not leave me entirely disappointed, however. He insisted that I take the afternoon to examine Paolo's manuscript page while he called on Signor Polani. A male perspective, he hoped, might shed a different light on the man's situation.

# xvii

The drudgery of Besina's days did not change over the following weeks. She was isolated and alone, and her heart screamed in pain every hour of the day. She hardly slept, images of what Uberto had done to her haunting her dreams. She lost interest in the projects that had previously occupied her mind. She abandoned the renovations of her house. She refused to make lace. She could no longer even take pleasure in the works of the poets she loved.

Nicolò had sent no word.

She knew he was waiting until more time had passed, that he did not want to do anything that might draw further ire from her despised husband. Yet to live without the comfort of Nicolò's words was like death itself, and Besina began to pray that God would take her from this miserable world.

Nicolò was not much better off. He cursed himself for not having left with Besina at once, though he knew such a thing would have led to certain disaster. They would have needed money, if nothing else. More than he kept on hand. Still, the knowledge that he'd come for his love only a quarter of an hour after her husband had arrived tormented him. His sadness was unbearable, and he would never be able to forgive himself.

So he immersed himself in the family business, which, though never overtly neglected, was not bringing in the money that it ought. Money was something Nicolò would make sure he always had enough of in the future. He would keep it near him, should Besina ever come to him again. He found he had a good head for the work and soon was turning considerable profit, significantly more than anything the family had seen before. So much, in fact, that before long he was one of the richest men in Venice.

His sisters pleaded with him to marry. That is, all of them but Lucia. She alone understood such a thing would never be possible for Nicolò. She alone knew that some things matter more than begetting heirs. He took Lucia's son, his nephew, named in his honor, into his business, grooming him to take over someday. In this young man, Nicolò placed all his hopes, so far as he had any.

He did not dare leave a message for Besina at Santa Maria dei Miracoli. He did not even dare watch from afar as she entered the church. Nicolò's heart broke, but nothing would be worse than bringing more harm to Besina. He could never risk that again.

Then, one day, more than a year after that terrible night, Nicolò received a slim package from a bookseller. Inside was a copy of The Divine Comedy. Hidden in the pages was a small slip of paper. And on it, three words:

Come to me.

# 18

After we left Signor Caravello's bookshop, Colin dropped me at the Danieli, where I looked in on Paolo and Brother Giovanni. They were deep in a game of chess and hardly noticed when I opened the door. I sent down for a pot of tea and applied myself to the manuscript page in front of me. I'd borrowed a magnifying glass from Signor Caravello but didn't start by using it. First, I read the page, as best as I could. It was from Canto V, when the narrator poet describes the Second Circle of Hell, where those guilty of the sin of lust are forced to spend eternity blown to and fro by vicious winds. The last line on the page was part of something the adulterous Francesca says to the poet:

No greater grief than to remember days
Of joy, when misery is at hand.

The words brought quick tears to my eyes. I brushed them away, refusing to succumb to emotion. Instead, I opened the copy of *The Inferno* I'd brought from Signor Caravello's shop and began to compare the text of the same passages in each, checking for any variation. There was none, which meant it was unlikely something had been hidden in the words themselves.

Next, I studied the illuminated image at the top left-hand corner of the page. It showed a fierce minotaur guarding the souls in his charge, a frightening look of menace on his face. I held the magnifying glass to my eye and bent close to the vellum sheet, but I found nothing unusual in the picture and so turned my attention to the border. Never before had I seen such delicate work. The brush used to fashion each miniature gold flower must have been tiny, and held with a hand steadier than one would think humanly possible. I started at the top, next to the box holding the great mythological beast, and followed the blue rectangle that enclosed the page, moving to the right, then down, then along the bottom to the left, and up again.

It was as if the world opened up for me. Hidden among the flowers were tiny letters, written with such flourish it was nearly impossible to discern them as different from the blossoms. Nearly impossible, but not. My heart racing with excitement, I started to copy them down, assuming I would reveal a code that I hoped would not be too difficult to break.

I began to suspect something different almost at once. The letters from the top and right side required no further analysis. I almost laughed as I looked at what I'd written in my notebook:

TITIAN

It was almost too simple. I continued to work my way around the border.

MOGLIEDIMANOAH

No code had been made from the letters. *Titian Moglie di Manoah.* I needed to find Titian's painting of the biblical story of the same name. I rejoiced that my mother had insisted on so many years of Bible study when I was a girl. Bringing with me my notebook and the magnifying glass, I set off for the Accademia, whose galleries were an obvious place to begin a search for the great painter's work. It was a short walk through busy places, so I felt safe going on foot. I cut through St. Mark's Square and rushed along the wide pavements, lined by expensive shops, that took me out of the piazza and in the direction of the museum. As I walked, I recalled the details of the tale of Manoah's nameless wife.

She was barren, unable to have a child. One day, the angel of the Lord appeared before her and told her this would change. She would bear a son. The angel's words were true, and the woman later gave birth to Samson, he of supreme strength like that of the heroes of the great classical myths, fit for wrestling lions.

A pity, really, that he let Delilah in on the secret about his hair.

I crossed the flat iron expanse of the Ponte della Carita near the gallery, barged into the museum, and begged to speak to someone in charge. Half an hour later, I walked out of the building, disappointed but not frustrated. The curator knew of no such painting. If it did exist, he was certain it wasn't in the Accademia. He gave me the name of a Titian scholar, whom I could find in the small gallery near the Frari church. I hired a gondola and was soon sitting across from an extremely serious young man wearing an ill-fitting pair of spectacles.

"Manoah," he said slowly. "Tintoretto painted a scene of an angel appearing to Manoah's wife, but I don't recall one by Titian. You are sure it's Titian?"

"I am," I said. "There is no possibility of mistake."

"Hmmmm." He pulled a tall, narrow ledger from the shelf above his desk. "It must not be one of his more famous works, or perhaps it is lost or destroyed. Or was never finished."

"I'm confident it was finished," I said.

He went through the ledger, page after page, then flipped back to the beginning. "Could it be called something else?"

"I don't believe so."

"I can't say I recall the story."

"She was Samson's mother," I said.

He smiled. "I know the painting. It is in Ca' Vendelino. Are you familiar with the location of the palazzo?"

•    •    •

Zaneta Vendelino, head of her still-influential family, was not home when I called, but her son, Angelo, introduced himself and welcomed me with effusive warmth. He was on the loggia, where a cooling breeze brought respite from the heat. His chair was turned so that he might watch the endless parade of boats on the Grand Canal below, and he was sitting with his long legs stretched in front of him, his feet resting on the marble rail above. He did not get up when he saw me but gave a brilliant smile and insisted I join him, to enjoy the breeze, the view, and the drink.

I took the glass of prosecco he offered. The only chair available to me was next to him, extremely close to his own. I scooted it over a few feet and took stock of the man beside me. He was extremely handsome. Dark blond curls framed a tanned, masculine face, and thick, impossibly long lashes lined his bright blue eyes.

"When my servant told me you had appeared at the door in search of art, I could not resist inviting you up in the hope you might teach

201

me something. My own lack of mastery of the subject is a source of much embarrassment. Yet I am too lazy to apply myself to the study of it. Do you make a practice of knocking on doors of palazzi in search of Renaissance treasure? I understand the English are very enterprising tourists."

"No, it's not something I do on a regular basis," I said. The cool prosecco and the breeze felt good. The combination of summer heat and excitement had caught up with me more than I'd noticed. My cheeks felt hot. "Your family owns a painting in which I have great interest. It's a Titian—a depiction of an angel appearing to Manoah's wife."

He raised an eyebrow and smiled. "As I said, I'm afraid I know very little about art. I would be more than happy, however, to give you a tour of the house, and you will, maybe, recognize the piece?"

"That would be lovely, thank you."

"It is unlikely there would be anything in here," he said, leading me from the loggia—only after we'd both finished our prosecco—and into the *portego*. "These are all portraits of my ancestors. Very distinguished, you understand. Count the members of the Council of Ten if you wish."

"An impressive collection," I said.

"You think?" he asked. "I think they're dour. When I inherit I'm going to pull them all down and replace them with something more pleasant."

"What will you do with them?" I asked.

"Don't be alarmed, Lady Emily," he said. "I am not destructive. There is a room upstairs that will make an excellent home for them. But I'd prefer to make the *portego* a lighter, more pleasant space to be. My taste in art runs more to the modern. Do you know the Impressionists?"

I made note of the contradiction, as he had earlier claimed little knowledge of art. The ensuing digression on the subject was extremely pleasant and proved him to be something of an expert on the topic. As I was well acquainted with a number of the painters in the Impressionist movement, I was able to give Signor Vendelino a wealth of information about them. He was particularly interested in the details of their studios. When he learned that Renoir had painted my portrait, he put his hand to his heart, threw back his handsome head, and sighed.

"If I could have him paint the woman I love," he said. "Nothing could be more beautiful."

"Are you married, signore?"

"Indeed I am," he said.

"Then your wife is a lucky woman," I said. "Your ardor is admirable."

"You flatter me, but don't quite hit the mark," he said. "My wife is lucky in many ways, but unfortunately it is not she who inspires my ardor."

I felt my face flush crimson. "I'm terribly sorry."

"Ah, don't be," he said, leading me into the next room. "It's not so uncommon a situation. Who doesn't share my plight?"

We made our way through countless rooms, including that in which Zaneta had received me when I last spoke to her. But no Titian. Well. At least not the *right* Titian. Then, not long after I'd started to worry we'd never find it, we turned into a splendid chamber, done in shades of the palest blue. There, on the wall opposite an imposing marble fireplace, was our quarry.

The canvas was large. In the center, a woman in a blue gown knelt, her face bowed. Above her and to the left, a lovely angel, clothed in a white gown and a scarf that nearly matched the woman's gown, hovered in the air. To her right was a large tree, part of the luscious garden in which the encounter was taking place. And there, attached to the frame, was a brass plaque identifying the work.

*Apparizione dell'angelo a Moglie di Manoah* —Titian

I stepped back from the painting, first wanting to take it in as a whole. Then I moved closer, dividing the canvas into small areas and analyzing them one at a time. I didn't notice what the painting concealed at first. The marks were hidden from my view until I pulled out Signor Caravello's magnifying glass and looked even more closely. There they were, clearly visible magnified, halfway across the scene: a series of infinitesimally small letters winding their way up and down both sides of the tree trunk and around all its branches.

"Will you help me?" I asked Signor Vendelino, passing him my notebook and pencil. "I'll say the letters and you write them down."

Soon we had a long string of letters. From there, it took very little time to decipher their meaning. Like the clue in the page of Dante, they were not encrypted.

I, Nicolò Vendelino, do here bequeath my estate in its entirely to Tomaso Rosso, only surviving son of Besina Rosso, born Barozzi.

Following that were two tiny signatures, their names printed in capitals after each: Nicolò Vendelino and Giulio Zorzi. This took me aback. I'd expected it to read Nicolò Vitturi. Yet here was a different N.V., Nicolò Vendelino.

Signor Vendelino laughed. I looked at him, and he only laughed harder, covering his mouth and shaking his head in apology. "Forgive me," he said, "but this will send my mother to an early grave. Just to see the names Vendelino and Barozzi together."

"Yes, I've heard of this feud between your families," I said. "Have you any idea of the origin?"

"That I do. It may be the only history I know. It was hundreds of years ago, when Venice was still a great republic, controlling all the seas. The doge had promised the Crusaders the Venetians would join their cause. Instead, he turned his ships to Constantinople and sacked the city. On the way back, some of the fleet was caught in a terrible storm, and a boat owned by the Barozzis overturned. Not far ahead of it was a boat owned by the Vendelinos. The captain saw the chaos behind him but did not want to risk his own men's lives. They did not go back and rescue the survivors. Unfortunately, the two men who did manage to cling to life and survive what must have been a dreadful night in the ocean, hanging on to debris, were brothers of the Barozzi family. They had watched their father drown and had been able to do nothing to save him."

"How dreadful," I said.

"Yes," he said. "The next morning the sea was calm, and they were hoisted from the water and into the very ship that the night before would offer no help. When dark fell again, and everyone else was asleep, the Barozzis took their revenge. They slit the throats of every Vendelino on board."

"So everyone is to blame."

"A disinterested party might think so," he said, "but neither the Barozzis nor the Vendelinos could be described as such. They have hated each other ever since. Through the next centuries, they fought each other whenever they could."

"Your mother still hates them?"

"Of course," he said with an engaging smile. "She is Vendelino, as am I. We would never receive a Barozzi into our home."

"Yet you laughed when you read the words," I said.

"Only at the notion that a Vendelino would leave money to a Barozzi. It would never have happened. Look, I do not hold with the past so much as my mother does. In another generation or two, no one will remember this feud. But during the age of Titian? This would have been impossible."

# Un Libro d'Amore

Come to me.

*The words haunted Nicolò, taunted him, even, as he strove to concoct a plan to reach Besina. He had his spies start to watch her again. Two of his closest friends knew Rosso, but he could not risk speaking to them, even in the most general terms, about his enemy. He did not trust himself to be able to hide his hatred.*

*Santa Maria dei Miracoli was the only answer.*

*Besina visited there, three times a week, as she always had, and as before, she stayed for nearly an hour each time. His spies could tell him that much, but no one could say whether she still climbed the marble steps to the altar, slipped behind, and checked for a message from him, hidden in the tiny crevice he'd found on the foot of one of the benches behind the altar. If she did, he could not imagine the heartache and pain it must have caused her, over and over again, to find nothing. Still, Besina would not doubt his love or fidelity. She would know that he had stopped writing only to protect her from her husband's rough hands.*

*Now, he hoped, enough time had passed for Rosso to be distracted by other things.*

*When Besina next stepped into the church the following week, the light seemed different to her. The pale marble of the walls, pastel hues divided by thick, strong bars of gray or ocher, were warm and aglow. True, the sun was shining, its light filtering through the clear windows that lined the nave and illuminated the space around the altar, but that was not out of the ordinary. She raised her eyes to the coffered ceiling and, as was her habit, counted the painted panels that lined it before she stepped forward.*

*She knelt and crossed herself as she took her customary spot at the bottom of the steps leading to the holy and miraculous altarpiece, not looking up until she'd confessed her sins to God himself, not to his priest on earth. She begged forgiveness and bowed her head again and prayed with a desperate fervor to Mary. The sun sent her shadow long across the marble stairs, and this time, instead of rising to climb them when she'd finished, she moved, slowly, on her knees, one step at a time, her lips forming the words of a silent prayer as she paused before she went on to the next. At the top, she prostrated herself before the altar, weeping.*

*She did not know how she could go on any longer.*

*When at last she lifted her head and rose to her feet, she almost went home without looking for a message from Nicolò. It had been long, too long, too many days and weeks and months with nothing hidden behind the altar. She started to turn away, thinking she could not bear to be disappointed yet again, but as she did, the serene image of the Virgin caught her eye. She seemed to smile.*

*Besina's heart pounded in her chest.*

*Today was different.*

She dropped back onto her knees, praying, her heart and mind at odds and confused. She loved Nicolò, but she knew this love was a sin. Yet here was Mary, smiling upon her.

Besina, almost without knowing what she was doing, rose again and stepped around the altar, to the left, to the place that held all the hopes of her heart. She sat on the bench. She lowered her hand, feeling the cool touch of marble against her skin. Then there was something else. A tiny slip of paper.

It was as if heaven itself opened up and a chorus of angels was singing in celebration. Never had Besina known such joy. She wanted to stay there, in Miracoli, and live forever in this moment. She pulled herself to her feet, steadying herself with a hand against the delicately carved marble that trimmed the walls around the altar.

She realized she could not wait any longer to read Nicolò's words.

She could not bear to read them in Uberto's house.

Bowing again before the altar as she passed it, she went down the steps and along the aisle between the rows of wooden pews. She sat in the last on the left. She opened the paper.

This time, Nicolò had not placed the note only a few hours before Besina would arrive. This time, he had come the night before and hidden his missive. But he had not left the church. The next day, after he'd spent a lonely night full of anticipation, no one watching Besina would have any idea that he'd entered the building. He sequestered himself in a room used for storage behind one of the two doors that led to the space beneath the altar. He hid himself in a corner, under a table surrounded by piles of stacked chairs, and he waited. He'd waited through morning mass and confessions. He'd waited what seemed like endless hours. He hadn't slept. He hadn't done anything but listen for movement at the door.

*Now, in the nave, Besina trembled, rising to her feet.*

*She walked toward the altar. She reached for the door on the left, adjacent to the statue of St. Francis. She pushed it open.*

*Besina fell into Nicolò's arms on the other side.*

# 19

Back at the Danieli, I tapped my feet in impatient anticipation of Colin's return, half inclined to rush to Signor Caravello's shop without my husband to share with Donata what I had learned. All this time we might have been searching for the wrong Nicolò! I couldn't wait to see my friend's reaction when I told her Titian had modeled the face of the nameless woman after Besina's. I had not noticed at first, but close inspection following my discovery of the hidden text in the painting had led to my conclusion. The woman's face was a mirror image of that on the portrait that had been vandalized at the Morosinis' villa.

After what felt like endless hours, Colin returned from his visit to Signor Polani and found me in the lobby, where I'd taken up residence at a comfortable table not far from the front desk. It was a glorious space, with high ceilings decorated with plaster roses and large chandeliers of Murano glass *a ciocca*. I was drinking a glass of cool lemonade when Colin arrived. He gave me a quick kiss, ordered a coffee, and told me he'd return as soon as he'd checked on Paolo and Brother

Giovanni upstairs. I sipped my drink with great impatience waiting for him to come back.

"No trouble upstairs." He slid close to me on the silk-covered settee. "How on earth did you handle Signor Polani on your own? I'm surprised you escaped with your honor intact."

"I assure you there was no danger of any other outcome," I said.

"I am not accusing you, my dear," he said, squeezing my hand. "Quite the contrary. He is all persistent charm. Not many ladies could be as strong as you."

"Not many ladies have husbands as handsome as mine."

He smiled. "You're bursting to tell me something, aren't you?"

"You can't even imagine," I said.

"I'm going to make you wait. This time, I'm going first." He sipped the coffee that had arrived before he'd come back downstairs, and then he pulled from his jacket pocket a packet of English chocolate-covered biscuits. "Before you accuse me of not drinking limoncello or something else you find suitably Italian, I will have you know Venice was the first city in the west to sell coffee. It may be, my dear, that I am even more Venetian than you."

"I'm glad to hear it," I said.

"Polani is an interesting character. Your instincts about him are quite right, I think. He claims not to care about his wife's near-dalliance with Barozzi, but man to man it was clear he was not entirely unaffected by the incident—and not because Barozzi had humiliated her."

"He was jealous?"

"He didn't like someone invading his territory. He doesn't truly believe his wife was the sole instigator of the friendship."

His smile was too bright. "Are you intoxicated?" I asked.

"No, but I've had more to drink than usual for this time of day," he said. "How do you think I managed to get Polani to talk?"

"You're a cad," I said.

"I'm a slave to my work." He grinned. "Polani told me he intercepted a letter that came to his wife from Barozzi. It was an invitation to go to the opera—after that first night at La Fenice."

"Do you think there was a relationship between them?"

"I spoke with Signora Polani as well," he said. "I think there can be no doubt Barozzi hurt her as much as he humiliated her."

"Leading you to conclude what?" I asked.

"That either of them might have killed him if they felt so inclined in the moment, but that their motives don't seem quite as strong as those of some of our other suspects."

"We may have to start considering an additional pool," I said. "I believe we've been searching for the wrong Nicolò." I recounted the events of my afternoon.

"There could an obvious connection, you know. Vitturi's daughter could have married a Vendelino."

"Vitturi's daughter did indeed marry a Vendelino."

"You located the missing records at the archive?"

"No, but I persuaded Angelo to show me the Vendelino family documents pertaining to the match. They've noted every birth, death, and marriage in a giant, leather-bound book that's trimmed in solid gold," I said. "When Nicolò Vendelino died, he had no children—he'd never married. He named his nephew, Nicolò Vitturi, his heir. One of Vitturi's daughters married a distant Vendelino cousin, and it was this man whom Vitturi named as his own heir."

"Why didn't he choose a Vitturi as his heir?" Colin asked.

I shrugged. "According to Angelo Vendelino it was because he knew Vendelino was the stronger name. More likely is that there wasn't a suitable male in the family to name as head."

"So why, if he had arranged a marriage that he thought would increase the family's power under a different name, would he have then changed his mind and left the estate to someone wholly unrelated to him, even by marriage?"

Sometimes gentlemen could be so naive it was almost painful. "Perhaps, my dear, Tomaso *wasn't* wholly unrelated to Nicolò."

"That's possible, of course, but proving it would be near *im*possible. I would like to see this painting," he said, studying my notebook, which was open to the page on which I had transcribed the text taken there from. "I can't imagine, though, that anyone would consider it a legally binding codicil to Vendelino's will."

"I agree you're most likely right, but it is signed and witnessed, at least in theory. It's not entirely impossible that a court would uphold it. Unlikely in the extreme, but not impossible."

"I shall consult the necessary solicitors. I don't suppose you fancy digging into the Vendelino family's dark secrets to see if any of them have reason beyond their supposed blood feud to want Barozzi dead?"

.   .   .

Angelo Vendelino was no longer at home when I returned to Ca' Vendelino, but his mother received me. A servant led me through the labyrinth of rooms to the salmon-colored one Zaneta favored, where I once again found the lady of the house on her chaise longue. She was reading *Le Château des Carpathes* by Jules Verne.

"One moment," she said, raising a slim finger but not looking up as I entered the room. I stood, awkward, for several minutes, not wanting to take a seat before she'd offered it. She kept reading.

And kept reading.

I was growing increasingly impatient.

Finally she shut the book and smiled at me. "There. A decent stopping place is essential or the entire experience of reading will be ruined," she said. "I hear you have met my son? He is a lovely boy, is he not?" She rose from the chaise and slipped the novel into an empty space in a glass-fronted case against the wall.

"He is—"

"We will walk," she said, clearly uninterested in my reply. "It is too fine a day to be indoors, and you have not yet seen my garden. It is the best in the city. I am one of the few Venetians who does not prefer marble to plants." She took me by the arm and led me back downstairs, through the atriums by the water entrance, away from the canal, and into one of the most beautifully landscaped places I'd ever seen. Not even a lush English garden could compete with what Zaneta had coaxed from the ground within the walls of her *cortile*. Larch and cypress shrubs stood in front of avenues formed by trees, fruit hanging heavy from their branches. The scent of honeysuckle filled the air, and banksia roses stood tall in every corner, their blooms a vibrant yellow. Dotted throughout stood tall marble statues in the classical mode, many of them Roman copies of Greek originals.

"I confess, Emily, I am less than pleased with what you discovered in my painting," she said. "I shall have to sell it, of course, which is a shame as I've always taken comfort from the serene visage of the woman it portrays. No one paints like Titian did."

"The woman is Besina Barozzi," I said. "It's the same face you would have seen in the portrait you sold to Signora Morosini."

"A tragedy indeed, and makes keeping it all the more impossible."

"You really do hate the Barozzis?"

She shrugged, as if such a thing were the most normal in the world. "Of course I do. I am Vendelino."

"Do you hate them enough to have wanted to see the conte dead?"

She threw back her head and laughed. "You are such a very serious lady, are you not? Want him dead? Well . . . I can't say I object to him being dead. Why shouldn't I? He was my enemy. But I understand the implication of your question very well, and no, Emily, I did not kill him."

"Forgive me," I said. "I don't mean to offend, but these are questions I must ask."

"Of course, of course—but you forget one thing."

"What's that?" I asked as we made our way along a charming garden path towards a collection of ancient sculpture.

"To kill him I would have had to touch him, would have had to plunge the knife into that repulsive flesh," she said, scowling. "I would never have done such a thing."

"What do you think of the message in the painting?" I asked. "Would you be prepared to give money to the Barozzis if it is found to be legally binding?"

"The money was to go to this, who did you say? Tomaso Rosso? Not a Barozzi."

"Rosso was Besina Barozzi's son. He died with no children of his own and left his estate to the man who was then head of the Barozzi family." I had checked the will at the archives.

"I would have no choice," she said. "I tell you, though, it will never happen. How would you even decide how much I should give? How do you convert sixteenth-century ducats to lira? Not that it matters. A painting—even one by Titian—cannot contain a will."

"Paolo Barozzi is bound to think otherwise."

"If Paolo Barozzi cares to set himself up for disappointment, that is of no concern to me."

"What would your son think if you were forced to honor the codicil?"

"First, Emily—and this is important—I would not have to be forced. The Vendelinos are an honorable family. If the codicil were upheld, there is nothing I could do but agree without complaint. What other choice would I have? To try to argue otherwise would be to dishonor my ancestor who, for whatever reason, saw fit—if indeed he did—to give money to those people."

"It would have a devastating affect on Angelo," I said.

"He would suffer. Of that there can be no doubt. But surely the court would not require that I hand over everything. That would be ridiculous. More likely they would determine a sum that would be considered adequate compensation for whatever Nicolò Vendelino had at the time."

"Would there be enough left for Angelo to see no change in his lifestyle?"

"You do not suggest that my son would have killed that man in order to preserve his future fortune?"

"No, of course not," I said, "but we must be realistic, Zaneta. Standing to lose a significant chunk of inheritance could be perceived as giving him motive to want the conte dead."

"Well, it doesn't matter, at any rate. Angelo was in Paris, at a reception at the Embassy of the United States, the night Barozzi died."

"You checked?"

"Of course."

"You must have been as worried about this as I was," I said.

"A mother always takes care of her son."

"He can prove this?"

"There is no question of that," she said. "The ambassador himself has already wired to confirm. I will not have Angelo embroiled in unnecessary scandal."

---

I headed straight for Signor Caravello's shop after leaving Ca' Vendelino, eager to tell Donata and her father everything I had learned. So eager, in fact, that I started speaking almost before I'd crossed the threshold into the main room.

"You're really sure?" Donata asked, her voice a whisper, as she motioned for me to speak quietly. "I am stunned. How could we have been looking for the wrong Nicolò?"

"This makes much more sense," I said. "Particularly as Nicolò Vendelino, ever loyal to Besina, never married."

"My father is asleep in his chair in the back room. Let's talk outside so we don't disturb him. But truly, isn't Signora Vendelino's reaction bizarre? I would have thought she'd refuse outright to even consider the possibility this new will would be upheld."

"Well, it's extremely improbable it would ever come to such an end, and she is perfectly aware of that. She can afford to be magnanimous." We sat on the steps at the edge of the canal in front of the shop. "The painting is unlikely to be upheld as a legal document. For one thing, how could it be proved the signatures are valid? It's a bit of a mess, but I don't believe the Vendelinos should lose any sleep over it."

"Yet you still consider Angelo a suspect?"

"I have to. Theoretically, he could have an extremely strong motive. At the moment, I'm more suspicious of Caterina Brexiano. There can be no doubt as to the effect Conte Barozzi had on her life."

"And Facio," Donata said. "Have you learned anything else about him?"

"Nothing. Colin has police all over looking for him. He's bound to turn up eventually."

"I am so frustrated to be stuck in this shop unable to help!"

"You've been plenty of help," I said, "and who knows? Perhaps we can work on changing your father's mind about keeping you close at hand."

"That, Emily, will not happen. The man never, ever changes his mind."

"I do have a project for you, if you're willing. We've got the eighteenth-century memoir that mentions Besina's letters. Do you think there's reference to them in any others? And what about those written by people who lived in Ca' Barozzi or Besina's husband's house? We know his name now—Rosso. It would be worth taking a look at anything you can find."

"I know nothing about any Rosso family," she admitted, "but my father will know something. I will see what I can learn."

I squeezed her hand and left her, knowing exactly where I needed to go next. If Besina's letters did reveal more about Nicolò's will, whoever had them might be in grave danger. As Caterina Brexiano was the last person to admit possessing them, I felt it only fair to warn her.

Perhaps that would encourage her to be more forthcoming about the details of the night of the conte's murder.

# Un Libro d'Amore

# xix

*In the small room beneath the altar at the Miracoli church, Nicolò embraced Besina, but he did not kiss her. Not in this holy place when she was another man's wife. He lit a small lamp and sat down next to her on the floor. Now, for the first time since all those years ago when her father had interrupted her planned escape, Besina wept. He held her in tender arms as she cried and he dried her tears when she was done.*

*He knew they did not have much time.*

*"Tomorrow," he said. "Can you find a way to leave the house?"*

*"No," Besina said. "It is not possible."*

*"The next day, then? I have everything arranged, even a house in Cologne."*

*Besina closed her eyes. It was too much pain to bear. "I cannot go with you, Nicolò. I have a child now. Tomaso. I cannot leave him with Uberto."*

*Nicolò slumped against the wall. "I knew of the child, of course, but had not realized that you felt—"*

*"It is not only the fact of the child's existence, Nicolò. It is his father."*

*"You cannot mean that you love him. I will never—" He could not find words.*

*"No, no. How could you doubt me?"*

*"I didn't doubt you," he said. "I only meant—"*

*"You are his father, Nicolò. His eyes are yours. I recognized them almost as soon as he'd been born. I had hoped, but dared not pray, that he was yours, that I would always have a part of you."*

*"Does Rosso—"*

*"He suspects nothing. He is only too glad to at last have an heir who appears strong enough to survive childhood. Uberto does not realize that could only come from a man other than himself."*

*"You called the boy Tomaso?"*

*"After my father."*

*"And he is healthy?"*

*"Yes," Besina said, "but we cannot leave him without protection in a house with a man of Uberto's nature. I realize I can exert very little influence over my husband, but I could not bear to abandon a child to him. Especially our child."*

*"We could take him with us." Nicolò knew she would not agree. It was too much of a risk to try to escape with a baby who might cry at any moment. All could too easily be lost, and there would be no way of hiding what had happened should they be caught a second time.*

*In fact, it was not fear of discovery that made Besina refuse. Tomaso deserved to live in Venice, deserved to inherit his fortune and serve the republic. He should have a life not spent in hiding. He was a Barozzi, even if not in name, and Besina wanted him to know her family, to know his heritage, not to live anonymously in a foreign city. Such a life might be better for her and even for Nicolò, but it would not be best for her child.*

"You and I, Nicolò, we can only have our words," Besina said. "Still, that is far more love than most people could hope for. You must write to me as often as you can. Your words and Tomaso are the only happiness in my life. Perhaps it is greedy to wish for more."

# 20

As my gondola glided through canals en route to Caterina, my thoughts turned to the other person the discovery of the painting could impact, another barren wife. Emma, unlike her ancient counterpart, stood little chance of divine intervention solving her troubles. Granted, I had no idea yet how Emma could be connected, but it seemed too much of a coincidence for there to be no relation. Could she have discovered the long-forgot codicil on her own? Did she think it might change her father-in-law's view of her? Did she even know what the old conte had counseled his son to do? Would an increase in capital have changed his advice to Paolo? It certainly wouldn't have changed the fact that Emma was still without child.

We were moving along a narrow waterway, too small for more than a single line of even the slim gondolas. The boatman behind us was singing, a mournful and beautiful melody. I smiled as I listened, lulled into a peaceful repose by the movement of the water and the sound of his voice. I loved Venice, loved its changing light and its curved bridges and the ethereal way the city seemed to float on the water. Most of all,

I loved how easy it was to imagine the city in Besina's time. In truth, it hadn't changed much at all. This was a place where history had not been lost, where it had not been torn down to make way for something modern and clumsy. It was said that if a sixteenth-century resident of the town were deposited in current-day Venice, he would recognize everything around him and be able to find his way through the *calli* without hesitation. I could well believe this claim.

By the time the boat approached the bordello, I was in far too pleasant a state of mind to have any interest in going inside. I didn't ask my gondolier to avoid the water entrance as I had before. Instead, he pulled up to it, and I called out to the young woman who opened the door to request that she summon Caterina at once. She looked confused, and I sensed an irritation in her reply, but before five minutes had passed, Caterina was sitting next to me in the boat.

"Where are we going?" she asked.

"Nowhere," I said and directed the gondolier to take us to the Grand Canal, down to the lagoon, and back again. "I wanted to speak to you privately. Not in . . . that place."

"And here I'd hoped you had a change of heart and were bringing me back to the Danieli. One gets used to that sort of comfort very quickly."

"You're awfully flip for someone in a precarious situation."

"Perhaps that is because I am confident in my innocence."

"There have been some new developments in the case," I said, "and I felt I should warn you. I know that you claim to have given the letters and the ring to the conte before he was killed, but, as you know, the letters have not been found. Information I have recently uncovered suggests that whoever does have the letters, assuming, of course, that person is not you"—I gave her a coy smile—"might not take kindly to anyone else who may have read them in their entirety."

"The usual channels of gossip," Emma said. "No one respects mourning these days. No one. You would think I'd have a reprieve from being its target during a time of grief, but apparently gossip knows no bounds."

"I know this is extremely upsetting," I said, "but there are other things we must discuss. If this woman can corroborate Paolo's alibi, then you don't have to worry that he'll be charged with murder. Surely that's a good thing?"

"I suppose."

"This brings me to the reason we called on you," I said. "Caterina Brexiano admits to having been in this house the night of the murder, and she says you saw her."

"I thought she was with my husband," Emma said.

"Perhaps that was later," I said. *Or a lie,* I thought.

"I don't remember any such thing. So far as I recall we had no visitors that evening."

"She says you were hiding, trying to keep out of sight, while she spoke to Paolo's father," I said. "She swears he was still alive when she left."

"Well, I don't recall any such thing," Emma said, "and I would like to believe I'd remember if I'd been hiding, particularly in my own house. Perhaps I was just at the other end of the room, minding my own business. Were they in the *portego*? It's enormous. I might not have even seen them. Whatever is the case, if she did see me, that would suggest she left before he was killed. I spent at least half an hour alone with my father-in-law on the loggia before I retired for the evening. We both drank limoncello and made up stories about the people in gondolas going by on the canal. It was our usual routine. Caterina Brexiano was certainly not there."

It was decent of her not to throw Caterina to the wolves, even though Emma couldn't remember being in the *portego*. If it was true she couldn't remember. I was getting tired of subterfuge, and none of this made any sense.

"We've learned quite a bit more about what your father-in-law was looking for," Colin said. "It appears that a man tried to leave his estate to Besina Barozzi's son. If that had been his intention, and it can be proved, it is possible that your husband stands to come into a not insignificant amount of money."

"He does?" she asked. "Is this true?"

"The question, Emma, is, would a fortune have made a difference in your own standing in the family? It would have taken financial pressure off Paolo, but would his father still have counseled him to abandon you?" Colin asked, not pausing as he circled the room with slow, measured steps. His words stunned me. I hadn't expected him to drop that particular tidbit of news on Emma.

Her reaction could be taken as evidence that she'd never heard this suggested before. She clutched a shaking hand to her throat. Tears streamed down her face. "You can't be serious. It is a lie—a lie! Paolo may have been upset, but abandon me? He would not have done such a reprehensible thing."

"The old conte thought he should have your marriage annulled," Colin said. "On grounds of you not being able to produce an heir."

All color had gone from Emma's face, and her whole body was visibly trembling. "I don't believe it. Not for a second. Not the conte. He wanted the marriage to work more than Paolo."

To someone cynical, her reaction could also be take as evidence of her guilt, as a sign that she was very, very afraid of getting caught. At that moment, however, I believed her—and as I watched her come unhinged in front of my eyes, I felt terribly, terribly sorry for her.

Colin frowned as he read the message the concierge handed to him as we walked into the Danieli. "A neighbor has positively identified Facio Trevisani's body. He was found in a barn on the grounds of the Morosinis' villa."

My heart sank. It must have been the young mother to whom I spoke, or her husband. I hoped for the latter. "What a senseless tragedy," I said.

"We don't know that yet, Emily," Colin said. "As soon as we're finished with Paolo we'll go investigate the scene. Until then, we can't draw any conclusions."

Paolo and Brother Giovanni were bent over a manuscript when we entered the room. The monk was carefully undoing the stitches that held the volume together. He'd already removed the heavy leather binding and placed it to the side.

"What is going on here?" Colin asked, crossing to them.

"We think this is where we will find the secret text," Paolo said. "There is hidden writing beneath *The Divine Comedy*. You can just make it out with the magnifying glass."

I stepped forward and looked at the top page of the book they were in the process of taking apart. Sure enough, there, extremely faint, were lines of text that ran perpendicular to Dante's poetry.

"Because vellum was so expensive, it was often reused. They would wash the old ink off, you see," Brother Giovanni said. "Which is what I'm going to attempt to do now. We just have to hope it won't also remove what's below."

"Are you certain this is a good idea?" Colin asked. "You're destroying a valuable book. Not just in terms of money, but in terms of the intrinsic artistic value of the illumination."

"There's no other way," Paolo said. "I have to know what it says."

"Shouldn't I have a say in that?" Emma appeared in the doorway behind us. "The book does belong to me, after all. I could have you arrested for theft and vandalism. You are wantonly destroying my property."

"Emma?" I asked.

"I had my gondolier follow you back here when you left my house," she said. "It's outrageous that you wouldn't tell me where I could find my own husband. Though I suppose, knowing what he is, one could question the wisdom of my wanting to find him."

"Emma, *cara,* I am so happy to see you!" Paolo rushed to her and took her in his arms.

She pushed him back. "I don't think so, conte," she said. "Not now that I know about your secret assignations and your extremely poor taste in ladies. What am I supposed to think about myself now that I know how base you are?"

"I have no idea what you are talking about," Paolo said.

Emma slapped him soundly across the face. "Why don't you ask your mistress if she might know what's upsetting me?"

Paolo stood there, silent, a great red welt developing on his cheek.

"I knew you had not been faithful, but to throw that sort of woman in my face—"

"*Cara, cara,* you are getting excited about nothing," Paolo said. "I have no mistress."

"Everyone is talking about it," Emma said, "and I had suspected for months. There's no sense denying the truth. You're the one who should've been killed, not your father."

Paolo's eyes drooped and he gave a sad sigh. "Who has told you these lies?"

"Only half the city," Emma said. "Caterina Brexiano? It was bad enough when she was just a medium, but now she is the lowest of the low in a brothel. How could you do this to me?"

"She was the only one who could help me, Emma," Paolo said, "but she was not my mistress."

"I won't listen to this tripe," she said.

"Nor will I." Colin had grown increasingly impatient during the course of this conversation. "Go sit in the other room and work this out at a considerably lower volume. I want to see what Brother Giovanni is doing."

The estranged couple, scowling, followed his direction. The monk continued his work.

"I have carefully studied each of the books," he said. "Every one has an older text, but I have found in this one—here." He carefully turned the pages until he'd reached one more than halfway through and then held up the magnifying glass to a particular spot. "You will see the word *Besina*."

It was there. Faintly, barely legible, and certainly all but invisible to anyone who didn't know to look for it, but it was there.

"I will use a mixture of milk and oat to dissolve the top layer of paint and ink. It is a gentle combination and may not be enough, but I want to work slowly in order to minimize any damage to what lies beneath."

"You're confident in the method?" Colin asked.

"Confident enough."

"Then proceed," Colin said.

Using a slim blade, Brother Giovanni cut the remaining stitches of the binding and pulled the thread from the pages. He opened the book—if it could be called that any longer—to the middle and then gently flipped the stack of unfolded pages so that he could start at the beginning rather than the middle of what we hoped would be a narrative of some sort.

Perhaps even a more easily defensible version of Nicolò Vendelino's will.

The monk dipped a paintbrush into the opaque mixture that filled a bowl in front of him on the table, and then, with great care, he started to wipe it over the vellum page. "If this does not work, there are stronger potions I can try, but they would likely cause more harm than good. I can't justify ruining this book unless there's a fair chance of finding something better on the pages."

It pained me to see the beautiful illumination begin to fade from the page. The ink came away less readily than the paint, but it soon became evident that Brother Giovanni's method was working, though extremely slowly. We watched him for approximately a quarter of an hour. In that length of time, he hadn't yet removed enough Dante that we could start to read what was below.

"We shall leave you to it," Colin said. "Tell my man outside if you require anything."

Emma and Paolo were still arguing in the next room. Colin and I left them to return to the Brenta Canal and see what remained at the site of Facio Trevisani's death.

# Un Libro d'Amore

Those few stolen minutes in Santa Maria dei Miracoli were all the comfort Besina had. Her life with Uberto Rosso did not improve. In the following years, she lost four more infants soon following each of their births. Rosso did not hide his disdain for her inadequacy, but he did not beat his wife again.

Not then.

Not until he found the small cassettina hidden at the bottom of one of the deep trunks containing her clothing. Not until he opened the cassettina and saw the letters she'd saved. Not until he began to believe his son's blue eyes might match those of whoever was the author of these lurid documents.

Rosso burned them all, but not before he'd stormed into the room where Besina sat, embroidering. He pulled her to her feet and flung the letters on the ground before her.

"This transgression will not be forgiven."

Besina did not reply. She did not cast stones of her own. She did not tell her husband she knew about all the courtesans, both the cortigiana

235

onesta *and the* cortigiana di lume, *the* onesta's *lower-class counterpart. She did not tell him they took his money but despised and laughed at him. She did not tell him she'd heard rumors about the strange requests he made of them. She did not think it was her place, because she did not question the world into which she'd been born. It did not occur to her to defend herself.*

*Instead, she dropped to the floor and covered her head as best she could with her arms, hoping to shield it from the bulk of his blows.*

*Rosso's anger blinded him to everything else. He did not stop his evil work on Besina until she no longer moved when he kicked her.*

*Much later, when she woke up to find herself being carried down the steps of her house by a servant, she commanded he release her.*

*She wanted to see Tomaso. To make sure Rosso had done nothing to harm the boy.*

*The servant did not obey his mistress. He did not so much as acknowledge her request. He carried her to the water entrance and put her in the family's gondola, closing the door of the felze only after he'd made sure the curtains had been pulled to cover the windows. Besina screamed and cried out, calling for Tomaso. No one came to her aid.*

*When the boat stopped after a short journey, her father stood at the water entrance of Ca' Barozzi, anger in his eyes.*

*"Daughter, what have you done to bring such shame to this family?"*

# 21

This latest trip along the Brenta River provided no respite from the heat of the city. I felt no sense of relaxation while we were on the boat, only an oppressive sense of anxiety and dread. My heart ached for Facio Trevisani. Colin, who knew my temperament all too well, took my hand and stood on the deck with me, not interrupting my silent thought.

On the outside, the barn in which Facio had died looked quaint and perfectly rustic, much like Marie Antoinette's hamlet at Versailles. It was the only such outbuilding remaining on the estate and, being situated in plain view of one of the gardens, could not be allowed to mar its surroundings. Its inside, however, was not so pleasant. Facio had left this world in a shabby, grim space, hanging from a rough beam. So far as Colin and I could tell, he'd climbed a ladder he'd leaned against a supporting vertical beam and crawled across the horizontal until he reached almost the middle. That's where he had tied the noose. He would have had to drop himself from there, after having placed the other end of the rope around his neck. There was no evidence suggesting anything but suicide.

"It's slim consolation, I know," Colin said, "but most likely his neck would have broken at once. He probably didn't suffer long."

"He suffered longer, and more, than most people could bear before he set foot in this barn." I couldn't stop shaking and was sick all over the floor.

Colin took me in my arms, wiped my face with his handkerchief, and carried me out of the barn. "It is a horrible thing, of that there is no doubt." He put me down on the trunk of a fallen tree and sat next to me. "Drink."

I took the flask from him and swallowed a swig of whisky. It burned my throat. "I know nothing can justify murder," I said, "but Conte Barozzi deserved to die for what he'd done to Facio."

"We don't know everything, Emily. We only have the sliver of information given by his neighbor, and we know the garden at Ca' Barozzi was a disaster. What if Trevisani hadn't been doing his job?"

"He still didn't deserve this."

"No, but it would make him take a share of culpability."

"I don't think he was responsible at all. You didn't see his home, Colin. They had saved and saved to buy a beautiful cradle for the baby. This was not a man who was lazy or afraid to work. He would have done whatever the conte wanted—and if that was nothing, who was he to argue? Colin, if you could see how these people lived . . ." My voice trailed into a sob.

"I know, my dear, I know." He put his arms around me. "The world is full of bleak injustice."

He indulged my grief for ten minutes and then insisted we return to Venice. I did not argue. There was nothing more we could do for Facio, save clear his name of suspicion if he had not murdered his former employer. The boat ride along the river and through the lagoon gave us the opportunity to decide what to do next.

"Look how Facio suffered from the loss of his job," I said. "What if the Vendelino servants heard talk of the possibility of the family's fortune being decimated? Could concern over their fate have prompted one of them to commit murder?"

"That seems a stretch, Emily. Besides, I don't think we need more suspects. We've plenty already."

"Bear with me," I said. "I agree it's far-fetched, but I think it would be worth at least looking at the people they employ and seeing if any of them has a connection to someone we're already considering."

"It can't hurt," he said. "Although it really would be relevant only if the codicil on the painting is recognized as legitimate."

"You and I understand that, but perhaps a servant, who hasn't had the benefit of an education, wouldn't."

"We can go if you like," he said, "but I'm worried about you, my dear. Let's stop at Caravello's shop first. You can talk to Donata. She'll help you deal with what you've just seen. I realize that sometimes I'm too callous about these things."

His idea was an excellent one, as I'd not managed to stop trembling since we'd left the barn. Donata threw her arms around me the instant we told her what had happened and took me to a quiet corner of the shop, leaving Colin and her father to a game of chess. She brought two chairs and placed them facing each other, close together.

"I locked the door so we won't be disturbed," she said. "Papà can miss business for a little while."

"It was so awful, you can't imagine," I said. My hands were cold, and my lips hurt because I'd bitten them until I drew blood. "The grounds of the Villa Tranquillità are stunning. In the midst of one of the gardens is a barn, lovely and quaint on the outside, left standing only to set a suitably rural scene. The interior is a most desolate, gritty place. A place that would make a person want to die."

"But Facio went there just for that purpose," Donata said. "It wasn't the barn that made him do it."

"I know, but if you could only see it. There's something about it. Not just the appearance," I said. "The structure is nothing out of the ordinary, but there's something to the atmosphere inside. Something evil."

"You don't think Facio was murdered, do you?" she asked.

"No. It was clearly suicide."

"You're certain? What if he knew something about Barozzi's death? What if the murderer lured him out there and killed him in a way that would cause no suspicion?"

"How?" I asked. "Colin is confident Facio did this himself."

"Could he prove beyond doubt that there was no one else present when Facio died?"

"I suppose not." The idea was disturbing. "The murderer could have had him at gunpoint and forced him to put the noose around his neck."

Donata nodded. "Perhaps that's why the place feels so evil."

"But Facio had done nothing to suggest he had sensitive information," I said. "We have no reason to suspect that he would have returned to Ca' Barozzi after he'd been fired, unless it was to murder the conte."

"You still believe it was suicide, then?" she asked. I nodded. "Do you think he took his life because of despair or because of guilt?"

"That I don't know," I said, "but I can't believe, given all the circumstances, that someone else would have forced Facio to kill himself. It doesn't make sense."

Donata smiled. "The color is returning to your complexion now that you're starting to think about the case again. I'm glad I could provide you with a way back to it, grim though it is."

"It's much appreciated," I said. "Your theory was an interesting one, but not realistic in this case, given the evidence."

"I don't have so much experience as you," she said. "No forced suicides. I'll remember that."

Knowing we could not afford to dawdle for too long, I thanked Donata and pulled my husband away from his game of chess. We bade good-bye to our friends and decided to make a quick stop at the Danieli to check on Brother Giovanni's progress before calling on the Vendelinos, but we never made it up to our room. Colin read the wire handed to him by the concierge and pulled me straight back to the water entrance, where he directed the waiting gondolier to take us to Ca' Vendelino posthaste.

.    .    .

On the way to the palazzo, my husband and I discussed strategy. I would open by bringing up the issue of the servants. Colin would take it from there. After she'd received us, Zaneta did not dismiss our request to look over her staff records, but she made no effort to hide the fact that she found it extremely troubling. "I do not like the implied accusation," she said. "I do not employ individuals with murderous tendencies."

"I would expect nothing less," I said. "It's really just to confirm nothing's amiss. One can't be too careful in these situations."

"Yes, yes, I suppose you're right," she said. "The housekeeper will assist you."

"Thank you," I said. We did not get up from our seats.

"Well?" she asked. "Is there something else?"

"I'm afraid there is," Colin said. "I've had a rather alarming telegram from the American Embassy in Paris. There was no reception the night of Barozzi's murder, and no one admits to having seen your son there anytime in recent memory."

"That can't be true," she said. "Angelo told me all about the party."

"He may have been lying to you, signora," Colin said.

"Angelo does not lie. Anyway, why would he have murdered that boor of a man? It makes no sense."

"It makes perfect sense if he feels his inheritance is being threatened," Colin said. "Men have killed for much less."

"Neither of us had spotted anything unusual in that painting," Zaneta said. "He had no reason to think he was under any kind of threat."

That might or might not be true. I remembered that in my initial conversation with Angelo, he'd first claimed no interest in or knowledge of art, then later revealed a passion for Impressionism. Why the inconsistency?

"We are not suggesting, Zaneta, that his guilt is a foregone conclusion," I said. "If we believed that, we wouldn't want to investigate your servants. Even so, we have to speak to your son, too."

"I don't know that he's home. You're welcome to inquire upstairs."

Angelo and his wife, along with their three children, lived on the second floor of the house. Zaneta explained that, as was customary, they were given the privacy one would expect had they lived in a building separate from his mother. Venetian palazzi were built for extended families. The head of the family and his wife occupied the first floor, his heir the second. Various unmarried brothers, should there be any, would be given bachelor apartments. In these enlightened (I apply to the word a sense of irony) and modern days, the same courtesy could be offered to the heir's sisters, should he have any. In the Renaissance, however, only one girl would be allowed to remain at home. She was given the task of helping to raise the heir's children. Any remaining sisters would either be married off or sent to a convent. If they were fortunate, they might be given a say in their fates.

The *portego* above the one in Zaneta's section reflected Angelo's tastes. A large painting of Venice, done in Impressionist style, hung in the room, as did several other smaller pieces by Monet and Sisley. Much though I appreciated the paintings, they didn't quite fit with the room's ornate beamed ceiling and heavy wooden doorways.

Colin strode without hesitation into the room, calling out for a servant. One appeared in short order, followed by a young woman who identified herself as Angelo's wife. She directed a maid to take Colin to her husband and then offered me a seat on one of the benches lining the long walls of the *portego*.

"I assume this has something to do with these unfortunate rumors about forgotten wills and families who can't stop blaming everyone else for their plight?" she asked.

"If that's how you'd care to describe it."

"I would," she said, "and I'm tired of it." She was a petite woman, curvy and moderately pretty, though not striking in any way. Detracting from her appearance was the scowl that seemed permanently etched on her face.

"Were you in Paris with your husband on his recent trip?" I asked.

"No, I've never had the slightest interest in travel. Why would anyone want to leave Venice?"

"How long was he gone?"

"I can't say I remember," she said. "It's so difficult to tell if he's here or elsewhere. In either case I see him virtually the same amount."

"How long have you been married?"

"Should I be counting the years?"

"It's a simple question," I said.

"Five. My eldest daughter is four."

"Had you ever met Conte Barozzi?"

"It's possible," she said, "but I have no memory of it."

"Where were you the night he was killed?"

"My youngest was suffering from a summer fever. I was up till sunrise watching over her."

"Was there a doctor present?"

"Good heavens, woman!" She stood up and backed away from me, her eyes fiery. "What are you suggesting? That I care about the Vendelino family so much that I'd kill for them? That my fate is so intricately connected to theirs?"

"Isn't it?" I asked.

"I have my own fortune," she said. "If my husband ever deserted me or if he came into ruin, he could not touch it. I don't need him half as much as he needs me."

"Do you have reason to believe he would desert you?"

"No," she said. "I use it only as an example."

It was an odd example, and one that set my mind going in an entirely different direction. Distracted and convinced I would get nothing else useful out of her, I excused myself and went downstairs in search of the housekeeper. Forty-five minutes later I held in my hand a ledger listing the names of every servant employed by the family in the past fifty-odd years. They had records of the same going back to the seventeenth century. Too late for Besina, but not for someone else.

When I'd finished, Colin was still entrenched with Angelo. I interrupted them only briefly, to whisper to him what I'd learned. He nodded and agreed that I should return to the Danieli. If my instincts were right, Paolo could be in a significant amount of danger. I only hoped he hadn't gone home. Before we left the hotel he'd asked if he was still being detained for his safety, and we'd told him no. At the time, it had seemed reasonable.

"I will confront Angelo," Colin said, "and follow you to the Danieli as soon as possible." He kissed me on the lips and slipped back through the half-closed door to the room in which the two men were speaking. I caught a glimpse of the Vendelino heir, his booted feet up on his desk. He was smoking a cigar and had an air of confident security about him.

I was half-expecting the concierge to hand me a message when I entered the hotel and so paused in front of his desk. He handed me an envelope. We knew the solicitor to whom Colin had spoken would be sending a reply soon; this was sure to be it. What I had not anticipated was the content of that reply:

Quite possible painting codicil could prove valid, especially if court could be presented with corroborating evidence.

This surprised me. I had expected something quite the contrary. This development made me even more eager to see what progress Brother Giovanni had made. But when I opened the door to my suite, I faced a catastrophic mess. Our belongings were scattered everywhere. As I went in further, calling for the guard Colin had stationed in the corridor, I saw that the monk lay unconscious on the floor and that all the manuscript pages were gone. Emma and Paolo were nowhere to be seen.

# Un Libro d'Amore

# xxi

*The pain in Besina's body was nominal when compared with that in her heart. Uberto had broken her arm and knocked three teeth from her jaw, but she cared not about that. What mattered was that he would not let her see her son. No one, having heard the charges her husband made against her when he went to the Doge's Palace to petition for divorce, offered her any support.*

*Infidelity was rife in Venice, but indiscretion would not be tolerated from a noblewoman.*

*Besina would not be allowed to see Tomaso again unless he chose to seek her out when he reached the age of adulthood. Uberto insisted on the terms. Even though he was no longer convinced of his child's paternity, Tomaso was his only possible heir, and Rosso wanted something rather than nothing. So far as he was concerned, Tomaso was his.*

*Besina's father, shamed by his daughter's actions, refused to let her stay in Ca' Barozzi, and so she was sent, with a legacy so minute she could only afford the smallest and barest of rooms, to the convent at San Zaccaria. Here, Besina would be forced to take Benedictine vows and promise to live out the rest of her life in pious study and prayer. For two years, neither any member of her family nor any of the many noble ladies she'd counted as her friends tried to see her. She was dead to them. They were embarrassed even to know her.*

*The ordinary rules at San Zaccaria were far from stringent. Many, if not most, of the nuns had felt no calling to dedicate their lives to serving the Lord. They were cast-off daughters who had been deemed not pretty or charming enough to squander the family dowry on. Or they were orphans, grown now and too old for the city's famous* ospedali *that took in girls abandoned by their courtesan mothers and noble fathers.*

*Besina's holy sisters studied music and wrote poetry, and some even took lovers and hosted parties, but she did none of this. She kept to herself, spoke very little to anyone, and asked for only one thing: a copy of Dante's* Divine Comedy. *It was not given to her. If she had the money to purchase it herself, the abbess told her, she could. But Besina did not have any money of her own. So she sat in her room, alone, staring out the small window. At first, Besina's reticence drew the attention of the other residents. Eventually they grew tired of trying to coax from her any semblance of friendship.*

*Unlike her fellow nuns, Besina was not allowed any correspondence. Her father had forbidden it, and the abbess saw fit to enforce his policy, as she did his insistence on allowing only family to visit his wayward daughter. Her family stayed away from San Zaccaria. Besina was left all alone.*

*Until Lorenzo came.*

# 22

The guard we'd placed outside the door to our suite insisted nothing unusual had happened. He had heard no disturbance. No one had entered the room. Yes, he had allowed the conte and contessa to leave, but Colin had told him they were free to do so if they wanted. The majordomo of the hotel assured me there had been no sign of disturbance in the lobby. I quizzed the gondoliers who worked in front of the hotel, across the pavement of the Riva degli Schiavoni. They had seen nothing unusual, but they had each only just returned from their latest trips and hadn't been back for more than a few minutes. A crowd of tourists waited to board their boats. Soon these gondoliers would be off and replaced by others. It was just like the people strolling by in front of the hotel. Constant turnover. It would be nearly impossible to determine who had been outside at just the right moment to have spotted our intruder.

Trying not to panic, I returned to our suite, where I was met by the hotel doctor, whom I'd had sent up to assist Brother Giovanni.

"No serious damage to the man," the doctor assured me. "A strong dose of smelling salts was enough to bring him around."

I thanked him and pulled a chair next to the settee on which Brother Giovanni was reclining. "What happened?" I asked.

"It was very strange, signora," he said, sitting up and rubbing the back of his head. "I was hard at work, as you know. The signore and signora were arguing in the other room. Eventually they stopped, although I can't claim to have been paying them much attention and don't know exactly when that was. I did, at some point, notice the absence of their strife."

"What then?"

"I wish I'd been more alert," he said, "but I was engrossed in what I was finding."

"Had you uncovered something significant?" I asked.

"It was too soon to tell, I'm afraid. My progress has been slow, as you know. Care is essential. I had revealed a few partial lines, but nothing that could help Paolo."

"What happened next?" I asked.

"As you may remember, I was working at the table in such a position that my back was to the door. I became aware of a figure behind me. It must have been the signore or the signora. Before I could turn around to look, whoever it was whacked me on the head with something. This, I think." He motioned to the fire poker tossed on the floor across the room. "Everything went black and I don't recall anything else."

"Please, sir, think very hard," I said. "Can you recall any detail about the figure?"

He did not answer at first, taking seriously my admonition that he ponder the question. "I cannot be certain, but I think he was dressed in black. I can see an image of black fabric, flowing black fabric, but I do not know if it is real. My impression was that he was very tall."

The plague doctor in his long black cloak.

Had it been Paolo all along?

"How often did the conte leave your company when you were in Padua?" I asked.

"We were together infrequently, signora," Brother Giovanni said. "He thought that the safest approach. He left me to my work while he did whatever it was that he did."

"Have you any idea what he was doing?"

"He only said he was following every avenue to seek information about whatever his father claimed to have learned."

"The partial lines you had uncovered. Could they have hurt Paolo?" I asked.

"No, signora. I saw the name *Besina Barozzi* and a mention of *beauty* but could not yet read anything else."

I heard the door in the next room open and then Colin's voice.

"What the devil?"

"A mess, isn't it?" I asked, joining him. Our papers and books had been strewn all over the floor. Cushions had been tossed from the settee and chairs. Every drawer in the desk was open, and our clothes had been torn from their hangers in the wardrobe. I quickly briefed him on what had transpired.

Colin nodded and took me by the hand. After giving firm instructions to the guard outside the door to let no one in or out, he took me downstairs. Within moments, we were back at Ca' Barozzi.

"My theory was completely wrong," I said, as we alighted from the gondola. "Thank heavens I hadn't yet acted upon it."

No servant greeted us at the Barozzis' water entrance. We mounted the stairs and climbed to the *portego*. There was no one there. Colin started in one direction, keeping his footsteps quiet, ready to search the house. Automatically, I did the same but took the opposite way.

"No,' he said, shaking his head. "Too dangerous. Stay with me."

We moved through every room on the first floor and saw no one. By the time we'd finished with the second and third, we'd stopped worrying about being quiet. By the time we were confident there was not a single living soul in the unlocked house save a motley handful of servants who seemed utterly unconcerned about their duties, we sank onto the marble steps near the canal, frustrated.

"They could have gone anywhere," Colin said.

"It doesn't make sense," I said. "Why would Paolo have stopped Brother Giovanni's work? If the hidden text contains Nicolò Vendelino's codicil, he stands to make enormous gains."

"Unless that's not what the text will reveal."

"If he knew that, he would have never let the monk start in the first place."

"Perhaps Emma learned something," Colin said. "Their argument could have been a ruse."

"Or perhaps we're on the wrong track entirely," I said, "and playing right into the hands of a murderous wretch. We need to find Caterina Brexiano."

*   *   *

Caterina was not at the bordello. One of her colleagues told us she'd gone to mass. Would we care to leave a message? I didn't believe the woman. I shoved past her, dragging Colin by the hand to the narrow back staircase that led to Caterina's room. She didn't answer when we knocked, and her door was locked. Colin pulled a slim lock pick from the inside pocket of his jacket and within seconds had it open.

The room was empty. We set to searching it at once, knowing our time was limited. Someone would be up to stop us soon, of that we had no doubt. Caterina's possessions painted a clear picture of her. Her gowns were beautiful and fashionable, and all had been purchased before her fall from grace. She had an ivory rosary and a pair of garnet earrings set in heavy gold in a style popular probably when her mother was young. She must have wanted to save them when she sold the rest of her jewelry. In her dresser drawers there were only two things of interest: a copy of the memoir given to guests at Hotel Vitturi and a deck of tarot cards.

"I don't really believe in her claim of being a medium," I said, "but let's suppose it's true. What if, through her communication with spirits, she determined that Paolo was not, in fact, to inherit anything. That he had no claim on the Vendelino fortune. He wouldn't like to hear that, would he?"

"No more than his father liked what Caterina had told him."

"Exactly."

"Which means?"

"I'm not sure," I said. "It doesn't impact the motive she already had to kill Barozzi, but it could have made her wish Paolo would disappear."

"I'm more inclined to say it must be Paolo who did it," Colin said, his usually smooth brow marred by deep creases. "I don't want to believe it any more than you, Emily, but it's time we faced facts. He fled after the murder. He's selling off family possessions. He's stolen some of those possessions. Now he's got Emma. The only question is whether she's in on it or his prisoner."

"He could have Caterina as well."

"True," he said, "and I do allow for the possibility that it's Caterina who has both of them."

"So how do we find them?" I asked. "They could be anywhere."

"I've got the police stopping trains and searching them. Their descriptions will be circulated throughout the country."

"What about ships?" I asked. "That's the easiest way to leave Venice."

"It is. I've asked that a general alert be issued to vessels in the area. We can hope the captains will take the threat seriously and look closely at all their passengers. Extra police will be sent to the docks, so if they've not boarded yet, they should be stopped."

"So what do we do?" I asked.

"We wait."

⸱　　⸱　　⸱

I was not convinced. Either that we should wait or that Paolo was guilty. Colin was adamant, however, that it was the most reasonable conclusion before us. They had fled, after all. I did not accept this conclusion and was returning to my earlier theory. I was convinced there was something to it. We went back to the hotel. I was sullen. Colin was resigned.

Brother Giovanni shouted a greeting as soon as we'd opened the door to the suite and called for us to come at once. The pages weren't all gone. His attacker had taken all of the still-bound books, and most of the sheets he'd unbound, but when he'd started to clean up the mess, he found a stack of them still remaining, including the first page on which he'd begun to work. He'd set it on top of a dressing table to let it dry a bit before he continued.

"Don't touch it, as the page is still quite damp," he said. "At least it's a start."

"An excellent start," I said, bending close to the table so I could read.

253

Besina Barozzi always knew she was not among the fortunate—
or unfortunate, depending on one's perspective—who could
rely on beauty.

A tear escaped my pooling eyes. I brushed it away before it could
fall on the vellum and cause harm.

"I've a sense now of what combination of milk and oat works best,"
Brother Giovanni said. "The work will begin to go more quickly."

"That's excellent," I said. "Let's hope that we'll be able to recover
the rest of the missing pages."

"It's possible we won't even need them," he said. "The document
you seek could be considerably shorter than *The Divine Comedy*."

"We can only hope." I left him to it, not wanting to cause any distraction, and went into the sitting room, where my husband had already started to make his way through the mess, starting at the desk.
"There's something not right in all this. I'm certain of it."

"Tell me what you're thinking." He looked me squarely in the eyes
and listened to everything I had to say. When I had finished he stood
up and paced for a few minutes before speaking. "I agree there is nothing tidy about this case. We need more evidence. Let's finish going
through our rooms, just in case this man who appears to come and go
unseen has, in his haste, left any clues to his identity. Then we can think
further about what to do next."

I focused my attention on our bedroom, but there was very little to
find there. The linens had been stripped from the bed, but there was
nothing under it. The drawers were pulled out of the two bedside tables and from the small writing desk that sat facing the window. Nothing had been in any of these drawers save hotel stationery, which was
now scattered through the room.

I moved into my dressing room. This was a mess and would require my poor maid to spend a great deal of time pressing gowns that had been left in a tall heap on the bottom of the wardrobe. I started to pick them up, one at a time, shaking each out before draping it over the back of a chair. As I worked my way through them, something struck me as not being right. The stack of gowns had been too high. I hadn't packed *that* many dresses.

I lifted the rest of them out with no regard to care, dropping them on the floor behind me. When the last was gone, revealing the wide cedar bottom of the armoire, I gasped.

There lay Emma, unconscious, a gag in her mouth, her arms tied behind her back, her feet bound.

# xxii

When her brother came to see her, Besina met him in a small room that had been designed for hosting visitors to the convent. She did not want him to see her own bare cell. She did not want to take him to the garden.

"Why have you come, Lorenzo?" she asked.

Besina had never been beautiful, but Lorenzo was shocked to see her now. Her face was drawn and thin, with harsh lines already etched on her brow. She looked far older than her years. He wondered if her hair was already streaked with silver. He could not see it beneath her veil.

"To beg your forgiveness." Lorenzo looked at the hard stone floor. "I should not have abandoned you to this."

"My daily life here is far more pleasant than it was in Uberto's house. Except for Tomaso."

"It is not right what has been done," he said. "I only wish—"

"You wish that I had never loved Nicolò Vendelino," she said. "You would rather that I had known no happiness than to have chosen so inappropriate a source for it."

"He wasn't your only happiness. You have a child."

"His child, Lorenzo. Uberto was correct in his deductions. No child of that man's could survive infancy. There is something evil in him that he passes to them. It keeps them from living."

Lorenzo winced. He had not really believed Rosso's accusations. He had not believed his sister would betray the man to whom she was bound by God. But he also remembered the condition she'd been in when she arrived at Ca' Barozzi in Rosso's boat. Her broken arm. Her bloody jaw. He cursed himself for judging her actions.

"My greatest sin was to love a man my family required me to hate because of some feud about which no one can recall the details. So instead of living with him and raising children, I was beaten, humiliated, and sent here," Besina said. "Now I no longer care about anything."

"That is a lie," Lorenzo said. "You still love him, and you love Tomaso."

"I cannot cry about them any longer. I have no more tears."

"I will help you, Besina. Somehow, I will help you."

Lorenzo was true to his word. He came back the next week, bringing with him a copy of The Divine Comedy. Besina accepted it with quiet thanks and a small smile.

"Look inside," Lorenzo said.

Besina opened the book. It had been printed in Venice that year, and while not so beautiful as an illuminated manuscript, the type was clear and bright.

"Further inside," her brother urged.

She flipped through the pages until she found it. A letter. Folded and sealed and far thicker than anything she or Nicolò could ever have hidden in Santa Maria dei Miracoli. Besina took it in her hands but did not open it. She would read it, back in her room, losing herself in the comfort of her lover's words.

"You will not be alone anymore," Lorenzo said.

# 23

Emma did not move when I spoke to her, or when I touched her face or gently shook her shoulders. I called for Colin, who came to my side in a flash. He lifted Emma's limp body from the wardrobe and carried her to the bed while I asked the guard outside our door to summon the doctor as quickly as possible. Brother Giovanni came into the room and, seeing the scene before him, fell to his knees and started to pray, quietly, in Latin.

Colin removed first the gag, then the ropes that bound Emma. He leaned close to her face. "She is breathing. Only just. Emily, would you . . ." His voice trailed off. I stepped forward and started to loosen her corset. She was wearing only underclothes, not her dress.

"Smelling salts," I said, trying to keep my hands steady. "I should carry them. Why don't I carry them? Just because I refuse to faint doesn't mean those around me will adopt a similar policy. Emma? Can you hear me?"

She did not respond.

"Colin, look around for clothing," I said. "Whoever did this might have left hers somewhere. She's taken Emma's."

A quick search yielded nothing. The doctor arrived and in a few minutes had revived Emma, who cringed and started to sit up the instant he wafted his smelling salts under her nose.

"I'm never traveling without them again," I said. I sat next to her on the edge of the bed and took her hand. "Who did this to you?"

"I don't know," she said, rubbing the back of her head. The doctor began to examine her scalp for abrasions.

"She'll make a full recovery," he said, holding her eyes open wide and looking closely at them. "I strongly suggest she focus on less strenuous sorts of activity for the near future. She has a slight concussion and will suffer from headaches for a week or so, but there will be no lasting effects."

"Where is Paolo?" she asked, her voice rough.

"We don't know," Colin said, stepping forward. "Can you tell us what happened?"

"We were arguing about . . . well, it doesn't matter what about, does it? Not anymore." She sniffed. "The door to the bedroom flung open and a hideous figure stood there, wearing one of those awful plague doctor carnival masks. She pulled a gun from the folds of her cloak and pointed it at me."

"It was a woman?" Colin asked. I had surmised as much the instant I saw Emma's state of dress.

"I didn't think so at first," she said. "The figure was so tall. Far taller than Paolo, and he towers above nearly everyone. Then she spoke, and there was no question as to her gender."

"Did you recognize her voice?" I asked.

"No." Emma shook her head, but the motion must have hurt. She cringed and lay back down on the pillows behind her. "She said she would kill me if we did not do what she told us to."

Brother Giovanni had finished his prayers and risen from his knees. Colin turned to him. "You heard none of this?"

The monk lowered his eyes. "I am ashamed to say that I didn't. I had made a point of ignoring their argument. I didn't notice when the tenor changed."

"I'm not surprised," Emma said. "Things were much more calm after she appeared. We weren't arguing anymore."

"What happened next?" I asked.

"She wanted the books. Paolo said she could have them, but it was as if she didn't believe him. That's when she came at me with the gun—but she didn't shoot. She hit me on the head with it. That's all I remember."

"She must have then come to you," Colin said to Brother Giovanni, who nodded.

"Then, keeping Paolo at gunpoint, somehow managed to get into Emma's dress and hat," I said. "Between her gun and the knowledge that she'd tied up his wife, Paolo would have been easily convinced to assist her and then to escort her from the room as if she were his wife. If she kept her face down, the guard wouldn't have noticed the switch."

"How did she get in?" Brother Paolo asked.

"Through the window," Colin said. "Much in the same way she did the night she killed the conte."

This did not sit right with me. "That would be impossible without someone seeing her. How would she have done it?"

Colin pushed farther the already open window. "All she would have need to do was affix a rope to the railing. It would be simple to get to the balcony and into the room."

"I still insist that someone would have seen her," I said.

"Someone probably did," Emma said, "but this is Venice. If she were in a carnival costume and made a show out of the whole enterprise, everyone would have thought it was a good laugh."

"So blatant as to not be suspicious," Colin said, frowning.

"Whatever the details, we need to find Paolo," I said. "As quickly as possible."

We did not wait for the police to reach the hotel. The staff and our guard would fill them in and give them whatever access they needed to protect Emma and Brother Giovanni. The trouble was that Colin and I did not agree on how to proceed. We each wanted to pursue a different avenue, and as we knew our suspect was armed, he would not allow me to set off on my own.

Which was irritating, but understandable.

"Do you think she will harm Paolo?" I asked.

"Quite possibly. He knows who she is, so he's a threat. She already faces one murder charge. Why not risk a second when it could mean you get away?"

"Where would she have taken him?"

"I think they're in the brothel," he said. "It would be easy enough to hide there. No one would take notice of her bringing in a man. We need to search it, top to bottom."

"Can we please leave that to the police?" I asked. "I think our efforts would prove more fruitful if we placed them in another direction."

He listened as I made my case, and then he stood, quietly contemplative. I knew not to interrupt him when he was in such a state. Finally, he nodded. "All right. We'll follow your plan."

"Thank you," I said. "It's just that we know the police can handle searching the bordello without any hitch. But this other . . ."

"I know," he said. "Only we could manage to pull that off. If we can."

*If I'm right,* I thought. *If I'm wrong . . .*

My heart was racing as we stepped into the gondola. If I were wrong, I would wreak havoc on an innocent life. Nevertheless, I didn't see that we had any other option. There was too much at stake. My nerves were on fire by the time we approached our destination. As we glided past the last church before we would alight from the boat, I closed my eyes and whispered a prayer.

Colin smiled when he saw this. "Becoming religious, are you? Take care or I'll send you to a nunnery."

This made me laugh. Which was just what I needed to cut through my anxiety and return me to a state of focused calm.

Signor Caravello waved when we entered the shop. He was speaking to two customers, and there was a third browsing the aisles. "Such good news, eh?" he called to us, smiling.

This took me aback. "Good news," I said, not wanting to reveal my ignorance.

"Donata told me everything after she read your note," he said. "I would never have agreed to let her go with you otherwise. I told her, no running about until after this bad business is all settled. And, so, it is settled. But did she mistake your meaning? She thought she was to meet you at the Danieli."

I didn't want to cause him any unnecessary alarm. "Yes, but she asked me to collect a few of her things for her. She forgot them in the rush."

"What things could she possibly need for a celebratory picnic in the countryside?"

"Books, of course," I said. "May I run up and look for them? I've set my maid to the task of styling her hair and thought I could save time by getting them for her." Now my heart was really pounding.

"Of course, of course," he said, turning his attention ι gentlemen at the counter.

"I expected her to be here," I said under my breath as Col. climbed the narrow stairs to the family's rooms. "Where else cou have gone?"

"Think it through," Colin said. "Bringing him here would ha caused complications. She needs to take him someplace where she ca finish the job."

"Unless I'm completely wrong and Caterina has both of them."

"We're not going to worry about that now," Colin said.

We made quick work of searching the rooms, especially Donata's bedchamber, looking for evidence, but found nothing. I grabbed off a table in her room the copy of *The Venetians* I'd seen her reading the day I met her. Sadness tugged at me. Closing my eyes to better focus on my thoughts, I went through every conversation we'd had—and then I knew.

"Facio," I said. "She's in the barn where he died, I'm sure of it. No false suicides."

"I don't understand."

"It's something we talked about after Facio's death, when you brought me to the shop. It's her only chance at not being held account-able herself. We have to stop her."

I didn't need to explain further to Colin. He took my hand and all but pulled me down the stairs. We called good-bye to Signor Cara-vello, waving the book in his direction as proof of the success of our invented mission, and leapt back into our boat. We made a brief stop at Ca' Barozzi, just to confirm they had, as we suspected, taken the fam-ily's boat. They'd left not in a gondola but in a larger craft, one suitable for travel through the lagoon.

We needed a lagoon boat as well and switched to one at a police station. The driver—captain, I suppose I should call him—was extremely competent, assisted by two able-bodied police officers. Soon the sails were raised, and we were making excellent time in the direction of the Brenta Canal.

Regardless of the skill of our crew and the mercifully steady wind that powered our journey, it was not a short trip. There was too long a distance to be traveled, and I was impatient. When at last we docked, Colin and I all but flew from the boat, hurrying along the path that led to the barn. The gray building soon loomed above us, and I felt my stomach turn, sickened by the memory of what had happened there. Colin, his voice quiet and calm, gave orders to the policemen who accompanied us. They would wait outside, ready to barge in should they be called upon to do so.

I took a deep breath and steeled my shaking nerves. Colin squeezed my hand and then dropped it. He opened the door, just a crack.

"Donata?" I called to her, hoping my voice sounded kind and concerned. "Are you there? Are you all right? He hasn't hurt you, has he?"

There was a rustling. The sound of silk skirts. Emma's skirts. "I'm all right," she said. I detected surprise in her voice. I wanted to make her think she could still get away free, wanted her to think we didn't suspect her. At least for long enough that we could get close to her without making her panic and possibly shoot Paolo.

"Is Paolo still with you?" I asked.

"He is."

"Barozzi!" Colin's voiced boomed in the open space. "Do not lay a hand on her."

"Wouldn't dream of it," Paolo said. He sounded scared.

"We're coming in," Colin said. He opened the door wide, looking back to nod at the waiting policemen before stepping into the barn.

Sunlight knifed through spaces between slats that formed the building's walls. Dust hung thick in the air, visible only when touched by the light. We moved forward slowly, letting our eyes adjust to the dimness inside. Colin kept a firm grip on my arm.

They were in the center of the cavernous space, Donata standing over Paolo, who was sitting on the floor, a piece of paper in front of him, a pencil in his hand. Donata's arms were at her sides, but I could see the gun in her right hand. Emma's dress fit her very ill and barely laced up the back.

"Paolo is composing a note," she said. She was very matter-of-fact. "He has a few things to say before he kills himself, you see. I don't want to influence him, of course, but wanted to offer my support, if you will."

Tears were streaming down Paolo's face. He was scribbling something on the paper, but his hands were trembling so violently I doubted the words could be legible.

"Put down the gun, Donata," Colin said. "That's your first step to finding your way out of this situation."

She laughed. "I'm afraid I'm not that naive, Mr. Hargreaves. It seems that Paolo is going to have to further indulge his murderous tendencies before he takes his own life." Now her voice cracked, just a little. "Which is really quite unfortunate, Emily. I always liked you. You shouldn't have come here."

"You can put the gun down," I said. I made sure my tone was calm, as Colin had instructed me. "You're in no danger, and we can help you."

"No one can help me," she said. "The days of that being possible are long since past. I know it all too well."

"There's no point making things worse," I said. "Something bad happened, yes, but I'm sure we can work through it, Donata. Do you need anything right now? We brought some water. It's awfully hot in here."

265

She was tempted, I could tell. Now that my eyes had fully adjusted to the darkness, I could see the sweat beaded on her face and dripping down her neck.

"I don't know how cool it still is, but water is water," I said.

"No, I don't need anything," she said. "We need to let Paolo finish writing."

"What's he writing about?" I asked.

"I told you already," she said.

"Yes, but I was hoping you could give me more details. You said he had a few things to say. I was only wondering what they are." Colin had told me it was critical that I make Donata think I was listening to her, and that she believe I was, within the bounds of the law, on her side. Only then could there be any hope of disentangling her from this situation without it escalating into violence.

"Paolo wants to take responsibility for what he's done," Donata said. "For ruining so many people's chances of happiness."

"That's an admirable thing to do, Donata," I said.

"So why don't you leave and let him finish?" she asked, raising the gun and pointing it at Colin. "Or do you need a little encouragement to do that, Emily?"

# Un Libro d'Amore

# xxiii

For seven years, Lorenzo carried letters between Nicolò and his sister, and for seven years, she entrusted him with her answers. He delivered them all to Ca' Vendelino, careful to make sure no one saw him outside the house of his enemy, not wanting his presence to draw the ire of any Vendelino cousin. He had promised Besina. That was all that mattered.

He attempted, over and over, to bring Tomaso to see her, but Rosso would never allow the boy to spend any time alone in his uncle's care. This did not surprise Lorenzo, but it did not stop him from continuing to try.

Then things began to change.

Besina's illness had come on gradually. At first she lost weight, but no one other than herself could see that. Her voluminous habit hid any signs of changes to her earthly body. Not even Besina thought anything was wrong for a great many months. Her appetite had disappeared, but she hadn't taken any pleasure in food after she left Rosso's house. To her, it seemed appropriate that her stomach had at last accepted the lack of interest that had long since taken over her mind. Her hair turned brittle, *but she credited that to no longer taking care to tend to it well. She applied no oils, no pomades. Her appearance did not matter.*

*She took no particular note of any of this until the pain began. It started in her legs, first the left, then, soon after, the right. Some days she could hardly discern it. On others, she could hardly bear to leave her bed. But no matter how great her suffering, she always managed to go to mass and always managed to say at least three rosaries every day.*

*Lorenzo expressed his concern when he saw her on one of those days where the pain all but paralyzed her. He wanted to send for a doctor, but Besina refused.*

*"It is the pain of my sins manifesting themselves in my body," she said. "God will not burden me with more than I can bear. Do you not see what I've already been through? How could this be worse?"*

*She took his hand and looked into his eyes. Lorenzo thought she meant to reassure him, but the result was not that at all. Her hand was small and bony, her skin like the thinnest tissue, and her eyes frightened him. The life in them, the brightness, the intelligence, had all started to fade away.*

*Lorenzo knew he must speak to Nicolò at once.*

*Nicolò did not know what to make of Lorenzo Barozzi's request when he received it. He did not much care about the feud between their families, but he knew he was alone among his brethren in his position. Still, Nicolò agreed to meet Lorenzo, to speak to him face-to-face, somewhere no one else would see them.*

*That evening, Nicolò ordered his boatman to take him to the cemetery island, where he found Lorenzo in front of the grave of an infant who hadn't been given a name. When Lorenzo told him of Besina's condition, when he told him that he believed she was dying, Nicolò fell to his knees and wept.*

*"We have both let her down," Nicolò said, pulling himself back to his*

feet and wiping his eyes with the back of his hand. "We now must do something to bring her comfort that will carry her peacefully through the rest of her life. We must save Tomaso from Rosso's influence, and Besina must know it. If she can believe our child is all right, maybe she will let herself heal."

The two men talked at length and soon had a plan. Nicolò would write to Besina at once. He would set her mind at ease. He would bring her peace.

He would end forever the feud between the two families.

None of their descendants would ever have to suffer for love in the cruel way they had.

# 24

Donata held the gun in front of her with two hands. She could not keep it quite steady, but it was definitely aimed towards my husband.

"Donata, there's no need for that," I said. "We're just here to talk and to help you."

"You had chance after chance to help me and you didn't bother," she said.

"Explain to me how I let you down, and I'll try to rectify the situation," I said.

"That's impossible now." Her arms bobbed up and down, as if the tension of trying to keep them—and the gun—level were too much for her.

"Of course it's not. You've done so much to help me. It's only fair I repay the kindness."

This made her laugh. "Oh, yes, I did help. I tried to get you to spend more time with the *Libro d'Oro*. Tried to get you to look through the marriage records before we had enough information to make such a task worthwhile. I helped to make sure you didn't learn too much.

But you had to go and uncover the Vendelino connection, didn't you? I should have known removing those documents from the archives wouldn't be enough. I never thought Angelo would have shown you his family's book."

"All that told me was that there was a connection between the Vitturi and Vendelino families, Donata. It's nothing to do with what's happening now."

"It made it possible for you to find everything. To know that Angelo could lose everything. To know that nothing, ever, would end as it was supposed to."

"You've known Angelo since you were five, haven't you?" I asked. "I understand your father was his tutor. I saw his name in the family's staff records. Did you live in Ca' Vendelino?"

"We did until Angelo's father died," Donata said, "and then his mother turned us out. Not because Papà wasn't an excellent tutor, but because she caught Angelo kissing me."

"But then you went to Paris and everything was better, wasn't it?" I asked.

"I missed Angelo terribly. He was my only friend, you see," she said. "The only one I ever had. His sisters didn't want anything to do with me, and I didn't like them much either. In Paris everything was different. No one cared that we weren't from a noble family. They only cared that Papà knew so much more than they did. They adored him there. They admired him. And I loved the university. We were surrounded by people like us, people who could discuss Dante and Shakespeare and who didn't expect me to want nothing more than dancing and fashion."

She still hadn't released her grip on the gun.

"Did you want to come back to Venice after your father retired?" I asked.

"I wouldn't have wanted to if Angelo hadn't come to Paris," she said. "He changed everything."

"When did he come to Paris?"

"It was three years ago. He found me—came to the university looking for my father. We walked along the Seine and fell in love all over again. He asked me to marry him but explained we would have to wait so that he could bring his mother around to the idea." Her voice broke.

"He must love you very much, Donata." I couldn't think of what else to say. Had she really not known that Angelo, even then, already had a wife?

"I told him I would wait as long as necessary. The pain of losing him the first time had never really faded, and I could not bear to go through it again. So I pledged my faith to him, and we . . . we . . ."

I looked at Colin. "Perhaps you should leave us alone. Some topics are not fit for gentlemanly ears."

"No." Her voice was sharp again, and she lifted the gun a little higher, more towards his head. "He's not going to move an inch."

It had been a misstep on my part. I shouldn't have strayed from talking about Angelo, but I so desperately wanted my husband out of the range of her gun. "What happened next with Angelo?" I asked, my tone gentle. "Did you see him again?"

"He came to me as often as possible. We pledged fidelity in the cathedral of Notre Dame, in front of God, and promised we would do so again in Venice, with a priest and our families. In every way that mattered, we were already married, and we spent every night in each other's arms."

Paolo was frozen in his seat. He'd raised his eyes from the paper and was watching Donata standing above him. It is not pleasant to see such terror on the face of a man.

"Angelo was lucky to have found you again," I said.

"So I thought. Then when Papà decided to retire, and return home, I rejoiced. Because Angelo and I would be together all the time."

"And were you?" I asked.

"Not all the time," she said. "Of course, I understood that would not be possible until the wedding I thought he was planning. Then in the market, soon after we had come back to Venice, I heard a kitchen maid talking about how Signora Vendelino was so difficult to serve, how she was so particular about what she'd let her children eat. I thought that was odd, that it was not something Angelo's mother would ever do."

"Did you confront her?" I asked. "The maid, that is?"

"No, but I looked into the matter and found out Angelo had been married the whole time."

"He has behaved in a most underhanded and despicable manner to you," I said.

"No, no, Emily, he has not," she said. "You see, when Papà and I left for Paris he didn't think he'd ever see me again. That's the only reason he agreed to marry his wife. He said he would leave her. He said that's what he was really waiting to do, but that it wouldn't be possible until his mother died. She would never approve of him divorcing and would disinherit him, and without his fortune, he couldn't support me."

I resisted the urge to ask her why she hadn't killed Angelo's mother instead of Paolo's father. "Signora Vendelino is in good health, is she not?"

"Good enough, but she is frail," Donata said. "Angelo had been afraid to tell me the truth because he thought I wouldn't wait so long for him."

"You were willing to wait, though?" I asked.

"Of course. You can set no time limit on love. But then—then that Barozzi man came to my father. Looking for help with his collection of illuminated books. Papa was busy with a customer, so Barozzi sat with me, telling crazy tales about how the Vendelino family owed him their fortune."

"Surely you didn't give his claims any credibility? He was nothing more than a deluded old man."

"He wasn't," she said. "I grew up in the Vendelino household, remember. There were stories, rumors that the servants still joked about. They said the Vendelinos had stolen everything from the Barozzis."

"That's nothing more than idle gossip," I said.

"Nicolò's letters weren't idle gossip."

"You found the letters he wrote to Besina?"

"No," she said. "I found a pledge, tucked away in an old copy of Dante's *Divine Comedy*. Two men, one identified as N.V., the other as L.B., initialed it, promising to end the feud in a manner that would forever join the families in a way more powerful and lasting than a marriage ever could."

"When was this? And where is it now?"

"I found it when I was a girl. I'd been reading the book and came upon it, and I always remembered it. At first because I liked the smell of the old paper and the feel of the ink on the page. Later, because it seemed romantic." She spat the last words.

"Yet this still proves nothing," I said.

"It was enough to give credence to what Barozzi was claiming. Enough to tell me I could not risk waiting to see what evidence he would find."

"Where is the letter now?"

"I burned it," she said. "I burned it with the letters Signor Barozzi was holding when I killed him."

My heart sank to learn that I would not be able to read the letters. "Why didn't you do the same with the page of Dante he had?"

"I didn't know he had it," she said. "Or I would have and we wouldn't be here now, would we?"

"Where did it come from?" I asked.

"I have no idea," she said.

"What about the ring? Why didn't you take that?"

"I didn't know he had that, either." The creases in her forehead deepened. "I didn't see it in his hand."

"How did you get the letter with the pledge from the Vendelinos' library?" I asked. "Was it still in the book?"

"It was," she said. "I asked Angelo to give me the book. He didn't mind. He remembered I had liked reading it, and he didn't want me to cause any trouble."

"Did he worry you were going to?" I asked. "Didn't he know you were content, that you trusted in his love?"

"Yes, but the baby, you see," she said. Her eyes grew wide and her lips trembled when her voice broke. "Our baby would change everything."

I tried to catch Colin's eye but couldn't get his attention. Donata was with child. That's why her figure was so curvy. That's why she'd had trouble fitting into my dress.

"A baby!" I said, reacting in the only way that would both be appropriate and, if I were lucky, provide just the distraction I needed. "How wonderful! Donata, I am absolutely delighted for you. This is such joyful news!"

This unnerved her. She lowered the gun, just a bit, and looked at me as if I were crazy.

"I'm so happy for you!" I plastered an enormous smile on my face, opened my arms, and stepped forward, enveloping her in a warm embrace. Then, with a swift motion I'm not sure I could ever again replicate, I knocked the gun out of her hand. Colin pounced on it, covering it with his body and then rising again fluidly.

He didn't have to point it at Donata. Defeat was written all over her face.

* * *

The police immediately took Donata into custody. They secured her on the boat and waited while we searched the barn until we'd found the bag Paolo told us she'd had with her. She hadn't hidden it, not suspecting anyone would invade the space before she'd forced Paolo to kill himself, but she'd flung it behind a moldering pile of wood. The manuscript pages were inside, wrapped in the long cloak she'd worn with the plague doctor mask, also in the bag. I felt something heavy in the bottom and reached nearly my whole arm inside to remove a ridiculously tall pair of cork-soled shoes.

"That is taking fashion to an extreme," I said.

Paolo, who hadn't stepped more than six inches from my husband's side since we'd saved him, cleared his throat. "They're called chopines," he said. "Venetian women wore them during the Renaissance."

Colin shook his head. "Far be it for any gentleman to try to understand ladies and fashion."

The trip back to Venice was tense and uncomfortable. As there was nowhere else to put her, Donata sat with the rest of us, a policeman on either side of her, her arms bound. Paolo kept as far away as possible from her.

"Emily, could I please have a word with you?" she asked. Her eyes were watery, and though I despised what she had done, I had once counted her among my friends. I asked the policemen to give us a few feet of space so that we could talk with some semblance of privacy.

"I know how terrible what I've done is," she said. "I wish I could go back and stop myself, that I could find some other course."

"If only such a thing were possible," I said.

"You have been so kind to me, far kinder than I deserve. I cannot help but think if I'd had a friend like you from the beginning, none of this would have happened." She turned her head to the water, where, in the distance, we could see the first signs of Venice. Tall bell towers rose over the red-tiled roofs of houses, and the domes of St. Mark's were coming into view. "I know I have no right to ask for more kindness from you or anyone, but I beg you to let me do one thing before I'm taken to prison."

"What?" I asked.

"I want to speak to my father," she said. "I want him to hear what I've done from my own lips, with my own explanation. He deserves far better than what I've given him. I lied to him so often—I wrote the letter you thought he'd sent to your husband, and I made sure he was expecting to hear from you about the ring so that when you came to the shop my manipulation would not be revealed. I stole out of the house so many times when he thought I was in my room. And then there's the murder. I must confess everything to him. Please let me shield him from the pain of having to listen to a stranger—or even you—tell him these terrible things."

It was a reasonable request, and one that would spare her father some measure of grief. "I will see if I can arrange it."

We looked at each other with tear-filled eyes.

"I'm so sorry," she said. "For how I betrayed you."

"You have my forgiveness," I said. "I just wish that it could do you more good."

No one objected to Donata speaking to her father. We stopped at the shop on our way to the cell where she would be held until her trial. The policemen waited just inside the front door. Colin and I came in farther, as we couldn't let her out of our sight, but we gave her enough space that she could have as much privacy as possible in the situation.

The old man, who still believed we were returning from a celebratory picnic, greeted us with a smile, standing and opening his arms to his daughter. As she started to talk, his shoulders slumped. He listened, bowing his head to hide his tears as she continued. Soon he was holding his head in his hands and Donata had put her arms around him. They were both sobbing.

I didn't care what I'd promised the police. I couldn't bear to watch anymore. I turned away, letting Colin make sure Donata did not try to escape. She didn't, of course. Eventually, we had to fetch her, tell her it was time to go. She cried all the harder, clinging to her father, but only for a moment. Then, resigned to her fate, she stepped away from him.

"I am ready," she said.

# Un Libro d'Amore

*Besina knew she was dying. The fact did not trouble her except in regard to her son. Poor Tomaso. She hated to leave him so totally, even though she could neither see nor speak to him. She had tried, again and again, to write to her son, but Uberto intercepted all of the letters, even those carried to the house by Lorenzo, and sent them back to her. He wanted her to know Tomaso would never read her words. He didn't want her to have the comfort even of false hope.*

*Nicolò and Lorenzo were changing that. Lorenzo had explained it all to her, though she found it hard to follow his words. Everything was difficult now. Pain blinded her to nearly everything else.*

*"I have named Tomaso as my heir," Lorenzo said, "and Nicolò is bestowing upon him the same honor. He will inherit the fortunes of both families, as he should, coming from them both as he does."*

*"But Uberto," Besina said, her voice weak and scratchy. "He will stop it."*

*"He cannot stop a legal inheritance."*

"*Tomaso,*" *she said.* "*He must know. He must know why this is happening.*"

"*We will tell him, Nicolò and I, when he is old enough to understand.*"

"*He must know,*" *she said.* "*He must.*"

"*I promise you he will,*" *Lorenzo said, pressing his hand softly on his sister's forehead. She could not survive many more nights, and he knew what he must do.*

*Besina had great faith in her brother. Nevertheless, she felt she, too, must do something to ensure her son would know the truth, even if something happened to Lorenzo. She called for her confessor and told him her story. She made him promise Tomaso would know.*

*The next morning, just after the sun had risen, Lorenzo came to the gate of San Zaccaria and demanded to see his sister. His request was rebuffed. He was not alone, the nun explained, he was with someone not from the Barozzi family. It could not be allowed, she said. Lorenzo had anticipated this response. He asked to speak to the abbess. When she came to the gate, he and Nicolò both gave her heavy bags of gold.*

"*I do not care what my father told you,*" *Lorenzo said.* "*You are well aware that my sister is dying. Have you seen any of the rest of my family come to offer her comfort and love in her final days? This man cares about her. He will be allowed to see her.*"

*Nicolò never was sure if it was the gold or Lorenzo's appeal that convinced the woman. Whatever the cause, she unlocked the door and ushered them both inside.*

"*She had a very bad night,*" *the woman said.* "*I do not think she slept at all. Prepare yourselves.*"

*Lorenzo went to Besina first. Today he did not read to her from Dante, as he usually did on his visits. He did not regale her with stories about* carnivale *or the latest gossip. Instead, he told her he loved her, and that no man could have a better sister.*

*Then he said good-bye.*

*He kissed her on both cheeks and on her forehead and backed away, his heart heavy. Nicolò stepped forward. Lorenzo retreated to the small window and stood facing it, wanting to give Besina as much privacy as possible.*

*Nicolò had not seen Besina since that last day in Santa Maria Miracoli, so many years ago. To him, even in sickness, her face was the most beautiful thing he had ever seen, and he prayed, thanking God for letting him lay eyes on it one more time before she was called back to heaven. He sat on the bed and took Besina's hands, her tiny, bony hands, in his.*

*"Being with you now, at this moment, is the most important thing in my life," he said. "I would give up everything else for it."*

*"Nicolò." Her voice was so weak he could hardly hear her, but he saw the muscles in her face moving. She was trying to smile at him. "My love."*

*"Never before has a woman been loved the way I love you, Besina," he whispered to her, leaning close, "and never again shall one be. I regret so much that I could not do more for you, that I let you down so terribly."*

*"No, Nicolò, you have never let me down. You're the only one who never has."*

*"This should have ended so differently," he said. "You should be surrounded by our children in a house that was always full of laughter."*

*"I can ask for no more than having you with me now."*

*Besina's breath caught in her throat, and it was hard for her to draw another. The sound alarmed both men in the room. They knew it would*

*ɔng. Nicolò looked at Lorenzo, his eyes sending a question, ask-*
*/mission. Lorenzo nodded.*

*Nicolò gathered Besina's frail body into his arms, wrapping around*
*her the soft blanket that covered the bed. He pulled her sideways onto*
*his lap and held her close to him. He showered her face with gentle kisses*
*and spoke, reciting from the poet they both loved.*

You've seen the temporary fire and the eternal fire; you have reached the place past which my powers cannot see. I've brought you here through intellect and art; from now on, let your pleasure be your guide; you're past the steep and past the narrow paths. Look at the sun that shines upon your brow; look at the grasses, flowers, and the shrubs born here, spontaneously, of the earth. Among them, you can rest or walk until the coming of the glad and lovely eyes—those eyes that, weeping, sent me to your side. Await no further word or sign from me: your will is free, erect, and whole—to act against that will would be to err: therefore I crown and miter you over yourself.

*They were the last words spoken to Dante by Virgil as he made his*
*way through* Purgatorio. *Besina, who had listened with a look of such*
*peace on her face, opened her eyes and tried to smile. "Are you releasing*
*me, Nicolò?"*

*"I am, my love."*

*He held her closer still, not letting her go until long after he felt her*
*shallow breathing stop and her body go slack. When the abbess, who had*
*watched it all from the doorway, came into the room, she laid her hand*
*on his shoulder, tears streaming down her face. Nicolò nodded, knowing*
*he had to put Besina down, but he could not bear it. He pulled her close*
*again and kissed the top of her head.*

Then, with the gentlest touch, he lowered her back onto the bed. He placed the blanket on top of her. He smoothed her hair. He closed her eyes, and he wept until he could weep no more.

There would never again be such beauty in the world.

# 25

After leaving Donata in the capable hands of the police, Colin, Paolo, and I returned to the Danieli, where Emma, still prostrate on our bed, burst into tears at the sight of her husband. Paolo's face and his white linen suit were covered with dust, but as soon as Emma was convinced he was unharmed, she demanded fresh clothes; I had left her with a nightgown into which she could change.

"I'm perfectly healthy," she said. "My head hurts a little, but it doesn't trouble me much. Not now that my lecherous husband has returned."

I couldn't decide if she was being facetious.

"Emma, *cara,* my love." Paolo took her in his arms. "I have never loved any woman but you. I may have made a mistake here or there in the past, but my heart never strayed—and you must believe me, Caterina Brexiano was never my lover."

"Then why were you spending so much time with her?" Emma asked. "Why were you with her the night your father was killed?"

"Because I actually did believe the things she'd told him," he said. "I think she can communicate with the dead."

"What about Margarita da Fiori?" Emma asked.

"She doesn't exist," Paolo said. "She's an invention of Signor Polani, who uses her whenever he needs a convenient excuse. I borrowed her from him because I was panicked."

"Did Caterina tell you about Besina's letters and the ring?" I asked. "Did you know she'd given them to your father?"

"No," Paolo said. "She kept those to herself after she'd found them in the hotel, but she used some of the information in them to tempt me with the idea of possible fortune in my future. I'm sure she had done something similar with my father, though I can't find any record of him having paid her beyond what she required for the séances she staged on his behalf."

"Did she ever tell you anything useful?" Emma asked.

"Not really," Paolo said. "It's a hopeless business."

"It's not hopeless anymore." Brother Giovanni had come out from the suite's second bedroom as soon as we'd returned but had not spoken until now. "I'm nearly done with the pages the villain left behind. There is a significant connection between the Barozzi and Vendelino families. Dare I hope you have found the rest of the manuscript?"

I smiled. "In fact, we have." I handed it to him.

"If I could trouble you all for some help, extra hands would mean we could finish this far more quickly than if you leave the job to me alone."

Colin and Paolo followed him at once. I helped Emma into one of my dresses but refused to call for the maid to do her hair. Some things can stand being delayed, and while being properly dressed is not one of them, catering to one's vanity is. We joined the others as quickly as we could and found that Caterina and the Polanis, responding to our summons, had also arrived. Colin had wanted to personally tell them they were no longer under suspicion, but we also had questions we wanted them to answer. Neither of us liked loose ends.

Brother Giovanni had reorganized the room considerably. The bed was pushed into a corner, and he'd asked for and received a larger table. It was around this that we all sat. Colin and Paolo were already hard at work, as were Caterina and Florentina. Signor Polani was doing an excellent job looking industrious, but he did not seem to be making much progress. Brother Giovanni gave Emma and me each a paintbrush and instructed us to dip them in the opaque mixture in a bowl in the center of the table.

"Do not work too quickly," he said, "and do not let your brush become too wet. You will soon get a feel for what you are doing, and then as one set of words disappears, you will be rewarded with another. You may use these rags to blot as you go."

It pained me to destroy the illuminated page in front of me, even though I knew I had to. As I watched the ink begin to dissolve, I wondered about the man who had written the words. A scribe, probably a monk, just like Brother Giovanni. He would not be well pleased if he could know his efforts were being erased.

No one else seemed troubled by our task. Colin described to Emma and Brother Giovanni all that had happened since we'd left them, and all that Donata had done up to that time.

"I do not understand how she got through the window here and at the palazzo," Emma said.

"She's quite strong," Colin said. "She rows for her father, you know, as they can't afford a gondolier. She used a rope to climb the wall. It wasn't difficult in the least. She employed a similar strategy when sneaking out of her house after her father had forbidden her to help Emily. She climbed down a rope from her bedroom. Her father never doubted that she was inside reading."

"I can understand that working, but here?" Brother Giovanni asked. "Are we to believe no one noticed her climbing up the front of the hotel?"

"Lots of people saw," I said. "Just as we suspected, she made a grand show of it. She was wearing her mask and cape and stopped to wave and shout at the crowd as she went. No one thought anything was amiss."

"What about the bit of canvas in my globe?" Signor Polani asked.

"She was carrying it with her from the time she cut it from the painting," I said. "Waiting for an opportunity to put it to use. As you know, she called on you alone—which is why you were able to tell me she was too smart for your taste—and when she saw the globe, she knew I would look at it. We'd discussed my fascination with old globes the first day I met her in her father's shop."

"But you, Emma," Caterina said. "I swear I saw you in the *portego* the night Signor Barozzi was killed. Will you admit it now? You stand to lose nothing."

"I wasn't there," Emma said. "I have no memory of it."

"I remember it vividly," Caterina said. "Mostly because your dress was so inappropriate for the season. Crimson velvet. I couldn't see it well, but I could make out the fabric and saw the way the color picked up the—"

Caterina swayed and started to lose her balance. Signor Polani caught her with an easy grace that suggested he had much practice at saving ladies when they had cause to faint.

"It was not you, Emma," Caterina said, making no effort to

disentangle herself from Signor Polani's arms. "It was Besina Barozzi, watching the scene from afar. She must have known something evil was going to happen that night."

"That's quite enough," Florentina said. "I'm tired of your ghosts and visions and lies."

Caterina mumbled an apology, and we all set back to work, all doing our best to come to terms with what Donata had done. Paolo and Emma were, of course, rightly angry with her and lamented that in Italy she would not be executed for her crime. Florentina and her husband, now free from suspicion of guilt, found the whole intrigue rather entertaining but did their best to hide the fact from the Barozzis. Caterina, still convinced she had missed her chance to speak to Besina's ghost, was sullen and silent. My own feelings were complicated. I had no sympathy for Donata's actions, but I was mourning the loss of a woman I'd come to consider a friend. I thought about her apology to me on the boat. It was not I from whom she needed forgiveness. Her betrayal of me was nothing compared to what she'd done to Signor Barozzi, and by extension Paolo and Emma. They would never be able to forgive her. Not that Paolo's father was ever given a chance.

Donata had recklessly destroyed lives because she could not cope with impossible love. I considered how many women, throughout the centuries, had been in situations equally—or even more—heartbreaking. So many of them came through with honor and dignity. What a shame, what a terrible shame, that Donata could not have found a way to do so.

We worked for the rest of the day. Caterina and the Polanis begged their leave before dinner, but the rest of us continued into the night, stopping only once to send for food to fuel us. The sky had turned the bright blue that comes just before dawn and the first hints of pink streaked wispy clouds when we finally finished.

"Now we must read it," Paolo said. "Something good has to come out of all of this. My father cannot have died for nothing."

"We cannot read straight away, I am afraid," Brother Giovanni said. "First, we must let the pages dry." They were scattered around the suite at the moment, covering nearly every flat surface. We'd had to call for extra towels on which to lay them.

"How long will that take?" Emma asked.

"An hour or two at least," Brother Giovanni said. "Maybe more. I want to be very careful. It's essential."

"You're right," I said. "We can't risk destroying this now."

"When the pages are dry, I will have to try to figure out the order in which they belong," the monk said. "That will be no small task."

"What should we do?" Paolo asked.

"Go home," Colin said. "All of us need to sleep, you included, Giovanni. The pages can dry, and then we can do the rest."

We were exhausted, not only from staying awake all night but from the terrible mental strain under which we'd all been operating. Paolo took Emma home while Colin installed Brother Giovanni in a room of his own at the Danieli.

"I do realize we need sleep," he said to me, after he'd returned to our suite, "but I am also in desperate need of being alone with you. Really alone. No one detained in the next room. No one under our protection. Just you and me and . . ." He looked at the bed and then he looked at me and then he began to unfasten the long row of buttons on the back of my gown.

*　　*　　*

When Brother Giovanni rapped on the door of our suite at three o'clock the following afternoon, I was dead asleep but sprang to life at once. Colin, who could make himself presentable more quickly than I, answered the door and settled into the other room to start piecing together the proper order of the pages. I followed as soon as I could, envious of gentlemen's clothing that did not fasten up the back and always require assistance.

Colin and I had not slept much, but I had the energy of a small child who has been given an endless quantity of sweets by an overindulgent uncle. I found this frequently to be the case after Colin's thorough and vigorous attentions to my person. There was an immediate period of inevitable and sweet paralysis after such interludes, when I could do nothing but sleep, but they did not last long, and once awake, I was awake.

My husband had a much more difficult time moving past said sweet paralysis. His eyes may not have been quite so bright as mine when I joined him and Brother Giovanni, but his efforts were focused and diligent. We didn't expect Emma and Paolo. We'd told them to sleep and then to wait for us. We would bring them the manuscript when we were done.

First, though, I wanted to read it.

Ordering the pages was an arduous task, at once tedious and tantalizing. We needed to put together sentences as if they were pieces in a puzzle but could not let ourselves be distracted by the words on the rest of the page. It was nearly seven o'clock by the time we'd finished.

"We should eat something and then go to Ca' Barozzi," Colin said.

"I'm not hungry," I said. "I want to read."

He understood my need. So while he and Brother Giovanni sat down to a quick dinner, I went to Caffè Florian, ordered a pot of tea, and read, knowing it would take some time for me to translate from the old Italian.

Besina Barozzi always knew she was not among the fortunate—or unfortunate, depending on one's perspective—who could rely on beauty. She didn't possess it. It was her mind, not her too-long nose or thin lips, that would have to set her apart from the profusion of stunning girls for which Venice was famous.

I was nearly at the end when they came to collect me, ready to go to Emma and Paolo. I said nothing, only held up my hand to tell them to wait. Tears streamed down my face. I'd never read anything so sad. When I finished, I collected myself and gathered up the pages. There still was work to be done.

# XXV

*Nicolò had already started to feel ill when he left San Zaccaria, but he put it down to grief. He had expected to feel no differently. It was only some days later, when he could no longer ignore the fever, that he began to worry. He wrote the changes to his will. He signed them, with two witnesses present: his nephew, Nicolò Vitturi, Lucia's son; and the man who for years had been the Vendelino family solicitor. Vitturi, in different circumstances, would have expected to be named Nicolò's heir. Nicolò thought it best to deal directly with his inevitable disappointment.*

*Nicolò had explained everything at length, and while his nephew did not much like the idea, he promised he would respect his uncle's wishes. It was not his own fortunes that concerned him, he said, but he wasn't sure it was wise to ally the family with the Barozzis. They could not be trusted.*

*In a different time, this would have amused Nicolò. Today it served to confirm he was doing the right thing. Enough of these feuds and vendettas. It was time for a new way.*

*Nicolò was not naive. He thought his nephew might give trouble,* might go back on his word. With great care and the finest paintbrush he could find, he made a small addition to a painting by Titian he had acquired some years before. A painting that hung in Ca' Vendelino. He hid the codicil in the scene. He signed it, and he had his solicitor sign it as well. The man promised that if any trouble ensued, he would direct the family to the message in this painting and to the copy of the new will hidden behind its canvas.

Two days later, Nicolò Vendelino succumbed to the fever that consumed him. He smiled as he took his last breath, knowing that now, at last, he would be with Besina.

It fell to me, Father Marco Grissoni, confessor of Besina Rosso, born Barozzi, to write this account, and I swear to its truthfulness. I have gone to great lengths to confirm from others involved the validity of those things told me by Besina the night before her death. She was wholly faithful in recounting her story.

Now, as directed by her, I will turn this book into another, before giving it to her son, Tomaso Rosso, so that when he is grown, he can know the truth about his mother.

# 26

Paolo grew increasingly frenetic as we started to read Besina's story to him after we'd arrived at Ca' Barozzi. He couldn't sit still. After a few minutes he interrupted, demanding that we stop.

"I can't take it," he said. "Please do not think me ungrateful for all the work you've done or uninterested in the plight of my ancestor. Someday, I will want to know more, but right now, all I care about is the end. What happened? Is there an inheritance for me?"

"There is," I said. I couldn't really blame him for wanting to cut to what mattered the most to him. He'd lost his father. He'd been through enough. I summarized Nicolò's actions and the pledge he and Lorenzo had made.

"So all we need to do is find the codicil?" Emma asked.

"Assuming it's still there, and assuming it will be upheld in court," Colin said. "Most likely you'll get something, but it's hard to predict what."

"Why are we sitting here?" Paolo asked. "Let's go to Ca' Vendelino."

Colin and I persuaded him it would be best if we went alone. There was still much bad blood between the two families, and Paolo's presence, demanding money, was unlikely to help the situation. Paolo saw the wisdom of this and agreed to stay behind. We also decided not to go at all until the following day, after we'd had time to do a bit more research on the fate of Nicolò's revised will.

Zaneta received us in the *portego* the following afternoon and sent for Angelo at once when she saw the grave looks on our faces. We told them everything that had happened in regard to Signor Barozzi's death, sparing no detail. Angelo did not look up from the floor once we told him what Donata had done.

His mother, on the other hand, was of a different mind entirely. She whacked her son soundly on the arm. "You foolish, foolish man," she said. "To behave in such a manner. To treat a woman in such a way. It is a disgrace."

"You sent her away," he said. "You didn't approve of her."

"Of course I didn't. I thought you could make a better marriage, and you did. You never once suggested you wanted anything else."

Angelo didn't say anything.

Zaneta narrowed her eyes. "You never wanted anything else, did you? This is no story of forbidden love. You liked Donata well enough and were happy to dally with her. You just didn't think she'd ever really come back to Venice, did you?"

"No, I didn't. She was happy in Paris."

"You had no right to do this despicable thing," Zaneta said. "I am ashamed. What will become of this child now? Your child, Angelo? His mother will spend the rest of her life in prison. Are you going to raise it?"

"No, of course not," Angelo said. Any sign of shame or compunction washed away from his face. "I could not ask that of my wife."

"No, you couldn't," Zaneta said. "You stupid, foolish man." She whacked him again.

"There is one other thing," Colin said. "Something you may not like to hear." He told them about the will. About the painting.

Angelo was incredulous. Zaneta sat forward in her chair and looked straight into my eyes. "Is this a valid will?"

"So far as we can determine, yes. Particularly if, as the manuscript suggests, we find the full text as executed by Nicolò's solicitor."

"Before we discuss this further, we ought to see if this codicil is still there." She all but leapt from her seat and stormed to the room that contained the painting in question. Angelo was right behind her.

"Mamma," he said, "surely this doesn't matter. We can fight this. Whatever some solicitor said about the validity of unusual codicils, there's no reason to give up. Surely the court—"

Zaneta stopped walking and turned to her son. "I do not care what a court says. I do what is right."

Colin lowered the painting from the wall and placed it facedown on a table after I'd cushioned the surface with a soft shawl. Using extreme care and a pocketknife, he removed the backing from the frame.

"I don't know enough about frames to know whether this one is the original," he said. The backing gone, we all stared at the canvas in front of us. Working from the bottom right-hand corner, Colin started to pull it away. "It's blank."

It was just an extra layer of protection—and there, behind it, was a folded and sealed document. None of us were in doubt of the contents. Colin handed it to Zaneta.

"Mamma—"

His mother stopped him with the sternness in her eyes. "This is mine to read and mine to make a decision about," she said. "Leave me, all of you."

There was no question we would respect her wishes. At least no question that Colin and I would respect her wishes. As for Angelo, I can offer no insight as to his thoughts or planned actions. My husband and I returned to the hotel, where we would wait to hear from Zaneta.

In the meantime, I asked Brother Giovanni to assist me in transcribing Besina's story so that it could be read without risking damage to the original pages. I assumed that at some point Paolo would want to see it, and I wanted to have a copy as well. We divided the work and by the end of the evening had made a great deal of progress. Before Colin and I had retired to bed, there was a sharp knock on our door.

"Signora Vendelino," Colin said. "What a surprise."

"I want to read this document you have," she said, "and I want to read it now."

"Of course." He invited her into the room.

"We've begun a transcription," I said, "but I imagine you would prefer to see the original, just to guard against any unintentional mistakes we may have made."

"Please," she said.

We set her up on the now clear table where only two nights earlier we'd worked so frantically to reveal the hidden text. She asked to be left alone, so we closed the door and waited in the sitting room.

Two hours later, Zaneta opened the door and stood in front of us, her eyes red and swollen. "I would like you to ask Signor Barozzi if I may call on him tomorrow at one o'clock. Will you do that for me?"

We agreed to set up the meeting. She gave us no indication as to what she planned to say once there. Expressing her thanks for all we had done, Zaneta took her leave.

---

The next morning, I sent notes to Caterina Brexiano and to Signora Polani to inform them of the closing details of the case. As for Signor Polani, I was content to let his wife fill in the details for him. Caterina would likely be in touch with Paolo. She would want to know the rest of Besina's story. That sorted, I settled back into transcribing the manuscript until a message arrived from the police station where Donata was being held. She wanted to see me. Colin and Brother Giovanni were perfectly capable of finishing our work without me, so I set off from the water entrance, not feeling much like walking. The day was exceptionally warm, and my spirits had taken a dive after I read Donata's note. Not because of something she had said but because of the havoc she had wreaked on so many lives.

The police offered me coffee and settled me into a small, dingy room. The sole window was covered with thick iron bars, and the only furniture in the space was a battered-looking table with four chairs around it. I sat in one of them and waited until an officer led Donata, her hands in restraints, to the one across the table from me.

"Hello." I hardly knew what to say.

"Thank you for coming. I know I don't deserve it," she said. "My father died last night, in his sleep. I'll never know if the knowledge of what I did killed him or if he would have died anyway. If it's the latter, I wish there had been some way to have spared him such pain in his final days."

My heart sank at the news, and I fought tears. "I'm so sorry, Donata. I liked your father very much."

"It's probably better this way," she said. "It would have been awful for him to live through my trial."

"Do you need any help with arrangements?" I asked.

"No, thank you," she said. "I have a lawyer, and he is taking care of everything. Everything that he can, that is."

"Is there something else?"

"Yes." She closed her eyes and took a deep breath before continuing. "My child, Emily. Obviously I will not be able to care for it. Angelo has already refused to have anything to do with it. If I cannot find a suitable guardian, the baby will be named a ward of the state and put in an orphanage."

I did not reply.

"Emily, I have let down every person who ever mattered in my life. I don't want to do the same to my child. I want him—or her—to have the education and the love of reading that my father gave me. That you could give, too."

"Donata, I don't know that I—"

"There's no need to answer now," she said. "I understand the enormity of the burden, and I will never fault you should you decline. All I ask is that you consider taking in my child. My father had some money. You would have all of that. As well as all of the books in the shop. I'd want them to be given to the child."

"Donata, I don't think it's wise at this juncture to be planning so far in advance."

"My solicitor has drawn up papers that would give you and your husband guardianship of the child. You don't have to sign them now or ever. Just read through them and speak to Colin. There's no rush to make a decision. It will be another five months before the matter comes to the forefront."

"We will discuss it," I said. "That is all I can promise you."

"That is all I can ask. Thank you."

I rose from my seat and started for the door. "Good-bye, Donata. I'm terribly, terribly sorry about your father."

When I returned to the Danieli, I hardly knew what to say to my husband. The transcription complete, Brother Giovanni had gone to mass at St. Mark's, so Colin and I were alone. We went to the terrace on the roof of the hotel, where not so long ago Donata had met us over breakfast.

"This is a conversation I never thought I would have," I said, unsure of where to begin.

"Easiest then to dive straight in," Colin said. "What did Donata want? For us to raise her unfortunate and abandoned child?"

"How did you know?"

"It wasn't a difficult guess."

"Her father died last night," I said, looking at the boats streaming past us, making their way to the Grand Canal.

"I am sorry. He was a good man."

"He was."

"He had a terrible daughter, though," Colin said.

"Yes."

"Do you suppose terrible skips a generation?"

"Skips a generation?" I repeated. "Are you suggesting . . . Can you mean? Would you consider taking in the child?"

"How could we not?" he asked. "What is the other option? Letting the poor thing languish in an orphanage?"

I did not reply.

"It is a lot to consider," he said, "but my initial reaction is to say yes. If there's a little bit of good we can squeeze out of an otherwise diabolical situation, I don't see how we can refuse."

"I couldn't agree more," I said. "It won't be simple, you know."

"It won't. Still, if anyone can force the dragon-like matrons of London society to embrace the innocent child of a murderess, it is you, my dear—and I can think of nothing I'd like better than seeing you rise to such a challenge."

# 27

Still somewhat dumbfounded by what we'd just agreed to do, we set off for Ca' Barozzi so that we would arrive in advance of Zaneta. This time, I hardly noticed the shimmering beauty of the Grand Canal. I was preoccupied with thoughts of Donata's child. When we reached the house, Emma and Paolo were aflutter with excitement, going so far as to wait for us at their water entrance.

"Do you think we'll get enough money from them to restore the palazzo?" Emma asked.

"Do you think they'll really agree to give us something?" Paolo's question was not only more within the bounds of taste, it was more realistic. "It seems too much to hope."

"It's impossible to guess," Colin said, "and there's no reason to try. You'll know the answers soon enough."

Emma had organized a lovely spread of traditional English pastries and tea along with a cold pitcher of lemonade to be waiting for her guests. She'd also chosen a gown that was demure and verging on elegant. Not at all her usual style.

"I want to make a good impression," she told me. "Put my best foot forward, as they say. Not that I suppose it will make any difference. Those Vendelinos are notoriously difficult, I'm told."

"Emma, the entire point of Nicolò's will was to put an end to the feud," I said. "Frankly, if you're bent on continuing it, you don't deserve any of his family's money."

"What about Lorenzo?" Paolo asked. "Did he keep his part of the bargain?"

"He did," Colin said. "He named Tomaso Rosso as his heir. The decision raised no eyebrows because Lorenzo had no children of his own. Sometime after Uberto Rosso died, Tomaso took the name Barozzi as his own. Hence you're having it."

Paolo nodded but said nothing. The room was thick with tension. Zaneta and Angelo's arrival did not improve the atmosphere. Not, that is, until Zaneta graciously accepted a glass of lemonade from Emma and began to speak.

"I have read Nicolò's will," she said, "and I have read Besina's story. There can be no doubt of what my ancestor's intentions were, and they were intentions of the noblest sort. I have consulted with my solicitor, not to seek advice as to how I should proceed but because I wanted to know what happened after Nicolò died. As we already are aware, Tomaso Rosso did not inherit any money from the Vendelinos. Instead, Nicolò's nephew, Vitturi, who witnessed the new will, became the head of the family. So far as we can tell, no effort was made by the family to honor Nicolò's wishes. Giulio Zorzi, the solicitor who oversaw the codicil, also oversaw Nicolò's estate. We can only imagine that this nephew of very dubious ethics paid the solicitor enough money that he was happy to forget about the codicil. I find this reprehensible."

"It is, Signora Vendelino," Paolo said. "However, if I may be so bold as to suggest, not an excuse for Vitturi's actions, but an explanation for them. Our two families have despised each other for hundreds of years. And why? Because something tragic happened during a storm after the sacking of Constantinople? The ensuing animosity would have made it almost impossible for the nephew to act in any other way. He'd been taught nothing but hate. Nor is it only the Vendelinos who are to blame. The Barozzis are just as culpable for having prolonged this feud. Today, as head of the Barozzi family, I would like to extend my apology to the Vendelino family for any and all offenses given to you in our name."

"Signor Barozzi, I am both impressed and grateful for your kind words," Zaneta said. "They make what I am about to tell you easier to say. I have decided to give you half of my fortune—and you shall have it now, not after I am dead, because we have seen too well how a person's final wishes may be disregarded." Angelo's face darkened as he listened to his mother speak. "I know it is impossible to gauge the precise amount your family would now possess had Tomaso received his rightful inheritance, but I hope you will agree that this amount"—she passed him a folded piece of paper on which I can only presume a figure was written—"will satisfy your desire to see justice done. To argue over it seems pointless. Tomaso and his descendants might have made more or might have lost it all. I hope you see I am trying to be fair."

"Signora." Paolo thumped his hand against his heart. "This is more than generous. I cannot thank you enough."

"I am only sorry that your father is not alive to see this resolution," Zaneta said.

"As am I," Paolo said. Emma had sidled closer to him, trying to get a look at the piece of paper. Paolo folded it and slid it into his jacket pocket. Angelo, sullen and silent, refused all refreshment and conversation.

I pulled Besina's ring off my finger, where it had been for the duration of our investigation, and held it out in front of me. What a journey it had taken over the centuries, from the Vendelino family treasury to the hand of Nicolò's forbidden love. His sister must have hidden it, along with Besina's letters, in the wall of her house. I wondered if she had done so after her brother's death. Had she ever intended to pull them out again? Or had she let them be lost, hoping that someone, someday, would stumble upon them? Caterina had been clever to discover them, and when she'd given them to the old conte, she had very nearly brought to a close the sad story of Nicolò and Besina.

"I'm not sure to whom I should give this," I said holding the ring out in front of me. "It seems you both have a valid claim to it."

"No," Zaneta said. "I now understand the Barozzis did not come to have it through underhanded means and recognize it does not belong to my family, but it must be yours, Emily. This peace could not have come without your intervention. Keep it."

"Yes," Paolo agreed. "Besina would want it."

Emma scowled and started to speak but was silenced by a glare from her husband.

"Thank you," I said. "Truly. It means more to me than I can say. I feel such a deep connection to Besina." Tears filled my eyes. "I only wish the peace between your families now could have happened at a time when it might have saved her from so much misery."

"That connection, Emily, is why you must have the ring," Zaneta said. "There could be no other outcome."

"We do have one other thing that belongs to you, Signora Vendelino," Colin said, passing her the page torn from *The Inferno* that Paolo had found in his father's pocket. "The rest of the book is in the library across from the Doge's Palace. So far as we can tell, the volume originally belonged to Nicolò, who must have removed it and added the message to Besina before donating the rest of the book to the li-

brary. According to library records, someone in the mid-seventeenth century reported the missing page."

"How did Signor Barozzi come to find it?" Zaneta asked.

"Someone—possibly Marco Grissoni—placed it inside the palimpsest that was to be given to Tomaso after his mother died. Unfortunately, Tomaso never knew the book contained anything beyond the text of *The Divine Comedy*."

"I feel stupid not to have made the connection sooner," Paolo said. "I'd always known there was a loose page in the book, but it never occurred to me that it didn't belong with that particular volume. When we gave it to Brother Giovanni while he was working to reveal the hidden text under our Dante, he recognized that it was not the same handwriting as the rest of the book and belonged with another one entirely."

"He took it upon himself to search out the original volume in the library," Colin said.

"That was good of him," Zaneta said. "I would like to keep the page, if you don't mind. Surely the library won't object, as it hadn't been given to them in the first place?"

"They've gone without it this long," Colin said, "and you're right, it wasn't part of Nicolò's original donation."

"I will trouble you no longer," Zaneta said, "but I expect both of you Barozzis at Ca' Vendelino for dinner Sunday after mass." With that she stood, pulled on her gloves, and left, Angelo trailing behind her.

"Well?" Emma asked after we'd watched their boat pull away from the house. "What did she give us?"

"What a disgraceful question, *cara*." Paolo frowned. "Suffice it to say we will never worry about money again."

I could see, in his eyes, what was unsaid. That they'd never worry about money, but that there also would never be another Barozzi. He

was the last male in the line. He and Emma began to bicker, but in a good-natured sort of way.

"Do you think they'll be happy?" I asked as our gondolier pushed away from Ca' Barozzi and I watched the elegant Gothic facade fade behind us.

"In their way," Colin said. "I'm more interested in your happiness, my dear. How are you feeling about the decision we made this morning?"

"Better and better," I said. "Terrified, too, but I think that's rather a good sign."

"I couldn't agree more." He put his arm around my shoulder and looked at the scene around us. "This is a beautiful city. Almost like magic, isn't it? Hasn't any business even being here and yet here it is, balanced on a forest of petrified trees pounded into the silt below the lagoon."

"I adore it," I said.

"As do I," he said. "I've sent the papers Donata gave you to our solicitor. He'll look them over and suggest any necessary changes. Now that we're done with our work, I think we should stay on until we hear back from him. Have a holiday. Travel by gondola and drink too much prosecco and wander in the narrow streets. What do you say?"

"It sounds like heaven."

"Then, when the solicitor replies, we can tie up any loose ends regarding the child, sign what needs to be signed, and go home."

That is precisely what we did. For eight weeks we meandered through the effervescent city, enjoying getting lost in its maze of streets as much as we enjoyed finding our way again. We looked at the great paintings of Titian and Tintoretto. We sketched bridges and palazzi both from canal-side cafés and from gondolas. We visited Santa Maria dei Miracoli, where I sat in the back pew and wept for Besina. It was so

easy to picture her there, in this beautiful church, a place of hope and love, yet a place that could not alter the tragic course of her sad life. Finally, we returned to Ca' Vendelino, where Zaneta had invited us to come see a portrait of Nicolò, whose handsome face was uncannily like Angelo's. Not only did they share a thick crop of dark blond curls, they both had the same bright blue eyes with lashes long enough to be the envy of any girl.

When the time came to board a steamer back to England, I found myself extremely sentimental as I watched Venice fade in the distance. If the root of nostalgia is pain, I was feeling it then. To leave such beauty is never easy, and I felt as if a piece of my soul were being ripped from me.

"It's like you're leaving your old home, isn't it?" Colin asked. "You know they say that when a tourist arrives in Venice and La Marangona is ringing in the campanile at St. Mark's, it is a mark of recognition. Recognition that the new arrival has the soul of some long-dead citizen of the republic. I seem to recall it ringing when we drew close to the city."

"How do you know it wasn't ringing for you?" I asked.

"Because I've been here on four previous occasions, and never once did the same thing happen. No Venetian soul for me."

I didn't reply. I couldn't take my eyes off the shimmering spot on the horizon where the city had just slipped from my view.

"We'll be back, you know," Colin said. He was standing behind me with his arms wrapped around my waist. "Soon, after Donata's child is born."

"I'm afraid you may have to come alone," I said.

"Will it be too hard for you to see her? You wouldn't have to, you know."

"It's not that," I said, glad that he couldn't see my face. "I might not be in a position to travel."

"Not in a position to travel?" he asked. "Why on earth not?"

"Perhaps position isn't quite the right word," I said. "*Condition* would be more accurate."

"Condition?"

I gave him a moment to digest what I'd said before I turned around to face him.

"Yes, condition. The real question is this: How will you handle the transition to having not only one child but two?"

"Emily, are you sure?" I'd never seen his face color so quickly.

"Quite. The hotel doctor has confirmed it."

"I didn't think . . . I never . . . I wouldn't even let myself hope."

"Neither did I."

"Oh, my dear girl, I could not be happier!" He picked me up, spun me around, and covered me with kisses, right there, on the deck, in front of everyone.

I knew, then, without question, that I was the luckiest girl in the world.

# Acknowledgments

Myriad thanks to . . .

Charlie Spicer, Andy Martin, Sarah Melnyk, April Osborn, Tom Robinson, and Anne Hawkins. A great publishing team.

Jesse Sheidlower, editor at the OED, for finding me a much-needed fifteenth-century word reference.

Dean Mayne, a.k.a. Charles Morgandy, for agreeing to show up in the nineteenth century.

Xander Tyska, for priceless assistance with Medieval and Renaissance research.

Brett Battles, Rob Browne, Bill Cameron, Christina Chen, Kristy Kiernan, Elizabeth Letts, Carrie Medders, Missy Rightley, Renee Rosen, and Lauren Willig. You guys are the best.

My parents, for continuing to read. And read. And read.

Andrew, for everything.